THE EVIDENCE

An addictive crime thriller that will keep you guessing

JODIE LAWRANCE

Detective Helen Carter Book 2

D1324621

JOFFE BOOKS

Joffe Books, London
www.joffebooks.com

First published in Great Britain in 2021

Cover art by Nebojsa Zorić

ISBN: 978-1-78931-884-5

PROLOGUE

Edinburgh, June 1976

Reggie watched Agnes enter the grimy, tobacco-stained living room of the flat, built as part of Edinburgh's post war slum-clearance scheme, a look of surprise spreading across her pudgy face as her eyes met his. If he had known she was going to turn up he would've had Moira tidy up before she left for work.

'What are you doing here?' Reggie asked.

'Nothing, I . . . Well.' She held up a small swollen cotton bag in her right hand. He noticed the bundle of keys in her other one. 'Just dropping off some food for Moira. She was hungry last time I visited and all you had in there was an old tin of carrots.'

'She said that did she?'

'No, but—'

'What food have you brought?'

'What's it got to do with you?' she asked, arching an eyebrow.

'I've not had my dinner yet.' Smirking, he wiped the hair that hung in damp rat-tails on his forehead. He had his feet resting on the edge of coffee table.

'This isn't for you.'

'Just drop the bag at the door and go.' Reggie squinted, struggling to see the television from the glare of the sun.

'Several large forest fires are burning in Dorset,' the news reporter announced just as Agnes clicked the television off.

'What are you playing at? The football is about to start,' he snapped.

'Shouldn't you be at work, Reggie?' She looked him up and down.

'Do you not know that there's a recession on? I got laid off.' She dropped her bag down onto the table in front of his feet, knocking a crisp packet onto the floor 'It's a good thing you've got someone to support you, eh?'

'You think you can walk into my house and speak to me like that?' Reggie asked, as he picked up his fag from a chipped tea plate. He took a long drag.

'I'm not scared of you,' she rebuked. She was wearing a pink top that made her look like she was a sausage about to burst, Reggie thought.

'Well, you should be.' Reggie replied, blowing the smoke out his mouth in the shape of an 'o'.

'If Moira wasn't out there working every hour, you'd be out on the street.' Agnes looked around the room. Reggie followed her gaze from the peeling mould-peppered wallpaper, battered pre-war furniture and the fist-shaped holes in the wall. The only modernish thing was the small black-and-white telly that sat between them.

'State of this place. My sister really married beneath her.'

'Right.' Reggie slid his feet from the table. 'No one talks to me like that.'

'After the accident, it wasn't just you that suffered the loss, Reggie. I loved him too.'

'Shut it.' He waved a hand at her. 'Don't talk about it.'

'No, you need to hear this. You've changed so much. You used to be . . .'

'Don't.' He looked away and stubbed out his cigarette. 'You were nice.'

'I'm not that person anymore.' He clenched his fists. 'Not after—'

'I loved him too, like a son.'

'Aye,' he scoffed. 'That's only because you can't have any of your own. No wonder no one wants you.' It looked like she was blinking back tears. Reggie smiled at the hurt that tightened her face.

'That might be true,' she replied. 'At least I haven't turned out like you though.'

Reggie scoffed. 'What do you mean by that?'

'Maybe this time, she'll leave you.'

'No, she won't,' he countered.

'I know what you did, Reggie.' She gave him a knowing smile and spoke to him with that almost sing-song tone she used when she knew she was scoring a point.

'What are you talking about?'

'I followed you.'

He made a clicking sound. 'You shouldn't have done that.' The pounding in his chest intensified. 'You're just jealous. Your husband wouldnae stick around.'

'That's not it at all.'

'Aye, and can you blame him?'

Agnes looked him up and down. 'You think Moira will keep you around when she finds out about your little bit on the side?'

'Whatever you think you saw. It's wrong.'

'Not this time.'

'No.'

'All the times you haven't let her go out of the house and see friends? And you were?'

'It's different, she's an alcoholic.'

'No, she's not.'

'I'm just trying to look after her. Do what's best for her.'

'You've never done that.' She stabbed a finger towards him.

3

'You can't tell her; she's had enough upset.' He motioned to the silver photo frame above the fireplace. 'You'd break her. She'd end up in the nut house.'

'She deserves a loving husband, not you.'

Reggie shook his head. 'I won't let you tell her.'

'You can't stop me.'

He grabbed her arm and pulled her towards him, feeling her warm breath on his face. She looked at him wide-eyed. Squirming, he tightened his grip. Squeezing his fingers around her arm, his fingers sank into her flesh. He could feel her heartbeat. She looked up at him, open mouthed. Terror draining the colour from her face. 'Just keep your big mouth shut, Agnes, that's all you need to do.' He spun her around towards the door to shove her out. He felt her body tighten, resisting him.

'This isn't going to help anything, Reggie,' Agnes pleaded. She twisted around so that she was facing him again and managed to wriggle her arm free from him.

'You're nothing but a pathetic bully, Reggie. You've hurt Moira. I've seen the bruises.' She looked down at the red hand mark that blotted her arm.

'You know nothing about me,' Reggie retorted, dragging a hand through his damp hair. He stabbed a finger at her chest. 'You wouldn't dare to put this on me, if you did.'

'I'm going to walk out of this flat.' She stepped backwards, holding her forearm. 'What's happened to you?' Agnes looked him up and down, loathing curling her lips.

'It's hardly surprising, is it?' He pulled away swallowing a painful lump that lodged in his throat. He wanted to look at the picture frame on the mantle again but resisted the urge.

She looked at it though, her features softening. The sweltering sun streamed through the billowing curtain, illuminating the dust in the air.

'Just get out,' he muttered. 'Get out before I do something that you'll regret.'

'I'm going, Reggie.' She shook her head and turned on her heels.

He listened to her shoes clicking on the bare floorboards in the hall, then the front door slammed shut.

Alone again. Reggie's heart roared in his chest, fire burning in his stomach. He clenched his fists and bit down hard on his lip until he tasted metal. He closed his eyes, trying to shift his thoughts. No good. He grabbed the table and upended it, the corner snapping and splintering on impact. Foamy lager leaked out onto the carpet. This was all her fault.

A thud filled the silence. He peeled back the nets and leaned out to get a look. A Ford Cortina was stopped in the middle of the street, the driver's side door was open. It took him a moment to notice it, for his brain to register what he was seeing. Agnes was lying on the street in a twisted heap, next to the metal bumper. The driver was kneeling by her head. The windscreen was shattered and sparkled in the sun.

'Call an ambulance!' the driver was shouting. 'Someone do something! Hurry please!'

For the first time that day Reggie felt a smile tug at his lips. Maybe his luck was finally changing.

CHAPTER ONE

November 1977

'Awrite, love?' A pensioner who reminded Helen Carter of Old Man Steptoe winked and flashed her a gummy smile. 'Fancy going for a wee drink?'

Shaking her head, she retrieved her warrant card from her duffle jacket. 'Not unless you fancy one down at the station.'

The old man waved a hand and disappeared into the pub.

She stepped back into the doorway of the takeaway for warmth, underneath a flashing neon fish sign. It had been a long time since she'd been out on a Friday night. She watched drinkers drift in and out of the bar opposite. A laughing couple holding hands brushed past her and into the takeaway. Helen slipped a glance at the queue; DC Terry McKinley was finally in the process of being served and was pointing to the menu above the server's head. The smell of chips drifted up her nose, making her stomach rumble. This would be the first thing she'd eaten all day, apart from a few leftover chocolate orange cremes. She blew into her hands and stomped on the spot, as the bitter evening breeze whipped through her.

'I've been looking forward to this all day.' McKinley handed her a newspaper bundle of fish and chips, and walked out onto the street. The chill made smoke of his breath. He was wearing a green cord jacket and a white shirt. The wind caught his blond hair and whipped it back and forth.

'You remember the sauce?' Helen asked, peeking into her parcel and tearing a bit of batter from her fish.

'Of course,' he smiled, peeling open his paper and stuffing a chip into his mouth.

'And the salt?'

'Aye,' his shoulder brushed hers, as he started down the Royal Mile. A Ford Escort trundled past, bouncing off the cobbles and releasing a plume of exhaust fumes into the air. A second pub to the left of them hit Helen with a burst of warmth, along with sound of cheers and drunken laughter and fag smoke.

'I'm glad I'm off duty now.' He motioned to where two drunken men staggered out, Helen dodged around them.

'I don't want to be dealing with that lot when it all kicks off,' he continued.

'Who is on duty?'

'I'm not sure actually.'

The mile-long street in the old town was lined with little independent shops, most of which she hadn't been in, and pubs. The ancient, spiralling buildings also housed a large proportion of Edinburgh's residents in tenements above. The street was punctuated by nooks and crannies, closes and courtyards. Behind them, Edinburgh Castle dominated the landscape. It was a downhill walk towards the North Bridge.

'How are you feeling?' McKinley chewed on a chip as he spoke.

'It's nice to be out. I was going stir crazy in there.' The warmth of her meal radiated into her hands.

'When I first started on the beat, I worked these streets.' McKinley bobbed his head towards an inky-blue police box across the road.

'I thought you came from Traffic.'

'I'm talking about before that.'

Helen thought back to her early days in Glasgow. It wasn't a time she'd enjoyed with the poverty from industries shutting, spiralling violence and razor gangs. 'Thanks for doing this.'

'What's that?'

'Just keeping me company, being here for me.'

'There used to be a lovely old woman in one of the tenements, she used to make us cups of tea and biscuits on a frosty night.'

'You'll not get anything like that now,' Helen chided.

'No,' he shrugged and slipped a glance over to the tenements. 'That old woman must be long dead now.'

'That's a cheery thought.'

'Sorry.'

'Don't be. I'm just in a weird mood.' She sighed and gazed up at the bruised evening sky. Any moment now it looked set to pour with rain. 'It does feel strange going back to work tomorrow.'

'Do you think you're ready?'

A police siren erupted from the quiet, Helen listened to it fade away, and she thought about what they would be attending to.

'My supper's getting cold. Fancy getting a taxi back to your flat?' McKinley asked.

'Do you not want to walk? We're not that far away.'

He blew out a sigh.

'Could get the bus?'

He turned to look at her and smiled, 'A bus might not let us on with these and don't worry, I won't keep you up all night.' He reached out and gave her hand a squeeze. It felt warm, comforting. The aroma of his *Hai Karate* aftershave filled the gap between them.

'You don't need to worry about me, you know.' Helen's stomach knotted, and her heart quickened.

He hesitated, as though he was thinking of what to say. 'You know that's not the only reason.'

CHAPTER TWO

Tina French needed to get home and look after her son, Ross. He'd had a raging fever before she left for work but they needed the money, so she'd had no option but to leave him there lying in bed, his forehead shiny with sweat and cheeks puffy and pink. His big blue eyes pleading with her to stay. Hopefully it wasn't that Russian flu she had heard about on the wireless. She buttoned up her woollen coat and picked up the pace, ice crunching underfoot. The overarching sense of unease trickled down her spine, which caused her steps to hasten.

The pub she worked in was on the outskirts of the housing estate. Normally, she'd cut around the scheme to get home, but not with the thick blanket of fog that creeped in. Maybe it was the cold that seeped through her jacket and made smoke out of her breath, but she was filled with a deep sense of foreboding. Adrenaline ran through her veins, and she shivered.

She looked around again. Most of the houses were in darkness, with their curtains drawn. Most people would be in bed by now. Candles flickered on the window ledge of one of the houses. Her heart palpitated, and her stomach twitched as she mustered the courage to slip another glance behind her. The street was deserted, as it normally was at this time of night. Just rows of pebble-dashed council houses on both sides. Her palms were clammy, and her handbag slipped in her grasp. They would've expected her in by now. A twig snapped, and it sounded like someone snapping their fingers.

Footsteps echoed behind her and she risked a glimpse over her shoulder — a man, head down, hands in his pockets. Tina crossed the road and started to run, her dress pulling her knees together. She stumbled a couple of times. When she looked back round again, she couldn't see his face and his hair was hidden under a hood.

Turning the corner, she lurched and crashed into the chest of another man who reached out and caught her arm, stopping her from tripping over.

'I'm sorry.' She spluttered and wiggled her arm free, her cheeks burning red. 'I didn't see you there.'

'Are you all right?' He looked at her with big brown eyes and smiled. A friendly smile that made creases of the corners of his eyes.

'I'm fine,' Tina said, stepping backwards to get some space.

'You don't seem it.'

'I am fine,' Tina repeated more forcefully. 'I just thought . . . There was someone behind me.'

The man stepped around her and shook his head. A look of concern furrowing his brow. 'There's no one there. It's dangerous out here at this time of night. Let me walk you home.'

'It's okay.' Tina held her bag to her chest and started to walk as fast as she could.

'I don't mind,' he broke into a jog to catch up with her. 'God forbid, what if someone was following you.'

'It's not far.' She slipped a glance at his left hand.

He must've noticed because he wiggled his fingers. 'My wife died of cancer.'

'I'm sorry,' Tina mustered.

'I don't think she'd be happy if I left you to walk these streets alone. Don't you read the papers?'

Tina didn't answer. She read them. It was less than a mile from where a prostitute had been murdered and dumped on wasteland, and the police didn't seem to be making any progress.

'You'll be doing me a favour, anyway. Giving me some company.'

'Are you sure?'

'My children are at a party overnight, and I don't know what to do with myself. It's their first time . . .' He walked along beside her.

'How many do you have?' she asked. He had a strong Edinburgh twang, but it sounded to Tina like he was putting the accent on.

'I just have the two little ones.' He slipped out a pair of black gloves from his pocket. 'It's so cold out here tonight, isn't it?'

'I guess so.'

'That's a lovely necklace.'

'Thanks,' she touched the gold cross around her neck. She could feel his eyes on her.

'Is it special to you?'

'Yes.'

He kept up with her pace, as they entered the path out of the estate. Trees lined both sides of the trail. Somewhere nearby an owl hooted in one of the trees. She looked up but couldn't see where it came from. This was the quickest way out of the estate. Presumably, it had been a railway line at some point, there seemed to be a lot of them around Edinburgh. Beyond this track, the bus stop was across the road. She slipped another glance over her shoulder; no one behind them. His breath quickened and they got halfway along the path when he spoke again.

'This won't take long, Tina.'

How do you know my name?' she asked, voice trembling.

The man looked around. 'This would be a nice place to walk in the summer.'

'How do you know my name? Who are you?'

'I've been watching you,' he replied. 'You weren't in the pub last week and I was starting to get worried.' He gave her a genuine smile.

'My son was ill. I need to get home to him, please.' Her heart thumped in her chest and felt like it was going to burst. 'I just want to get home to my son, that's all.'

'I didn't want you to leave after all my planning.'

'What planning?'

'You don't remember me, do you?' he asked.

'Should I?'

'You laughed in my face when I asked to buy you a drink.' He whispered into her ear. 'I saw the look of disgust on your face for me.'

'I didn't . . . I don't . . . I don't remember doing that?' Shook her head. 'I wouldn't, I'm not like that.'

'Exactly a month ago now.'

'I don't drink with customers. I just do my work and go home.'

'You think I'm weak and pathetic.'

'No, it's not that, we can go get a drink tomorrow then, if that's what you want? Please, I have a son that I need to get home for.'

'I really like your hair. You should wear it down more often.'

'Stop, please.' Tears stung the back of her eyes.

'There's just something inside me.'

Tina swallowed hard, her eyes darting everywhere, tears stinging. Ross would be waiting for her. She thought of him tucked up in bed with his teddies. This couldn't be happening to her. She could see the streetlight at the end of the path. If she could get to the main road . . .

'I tried to stop.'

'Then stop.'

'I can't,' he shrugged.

'Everything is in your control,' Tina pleaded.

It was now or never. She ran. Pounded the tarmac as fast as she could. Puddle water soaked through her shoes. Her knees burning. Gasping for breath.

He grabbed her by her hair. She screamed but no sound came out. She kicked and thrashed. Bit down on flesh. He yelped. She punched out, connecting with his ribs. No use. He pulled her around, ripped her necklace from her throat and shoved her down onto the concrete. Pain shot up her legs and spine.

Why was he doing this to her? What had she done to deserve this? A sob burst from her throat.

A moment later, the mallet silenced her.

CHAPTER THREE

Detective Sergeant Helen Carter awoke from another nightmare and sat up, rubbing her damp forehead. Pain shooting through her ribs and spine. She gritted her teeth and waited for the pain to ease. There was no noise coming from the flat — aside from the ordinary everyday sounds you'd expect. The heating system groaned, and footsteps creaked from the flat above. She clambered from the bed and grabbed her dressing gown from the chair, wincing as she slipped it over her shoulder. It was still dark outside as she headed towards the kitchen. Swallowing hard, her throat felt like sandpaper. According to the clock, it was eleven thirty and she had been asleep less than an hour, but even that was good going for her. Her pain medication was sat on the worktop along with the remnants of the fish and chip dinner that she had shared with Terry McKinley. Someone cleared their throat behind her, and Helen jumped.

'You gave me a heart attack!' Helen exclaimed.

A smile twitched McKinley's lip. 'Sorry.' Exhaustion dimmed his lilac-blue eyes, and he was rubbing his neck like he had fallen asleep in an awkward position. His overgrown strawberry blond hair flopped onto his forehead. 'Thought I'd come through and see how you were doing.'

'I thought you were going to go home once I went to bed.' Helen knew with his six-foot frame he wouldn't get any sleep on her two-seater sofa.

'I was, but you seemed in so much pain, I didn't want to leave you.'

Helen winced. 'I'm fine.'

'You don't look it.'

'Terry, you should go home. Get some sleep.'

He shook his head. 'No chance.'

Helen relented. 'Fancy a drink then?' She hobbled to the cupboard. 'I've got tea, coffee, or something stronger perhaps?' Her eyes fell to the bottle of Blue Nun on the bottom shelf.

'I'll give that a go.' He motioned to the bottle.

Helen rummaged through the cupboards for a packet of biscuits she kept for visitors and arranged a couple of Jaffa Cakes on a plate.

'Take a seat.' She motioned to the mahogany table behind her.

'Are you still planning on doing this place up?' He made a show of looking around the kitchen.

'I might sell it,' she replied. 'But it's close to work.'

McKinley took a seat. He rested his arm on the radiator.

'Ted always hated this place,' she explained, pouring the drink into two glasses. 'I was meant to move into his townhouse. I was round there a lot of the time anyway.'

'Is it over with you two?'

'I can't see any way back now.' She handed him a glass and forced a smile. 'I think leaving him at the airport was pretty final.'

He took a sip and looked like he was thinking of the right words.

'It's fine,' she carried on. 'It would've been a mistake to marry him. At least we didn't get that far.' Helen sat down opposite him but didn't bother with her drink. It wouldn't mix with her medication anyway. 'He made it pretty clear that if we were going to tie the knot then I'd need to leave the police.

For a moment I was tempted . . . but I've worked so hard to get to where I am. Waiting for Ted to come home every evening, having his dinner on the table — it just isn't me.'

McKinley took another sip, looking like he didn't know what to make of it all — either the wine or what she was telling him.

'What about Sally?' Helen asked, between mouthfuls of biscuit. 'I don't think she'd like you being here.' It wasn't the first time she'd broached the subject, but she still wasn't quite sure if they were completely off.

He shrugged. 'I wouldn't worry about her. This is quite nice,' he said, holding up his glass. 'Quite fresh.'

'Ted likes it . . . a bit too much sometimes.'

'Aye.' McKinley slid the glass away. 'I heard he had a reputation for that.'

'Unfortunately—' Helen retrieved the empty glass — 'he needed it when work got too much for him.'

'I'll get that.' McKinley took it from her hand.

'Thanks, there's more in the bottle if you want it.'

'No, it's all right.' McKinley replied, rinsing the glass in the sink. 'It's not really my thing.'

'Ted might've left a bottle of something else in the cupboard.'

McKinley shook his head. 'I keep thinking about what happened after the picture house murder.'

'So do I.' Helen tugged at a crease in her dressing gown.

He placed the glass on the drying rack. 'You haven't been the same since.'

'I don't want to think about it really.' Helen muttered.

'I'm sorry, I didn't mean to,' he sighed and sat back down. 'I just thought—'

Helen tucked a stray strand of hair behind her ear. 'I thought I was going to die.' Helen's eyes narrowed. 'Slow and painfully. I know you think I should talk about it, but I can't. Not yet.'

McKinley sat back in his chair and placed his hand on top of hers. 'But you didn't.'

'That's something I suppose.' Helen blinked back tears and looked up at the ceiling. 'I'm going to go back to bed and get some sleep.'

'Good idea,' McKinley replied. 'Do you have to go back on shift tomorrow?'

'I can't put it off any longer.' She flicked a glance around the dated kitchen, from the old-fashioned tiles that looked like they belonged in some Victorian bathroom to the fat-stained net that hung against the window. 'The longer I leave it, the harder it'll get and DI Craven is not as sympathetic as you.'

McKinley arched an eyebrow.

'I just want to get on with things now and put all this behind me.'

McKinley didn't look convinced. 'Have you heard anything more from that Stanley?'

Helen shook her head.

'I thought he'd disappear.' McKinley sighed. 'He seemed like that type that was always on the move.'

'Maybe. He wasn't charged with anything and there was nothing left to say.'

'I suppose.' McKinley stifled a yawn.

'Let's try to get some sleep.' Helen brushed crumbs from the table and stood up. 'I've got a double bed. You won't get any sleep on the sofa.' She motioned to the kitchen window. 'It's started to rain now.'

CHAPTER FOUR

'This is the only way. It will work. I promise you,' he rubbed her shoulder.

'I don't know.' Moira McKenzie shrugged him off, a frown creasing her brow. She rubbed the condensation from her wine glass and blew a stray strand of mousy brown hair from her face. A classical record spun on the turntable; she didn't know the name of it. Elvis was more her thing. Most of the music from the record was being drowned out by the heavy rain that battered the windows. She swallowed hard to push back the words that wanted to spill from her. She took another sip of wine. 'I think Reggie suspects,' she muttered. 'No, I'm sure he does.' She could feel the familiar burn at the back of her eyes and the butterflies in her stomach. Reggie's words echoed in her ears. *Worthless. No one would ever want you. Mutton dressed as lamb. Pathetic.* Each one like a punch to the gut and he was right.

'Are you sure?' he asked, in that soft voice that always made her want to spill her guts to him.

She considered the question. 'It's been so hard since Harold died. I didn't think I'd find any kind of happiness again, but I have with you. Something always goes wrong, every time I'm happy.' She tore at a nail until it stung.

'There is no way he can know. You're just putting your own guilt onto him. It's natural.'

She nodded. 'I keep thinking about the time we had a picnic on the pier. It was just so warm, and the sea sparkled. I've never seen it like that before.'

'Well, we can do that again. I even want to take you to New York.'

'I've never been on a plane before.' She sighed. 'I've never even been abroad before.'

'Oh, you'll love it, I know you will.'

'I can't. If Reggie does know, he'll kill me.' Moira shook her head. 'You really don't know what he's like.' She pulled back her sleeve, showing a green-blue bruise around her wrist.

'Oh my god!'

'It's in his eyes.' She paused to think of the right words. 'The way he looks at me. It's hard to explain.' She shivered thinking about his moods and how quickly they could change.

'A man like Reggie.' He grimaced. 'He would do something if he really suspected. No,' he reached out and squeezed her hand, 'that's just the guilt talking. You're just feeling guilty because you're finally happy and you deserve to be.'

Moira sighed and looked at the crystal chandelier that hung above them, and the oil paintings that adorned the walls. She'd never imagined herself in a lovely townhouse like this, with big bay windows and a garden, on the other side of Edinburgh.

'No. I can't do this.' She put her glass down on the coffee table. 'I need to go home.'

'Don't.' He looked at her wide-eyed. 'I don't understand—'

She dragged the heel of her hand down her face. 'We're both married. This can only end badly.' Moira stood up and lifted her jacket from the coat stand. 'What happens when your wife is back from her mother's?' Her eyes pleading with his, willing him to say the words that she wanted to hear. Say something to stop her going home. She swallowed back the painful lump in her throat. 'When your wife gets back, I'll be forgotten.'

He lowered the volume on the record player, shaking his head. 'That's not true. I just don't want to tell her about us until she gets better. It would knock her back . . . We've been through all this. I promise, once her treatment is over.'

'Do you even think she'll get better?' Moira asked, slipping on her jacket. 'You didn't think so before.'

He stepped towards her, arms outstretched. 'Don't be like that. I can't just walk away from her now and you wouldn't want me to.'

'I should go.'

'I meant everything I said earlier.' His cool fingers brushed against her hand. 'Will I drop you home, then?' He frowned and his forehead creased in that way she liked. 'We can meet for dinner next week. We could go to Aperitif again?'

She looked away. What was she thinking, a good-looking, educated man — what the hell would he see in her? This was like a dream and all dreams end when you wake up to reality. Dreams become nightmares. Buttoning her duffle, she forced a smile. 'Drop me home.' She kept her gaze on the red carpet and blinked back tears, not wanting to look at the wedding photographs that adorned the mantelpiece and the pictures of his wife that always seemed to be staring at her.

'If that's what you really want.' He picked up his keys from the coffee table. 'I wish you would stay, though.'

Moira twisted the thin gold band on her finger. 'I can't.' She should be home waiting for Reggie.

'After all the things you've told me he's done to you. All the hurt he's caused you. It's only going to get worse. He'll never change.'

'What else am I meant to do?'

'Let me protect you.'

'He'll never let me leave. He'd kill you and then me.'

'Then let me help. I'll take my chances with a man like Reggie.' He stroked her cheek with the back of his hand. 'I'm not scared of him.'

'You should be.' She pulled away. 'Take me home.'

* * *

20

Moira clambered out of the Rover a few streets away from the flat, despite his protests that it wasn't safe. Reggie was right, anyway. She sobbed. No one would want her. She reached into her pocket for her tissues and dabbed at the mascara that trailed down her face. Reggie would probably still be at the pub, so there would be enough time to get cleaned up before he got home. He was always there on a Friday night before he'd come home reeking of lager and overly friendly. It was the only time that he would be nice to her now.

Shivering, she wrapped her arms around her body. Rain seeped through her trousers and trickled down the nape of her neck. She sniffled and looked over her shoulder. She was enclosed by council flats on both sides of the street; only a few lights were on and the lamp posts glowed orange but didn't seem to cast much light. The screaming howl of a fox filled the silence and she whipped around but couldn't see anything. She walked faster towards home. Her stomach twitched when she looked up at her flat and saw the bathroom light on.

Moira closed the front door. Rushing water and banging pipes trailed from the bathroom. The door was ajar and she crept towards it. She saw Reggie hunched over the sink scrubbing at his arms with a pink towel. Strange, as she couldn't remember them having any pink towels. The sleeves of his white shirt rolled up to just underneath his elbows and his brown hair flopped over his forehead. She stood at the gap in the doorway. The sink was stained red. His head snapped towards her. Moira gasped and stumbled backwards.

'Why are you back? I thought your mother was sick,' he snarled.

'Oh my god! Are you hurt?' Moira mustered, feeling the bile rise in her throat, as the metallic smell drifted up her nostrils. There was something about the sight of blood that just made her want heave or pass out.

Reggie shook his head. 'Nothing for you to worry about.'
'How?'

'You dinnae want to know,' he spat and threw a towel at her. 'Wash this.'

'I can't,' she sobbed.

'Get it washed in bleach and clean in here too.'

'How did you hurt yourself? Have you stopped the bleeding?'

'As if you care.'

'Where are you bleeding from? You need to go to the hospital. Have you called the police?'

'Am I on *Mastermind*?' He clenched his jaw. 'Just dae as you're telt before I lose my rag.' He stabbed a finger at her. 'Make sure you mop the floor in here too. I need it all spotless.' He shoved past her and she heard the bedroom door open.

After she had cleaned the bathroom, Moira peeled her jacket from her shoulders and slumped down into the arm-chair. Her knuckles were stinging from the cleaning fluid that left her hands red and blotchy. By the time she had finished and done the washing, Reggie had gone to bed. She closed her eyes and heard the soft mumbles of his snores. How could he sleep after what she had just cleaned up? She couldn't follow him to bed, that was for sure. She climbed up from the armchair, grabbed a half-empty can of Tartan from the dresser and downed the warm lager in one gulp, and her eyes fell to the *Evening News* that lay next to it.

Picture House Murder Solved.

She needed another drink. Crushing the can in her hand, she wandered through to the kitchen. Her temples throbbed, and even though the blood was gone, she could still smell it, taste it, every time she swallowed. She envied Reggie. The way he never had trouble sleeping, never seemed to have trouble forcing any of the horrible things from his mind. She picked up a bottle of red from the worktop, poured some into a mug and sat down, glancing at a couple of books she'd got from the library which were lying in the centre of the table.

Reggie cleared his throat behind her. She had her back to him but could imagine the look on his face if she'd woken him up. From the corner of her eye, she could see him take a step forward.

'What are you doing up?' he asked, his voice soft.

'I . . . couldn't sleep.'

He placed his hand on her shoulder. 'It's no' good for you.'

'I'll go in a minute. I've finished the bathroom.'

'I'm sorry,' he frowned, crinkling his nose. 'I shouldn't have been so . . .'

Moira straightened. 'It's fine.'

He grimaced as he sat down opposite her and rubbed his side. Two red scratches peeked out from under his sleeve.

Moira glared at him. He looked like he was thinking of what to say next. She made a move to stand.

'Wait.' He put his hand over hers. 'We both need to be honest with each other.'

The hairs on the back of her neck bristled.

'What happened tonight . . . well, it was because I was so upset about your affair.' He carried on. 'It's broke my heart. This was your fault.'

'I'm not—'

'Don't. I saw you. I saw you with *him*.' He jabbed at his temple. 'How do you think that makes me feel?'

'What are you going to do?' She felt her body tighten ready to take the blows he'd often rain down on her.

'Nothing.'

'Nothing,' Moira scoffed.

'Nothing — if everything stops.' He reached into his dressing gown pocket and pulled out a little gold chain with a cross. 'I got you this.'

'Why?'

'I want to try again. I want us to be like we were before.'

Moira made no move to take the scuffed little chain. 'Where did you get this?'

'I know it's not much.' Reggie looked like he was trying to be careful with his words.

She wasn't even religious, nor was Reggie. They'd only got married because she'd fallen pregnant, and it was the done thing.

'It might not be your ideal bit of jewellery, but it was all I could afford.'

'No, Reggie, it's—'

'Everything that happened tonight wouldn't have happened if you'd been a decent wife — the wife that I needed. I wouldn't have been so angry . . .'

'I'm sorry. I can't do this.'

'You're always sorry.' He stood up and walked over to the window, keeping his back to her. 'I try so hard to make you happy. Given you everything.'

She saw the peeling wallpaper, along with the space in the kitchen where the washing machine used to be. 'I made a mistake, Reggie. It won't happen again.'

'Why have you always got tae annoy me, Moira?'

'I don't mean to.'

Reggie picked up the photo of their son on the windowsill, brushing dust off the silver frame with his thumb. 'We had everything then, eh?' He put the photo back. 'He wouldnae be happy with the way you're behaving.'

'I miss him too, Reggie. Not a day goes by—'

'Nah,' he scoffed. 'It doesnae matter now, does it? He's dead. Nothing's going to change that. Nothing will bring my boy back.'

He turned to face her, a sneer twisting his lip.

'Reggie, please. Let's just have a quiet night.'

He tutted and grabbed one of her books from the table. He flung it against the wall where it landed with a thud in the sink. Smiling, he picked up the mug of wine from the table and emptied it onto her lap.

'Sorry, Reggie. I don't want you to be upset.' The wine seeped through her denim skirt and soaked her legs. 'I'm so sorry.' She sobbed. 'I've struggled since Agnes's accident. I really have.'

Reggie had his hand braced to slap her. 'You don't think I have too? I'm the one that saw her get run over.'

'I'm sorry, Reggie. I'm clumsy.' She shook and swallowed back tears. 'I'll stop and do anything you want. Just don't . . .'

'I know,' he snarled and knelt in front of her, putting his hand on her shoulder on top of the bruise. 'You know just how to wind me up. You're trying to play games with me.'

She bit down on her lip. Ready for the familiar sting.

'You're always daeing ma heid in.' He squeezed her shoulder as he stood back up.

The dog in the flat below was barking wildly.

'Do you want me to get you a drink, Reggie? We can see if there's a film on the telly?'

'A drink? That's your answer to bloody everything.' He rubbed a hand through his perm of black hair. 'You know I dinnae like you drinking, but you do it anyway. You know I don't think it ladylike behaviour.'

'It was just an idea, Reggie.'

'You always have to have an idea, don't you? You cannae have a bloody good one, though, can you?'

'I'm sorry.' Moira clambered up and moved towards the sink. He followed her. She put the mug in the basin and ran the dishcloth under the tap to clean her skirt. The maroon stain wouldn't budge.

'I didnae mean to say that you dinnae have good ideas. It's just been bad at work. The production's no' where it's needed and now, we've lost another contract.'

She nodded and dabbed her skirt. He never lasted more than a few months at any job. 'But you've lost contracts before and we've got by. Indestructible — that's what you said. We always get by somehow. We can ask my mum and dad for some money to tide us over like before.'

'Why? What hiv you been saying to them?'

'Nothing.' Moira shuddered.

'You better keep it that way.' He stabbed a finger into the small of her back. 'I'll find the money fae somewhere. We're no' doing that again, I ken you dinnae understand all of this but it's different this time. It really is.'

'I'll help you Reggie, whatever you need.'

'I'm not going to let you leave, Moira. Marriage is for life. Till death do us part.'

CHAPTER FIVE

It was now or never. Helen sighed, standing in front of the mirror, surveying her reflection. The water for the shower rumbled through the pipes and she could hear McKinley banging about in the kitchen. If he was looking for breakfast, he wasn't going to find much. She stepped closer to the mirror, her skin was dry and blotchy from the icy wind that whipped through the city. Lack of sleep hadn't helped the purple bags under her eyes. McKinley had snored and tossed and turned for most of the night. She slipped on her brown slacks with the loose waistband and teamed it with a baggy yellow sweater. Comfort over fashion today. A quick coating of eyeshadow, mascara and red lipstick, and she was good to go. She slipped on her jacket as she headed into the kitchen with the dregs of her coffee, her heart began to race. She rubbed a clammy hand through her hair and felt her throat close. A glass of water, that's what she needed. She ran the tap and held her hand under the cool water, the bottle of Valium caught her attention. She poured a glass of water then slipped down one of the pills. Her breath quickened. Blood rushing to her ears. She slumped down in the chair, closing her eyes, praying for the pill to take effect.

'Was going to make some toast but there's no bread.'

Helen dragged a hand down her face. 'I've not been shopping in a while.'

'I'll see you at the station. I need to pick up some stuff and change before the start of my shift.' He slipped on his jacket.

When she was finally alone in the flat, Helen crossed to the worktop and dumped a teabag into a cup, the headache behind the back of her eyes easing.

* * *

Already running late for the start of her shift, she hoped that she'd be able to pick up the pace once she got past Bruntsfield and the morning rush hour traffic. Helen slipped the car into second gear, then stopped at some roadworks. She drummed the steering wheel. Traffic in Edinburgh was over-congested, and there constantly seemed to be roadworks and building going on in every other street. Giving up on that, she clicked on the radio. The morning news bulletin intermixed with static filled the Mini. Cars snaked around the curve in the road, then split into two lanes as they got further along towards Lothian Road. Rain sprayed the windscreen. She took the right onto Princes Street and was slowed by a double decker bus that pulled out, causing her to brake hard. It was going to be one of those days.

Turning into the station, she cursed under her breath. In her usual parking space sat a rusted lime green Ford Cortina. She knew who it belonged to, DC Randall. Helen winced. She had been hoping to avoid him this morning. He was normally on the graveyard shift. He was one of those officers that had seen it all, done it all and knew it all. Too bad he still had the poorest arrest record. Circling around, she found a space on the far side of the car park next to a van. Fettes police station was just over three years old, an ugly concrete flat-roofed lump of a building. From this angle she could see the CID window. The blinds had been raised and the window opened a crack.

She grabbed her handbag from the passenger seat and threw up the hood of her duffle coat, as the wind blew the morning drizzle against her face. It felt like a mile walk before she was inside the warmth of the reception area. The staff sergeant, Robert Keaton, looked up as she passed the reception and gave her a nod. It wasn't much of one but still, that was a first.

Chatter from the CID room leaked out into the corridor. Helen had her hand braced on the handle. She took a deep breath to steady herself from climbing the three flights of stairs. The door swung open, and she met eyes with a flustered-looking Detective Inspector Jack Craven.

'You're late,' he brushed past her. He was wearing his tweed jacket with the elbow patches, and his brown hair looked windswept. It didn't look like he'd been in the office long either. He was closely followed by DC Terry McKinley, who gave her a smile.

'What's going on?' Helen asked.

'Keep your jacket on', Craven replied, carrying on down the corridor. She had to jog to keep up with him.

'There's been a body found.'

'Call came in about ten minutes ago.' McKinley added, as he scrambled to slip on his oversized jacket, an old-fashioned looking parka which was at least a size too big.

Grimacing, Helen held pressure to her ribs as she was forced to take the stairs two at a time to keep up.

A few minutes later and they were bundled into the Ford Granada, wheels spinning as they shot out of the car park. Helen was thankful to get the front passenger seat, as she could see from the rear-view mirror that DCs Randall and McKinley looked sandwiched together, and Randall was elbowing McKinley for space. She kicked away some of the Marathon and Opal Fruit wrappers that stuck to her boot in the footwell and squirmed in the seat, struggling to find the most comfortable position. It wasn't long before the smell of wet dog tickled her nostrils and Helen rolled down the window a crack.

The car juddered as Craven pressed on the accelerator.

'How far away is it?' Helen asked.

'About twenty miles or something,' he fished in the pockets of his jacket, pulling out his cigarettes, fumbling with the packet.

Her shoulders tensed, ready to grab the steering wheel as the car jutted to the right then left. She folded her arms to resist the urge.

Relief prickled Helen when twenty minutes later he took a left turn onto a single-track gravel road. The derelict hospital was just at the end of this one, according to the *A-Z* spread out on the dash.

A long, single-storey, run-down building came into Helen's view. It looked like it sprawled off for miles in both directions. The bushes around the entrance had been left to grow wild, and roof tiles had fallen onto the path. The main hospital had been constructed around a hundred years ago as a tuberculosis sanatorium but had since been shut down.

There were a couple of other, more modern-looking buildings around the main one, with smashed windows and cracked brickwork. The roof of one of these side buildings had completely collapsed, leaving only the chimney stack. All the windows of the main building were boarded up, and the door was covered with a guardrail.

According to the newspapers, this land was going to be used for a new village, but no work had taken place as far as she could see. She read, '*DANGER! KEEP OUT!*' and '*WATCH OUT! GUARD DOGS PATROLLING*'. However, the signs hadn't put off the local kids who were still sneaking onto the grounds on Saturday nights. According to the graffiti, '*Stevie Boy wiz here*' just last week.

They drove through the entranceway, churning up gravel. A couple of stray bits cracked off the windscreen. Overgrown bushes, bits of rubble, glass bottles and wrappers lined both sides of the road. Around the back, two uniformed officers stood guard, their car partially blocking the track. Craven stubbed out his cigarette and parked up next to an old wooden hut. Somewhere nearby, a train rumbled past.

'Right, where's the party?' Craven asked as he climbed out of the car.

The ground was soggy from the morning's storm and mud squelched under Helen's boots as she trudged up the track. Scenes of crime officers had cordoned off both sides of the road. A raindrop hit the back of her neck, and she rubbed it away. The earlier downpour would've also washed away a lot of evidence, she thought as she looked up at the ashen sky.

On entering the hut, she absorbed the sight in front of her. Previously, the dead woman had been wrapped in plastic sheeting. Now, she was enclosed in a body bag. From what Helen knew about the stages of decomposition, it didn't look like she had been dead long. Rigor mortis had finished in the corpse. So, she guessed she'd been dead a day or two at the most, but the SOCO would be able to give a more accurate guess of time of death. The smell of it stung her nostrils, a sickly scent that clung to everything. It was a combination of rotting fruit mixed with the aroma of a meat-rendering plant.

Helen had to force herself to keep looking at the woman in the open bag. The woman looked to be in her late thirties. She had no jewellery, no tights, and a pair of black plimsolls on her feet — or were they jazz shoes? Helen was sure that's what they were called. She looked like a dancer, doll-like. She was wearing a white knee-length dress with a daisy pattern. She didn't know much about fashion, but the dress looked old. It was like something her mother used to make for herself from old curtains. The woman's nails were perfectly manicured with a pale pink nail polish but the cuticles around them were bitten, and there were no obvious fibres underneath them. Bruises peppered her bare arms. She was so skinny, the elbow and shoulder jutted out of the skin. Her narrow lips were blue, and her neck had a thin red-purple bruise around it and there were nicks at both sides of the neck. Maybe she'd been wearing a necklace? The whites of her eyes were streaked with red. Her face looked puffy. Her wispy blonde hair clung to her forehead and was matted with blood.

The pathologist, Alex Winston walked towards them. Sweat pooled under the armpits of his white shirt. He was a portly man in his late fifties with a tendency to be overfriendly.

'Have you not retired yet?' Craven brushed past, taking in the scene.

'I could say the same to you, Jack.' Alex Winston gave a half-smile.

'Was there any ID on her? A jacket or a bag perhaps?' Helen asked.

'No, nothing, but uniform is out searching the woodland so who knows what they'll find,' Winston replied. 'There's miles of forest at the back of these old buildings.'

'What can you tell us?' Craven interjected, stifling a cough.

'Not much more than you'll already know. She has a depressed skull fracture, but I'll need further examination to determine what caused it.'

'Aye, but if you were to take a guess?' Craven asked.

Winston tutted. 'A hammer, perhaps. Something like that. There's also multiple contusions on her body.'

A crime scene photographer moved around capturing the body from different angles with expert precision.

'So, it's likely she put up a struggle then,' Helen stated, taking a step back. She had seen enough.

'Could they have happened after she died?' Craven asked. 'All these marks?'

'It's unlikely — it's difficult to bruise a corpse — but not impossible.'

'What about the ligature marks?'

'There's some grooves in the neck area.' He pointed a tobacco-stained finger towards the area. 'So, I'd say she was also strangled with something thin. A cable or cord, perhaps.'

'Could that be the cause of death?'

Winston frowned. 'I can't say for certain yet. I think it was more likely the head wound that would have been the fatal blow.'

Helen moved away for air. The wind caught her hair and whipped it across her face.

A uniformed officer who looked like he had just walked out of the police college waved a hand and offered a faint smile. 'Sorry,' he apologized. 'But I've got the details of the couple who found the body. They're waiting in the van. The girl's getting a bit overexcited . . .'

'I'll go and see.'

'Thanks.'

'What're their names?'

He looked down at his notes. 'Derek Archer and Kim Black. They're both local.'

CHAPTER SIX

'Just breathe.'

The girl, who looked no older than about seventeen, sat in the passenger side of the van, hyperventilating wildly. Her hands grasped at her blouse.

'Take a deep breath. One. Two. Three.' Helen motioned to her own breathing. 'One. Two. Three.'

The girl nodded, her face deathly white and her breath raspy. 'Keep going.' Helen guided as the girl's breath slowed and a sob broke from her body. Her brown eyes were blood-shot, and mascara and sparkly blue eyeshadow trailed down her face.

After a few more minutes she was able to speak. 'I've never seen a dead body before.' She wailed, her voice rising. 'I nearly tripped over her!'

Helen placed her hand on the girl's and softly squeezed. 'You're doing really well, just keep focussing on breathing. Nice and easy, okay?' The girl nodded and Helen turned her attention to the boy who looked equally pale but was at least calm.

'Are you able to tell me what happened?'

He nodded. 'I wish we hadn't bothered going out now.' He shoved a stray strand of brown hair from his eyes. He was still wearing his school shirt, which was unbuttoned at the collar, the shoulders specked with make-up.

'So, you went into the hospital grounds?' Helen prompted.

'A few of us like to mess about in one of the buildings over there.' He replied, tearing at a nail. 'Have a laugh.' Derek Archer cleared his throat. 'I got locked out my house, my mum's not back until late. So me and Kim were hanging about until then. That's when we found her.'

'Exactly how did you find her?'

'We were mucking about. I chased Kim up the grass and she tripped over . . .'

Kim retched at the description and Helen let go of Kim's hand just in case. 'You've both been really helpful, and this is almost over. Did you see anyone else near the scene or anything out of the ordinary?'

Kim covered her mouth.

'No, no one was around.' Derek looked to Kim for confirmation, who just nodded.

Helen made her way around the van, as she heard Kim retch again. Helen grimaced, and felt the bile rise in her own throat. The same uniformed officer that had asked her to speak to the couple smiled at her as he approached. 'You did a really good job of calming her down, I couldn't even get her to confirm her name.'

Helen sighed. It wouldn't be something that Kim would get over easily. She had learned that the hard way. The names you forget over time, but not the faces.

'Have you seen anyone hanging around the crime scene?' It wasn't unheard of for the killer to return to the scene of the crime. Sometimes she couldn't believe the number of people that would try and get past the police tape to take a shortcut home or to rubberneck at what was happening.

The officer shook his head.

'Over here!' Another constable shouted from the side of the main hospital building. He had his arm in an industrial bin and was rummaging through the contents. 'I've found something.'

Craven got there first and was peering into the bin as Helen got close. 'What have you got?'

'They don't pay me enough for this.' The constable grimaced, retrieving a small faded black leather handbag first, then a cream-coloured wool coat He held them away from his uniform and his gloves dripped water. 'The lid was up on the bin, so it's about a quarter filled with rainwater.'

Craven slipped on gloves and took the bag, holding it up until it stopped dripping. He lifted the flap and pulled out a brown leather purse. Helen put on her gloves and took it from him. A few coins, and a small black-and-white photograph. She held up the picture to catch the light. A dark-haired woman smiling with her arms around a little boy. It looked like his first day at school.

'The photograph is quite faded, but this looks like our victim.'

Craven carefully unfurled a soggy piece of paper from the bag. 'Well, if it is her then I have an address. Her name is Tina French.'

CHAPTER SEVEN

Helen kept her attention on the window until Craven parked in front of a pebble-dashed council house in the middle of a row. The house in question had a black front door with plants lining the path to the doorway. A child's bike was propped up against the wall, under what looked to be the front window. No lights were on. A vase of half-dead roses stood on the window ledge. Helen waited for a moment to gather her senses. She took a deep breath, then climbed the steps to the property. She could hear her heart thumping in her ears as she rattled the letter box. Craven cleared his throat.

A woman in her late sixties opened the door. Her wispy grey hair was pinned up with a gold hair clip and she wore an oversized green knitted cardigan. Her face dropped when she fixed eyes on Helen and Craven.

'No, you've got to be joking.'

Helen produced her warrant card. 'I'm DS Carter and this is DI Craven, can we come inside?'

'What's happened to Tina?' She slipped a tissue from up her sleeve and rubbed her nose. 'Please tell me she's okay.'

'It would be better if we could talk inside.'

'Please just tell me what's happened, where is she?'

'It would be best if we came in.' Helen took a deep breath as she crossed over the threshold. They followed the woman through to a narrow kitchen where a half-empty mug of tea and a tinfoil ashtray with three butts in it stood on the table. The window was open, and outside a couple was chattering, followed by laughter which filled the kitchen before it faded away.

'Please take a seat.' Helen guided the woman to a chair at the kitchen table.

'Are you any relation to Ms French?' Helen asked.

'I'm Tina's aunt. Please don't tell me she's been hurt.'

'What's your name?'

'Rita.'

'I'm really sorry, Rita.'

A sob escaped her frail frame. 'When was the last time you saw Tina?'

'She works in a pub; she normally gets home late, but she didn't come home last night. I phoned the police, but they said there was nothing they could do as she was over twenty-one . . .'

Helen produced the photograph from the purse and placed it on the table. 'Is this Tina?'

She picked up the evidence bag and smoothed out the plastic. Tears streamed down her cheeks. 'That's Tina. It's her favourite photograph.'

Helen exchanged a glance with Craven.

'What's happened to her?'

'I'm afraid we've found the body of a woman matching Tina's description in some derelict hospital grounds not far from Edinburgh.'

'I don't understand.' She twisted around to see Craven. 'It wasn't some kind of accident?'

Craven cleared his throat. 'No, it looks like she was the victim of an assault.'

'I can't believe this, no one would want to hurt her. She's such a lovely girl. Just ask anyone. How could this happen?'

Helen struggled to find the right words. 'Do you have a recent photo of Tina that we could have?'

'There's some photos in the little tin up there.' She pointed to a shelf in the kitchen area.

'Thank you. Do you want me to make you a fresh cup of tea?' She felt the kettle with the back of her hand. It was stone cold.

Rita nodded, and Helen filled it from the tap. The sash window above the sink looked out onto a small drying area and a block of flats with balconies.

'Where is the pub that Tina was working in?' Helen asked.

'It's not too far away. The Weary Traveller.'

'I know it. It's near the docks,' Craven admitted.

'Had Tina mentioned anything out of the ordinary? Anything at all, no matter how small.'

'I can't think of anything. It was just a normal day.'

'That's okay, I understand.' Helen replied, softly.

'I can't believe she's not going to just walk through the door.' Rita trembled. 'She worked so hard to keep this house going and pay the bills.'

'Are you able to come with us to help with identification? Or is there another family member or a friend we could ask, perhaps?'

'There's no one else, just me and Ross. He wasn't well yesterday but I sent him to school this morning to keep him occupied,' she rubbed tears away with the back of her hand. Helen placed the mug of tea in front of her.

'I don't know what I'm going to tell him.'

'Where's Ross's father?'

'Him. He ran away when Ross was little, some tart he met at work. We haven't seen hide nor hair of him since. He'll not care. I wouldn't bother with him.' She picked up the mug of tea but made no move to drink it. She made a noise, something halfway between a snort and a hiss and broke down, letting go of the mug. Helen managed to catch it before it dropped.

Craven handed Rita the box of tissues from the windowsill. Rita pulled a bundle from them and blew her nose noisily, her hands clutching at the bunched-up tissues afterwards as she peered up at him with bloodshot eyes. She reached out for his arm. 'Will you find who hurt her?'

He nodded solemnly. 'We will do our best to get justice for you.'

'I want to see her,' she replied, standing up. 'I need to see her.'

Her face had drained of colour, looking almost translucent under the unforgiving kitchen lights, and Helen had a hand ready to catch her in case she collapsed as she led her to the back of the car.

CHAPTER EIGHT

The Edinburgh City Mortuary in the old town was a short drive from the station, in theory, but as rush hour traffic started to take hold, they struggled through the temporary traffic lights, roadworks and one-way streets towards Cowgate. Rita stared silently out the window, looking like she'd aged ten years since she got into the back of the Granada. Her hands were trembling, tears trailed her cheeks as she stared out the window. Helen wound her window down a crack and closed her eyes as the gentle breeze cooled her face.

A shaky sigh heaved from Rita as they parked around the back behind a small silver chimney stack and a private ambulance. Many would pass by this structure and not realize what this building was for.

A nondescript brown block with small window at the front, it was obscured by a wall with graffiti scrawled across it and black fencing. The only giveaway was the small brass plaque on the right-hand side of the door, but you'd need to look closely to see it.

The mortuary assistant was usually overly chatty, but he must've understood the look that Helen was giving him because today he was quiet, leaving the morgue eerily silent.

She swallowed; she could taste the antiseptic as they walked to the viewing room.

It would be easy to forget that this room was inside a mortuary. The air was controlled to be ambient and so that no smells would leak through. The lighting was soft and there were modern orange comfy sofas, chairs and a teak coffee table. Helen helped Rita into the room, followed by Craven. They stood in front of a window nearly the size of one wall that was covered with a black blind from the other side and waited until Rita finally gave the nod that she was ready.

Helen wanted to look away as the attendant pulled the sheet down. Instead, she watched realization dawn on the aunt's face — her lip trembled, and tears filled her eyes. Rita was shaking her head wildly, convulsing. Sobbing. The attendant covered the body.

'That is Tina,' Rita cried. She would've collapsed into a heap on the floor, but Helen managed to catch her and slip an arm around her waist to keep her upright. 'No, no, no, that's my Tina,' she sobbed. 'That's my Tina.'

'I'm so sorry for your loss.' Helen led Rita away.

'She was so young. She had her life ahead of her. Why would anyone do this?'

Outside Craven patted down his pockets for his cigarettes, then offered one to Rita. She took a long drag before speaking. 'I've pretty much looked after her since she was ten years old. Her life keeps flashing before my eyes, every time I close them.'

This was without a doubt the worst part of the job. Helen shoved her hands in her pockets for warmth and stepped back. The smoke did nothing to help the nausea in the pit of her stomach. Rita took another cigarette as she climbed back into the car, but even putting it to her lips proved a struggle.

* * *

Thankfully, Reggie was sparked out on the sofa, snoring. Moira inched forward and lifted his half-eaten plate of fried eggs and chips from the table. She went to pick up his fork but caught the top of his lager can with her elbow and knocked it onto the floor. A lump rose in her throat, as the lager gushed from the can. She found herself holding her breath until Reggie made another murmur in his sleep. She turned to head into the kitchen with his plate when she saw him sit up from the corner of her eye.

'Trying to kill me, were you?'

Moira took a breath to steady herself, then turned to face him. 'I'm sorry.' She looked down at the egg yolk, mixed with tomato ketchup. 'You've eaten most of it.'

'Those chips are whiter than a ghost and those eggs were raw.'

'I thought that's how you liked them?'

'What, I like food poisoning now, do I?'

Moira shook her head, eyes burning. 'No, I'll do better next time.'

'Eat it.' Reggie sneered, rising to his feet. 'That's the only way you'll learn.'

'No, please. I hate eggs, you know that.'

He tugged the plate from her hands and thumped it back onto the table, dropping a chip onto the floor. 'Don't make me tell you again.'

CHAPTER NINE

That evening, a burst of rain soaked Helen as she headed back into the station, a throbbing headache niggling behind her eyes, a combination of hunger and dehydration probably. She swallowed hard in an attempt to ease the dryness in her throat. After they had taken Rita back home, Helen had gone back to her own flat for a couple of hours to rest but she couldn't sleep, and it sounded like her downstairs neighbours were having a party, judging from Boney M.'s Rivers of Babylon that they were blasting out on a loop. It didn't matter anyway, she wanted to go back through the files for Tina French. There must be something that she was missing.

Sweat intermixed with cleaning fluid hit her as she entered the station. Sergeant Keaton was at the desk, squinting at paperwork and slurping a cup of tea, he didn't bother to look up as she passed.

Her stomach rumbled again, so she took a detour downstairs to the canteen for coffee and a sandwich. Helen eventually headed back up to the CID suite, the last packet of tuna sandwiches in hand, not her first choice but it was all that was left after the dinner rush. She dropped the food onto her desk. During the early evening, it seemed that most officers were at their desks, and despite the window being open — and that was only because the catch was broken and it wouldn't close properly — the air still hung thick with smoke. Even the white paintwork around the windows and doors had started to yellow.

She pulled her chair out to sit down and that's when she noticed them, on top of her paperwork. She bit down hard on her lip as she lifted the feather duster on her desk, along with a pair of handcuffs. She looked around the room but no one looked up as she held out the manky old thing with her thumb and index finger. Randall was at his desk, smoking a cigarette. McKinley wasn't at his desk, but his jacket was draped over his chair, so he was still in the department. DC Bell was at the filing cabinet by the door.

'Anyone want to claim these?'

She noticed a smile twitch the corner of Randall's mouth, but he kept his eyes down. Bell turned his head and shrugged.

'Last chance? Anyone?' Helen rolled her eyes and dropped the duster into the waste bin. 'I thought we were past all this rubbish.'

'Someone was probably only having a laugh.' Bell muttered.

'Well, I'm not in the mood for it,' Helen snapped back.

Randall cleared his throat and she shot him a look, daring him to say something.

Brushing the dirt off her desk, Helen sighed, losing her appetite for her sorry-looking sandwich. She peeled her soggy jacket off and placed it on the back of her chair. Stifling a sneeze, she opened one of the folders she had requested and flicked to the crime scene photographs of Tina French. A lump formed in the pit of her stomach. Was it just an opportunistic killing by a stranger? What had driven the murderer? Helen pulled out a close-up of the victim's torso and arms. The perpetrator was most likely male, considering the victim had been moved and the violence used against her. Both those things would require a great deal of strength. The victim had been placed on a plastic sheet and positioned with her arms by her side. Helen considered this. In her experience, the posing of a body could give away a valuable clue as to the motive, but not this time. She hadn't been posed to shock or degrade. Helen flicked the image over and sighed.

The killer had left the victim out in the open — somewhere she would easily be found. There might be a lull, but Helen's gut instinct told her to expect another killing unless he was captured shortly. The next image was of the inside of the bin — the items they'd found there. Why did he bother to do that?

Bell slammed one of the filing cabinets shut and Helen looked up.

'Sorry, it was jammed,' he muttered.

Randall was frowning now and scribbling something down with a pencil in one hand and a fag in the other. Some folders were open in front of him. He looked up and met eyes with Helen then muttered something under his breath.

She had hoped this was going to stop from him. The snide comments and dismissive attitude that he didn't use on other members of the team. Helen's nickname for him was Jekyll and Hyde. Although he was one of those cops that knew Edinburgh inside and out, and all the criminals in it, and was also one of the longest-serving officers in the department, he was lazy and only ever seemed to do enough to get by.

Helen looked away and flicked to another photograph, a full-length shot of the victim. The pub and the hospital were about twenty-five miles apart. So, whoever murdered her would have to have had access to a vehicle. Swallowing to get rid of the taste of her coffee, she pushed the mug away, it tasted more like chicory than actual coffee and that would do nothing for the tension that was building against her temples.

Helen's desk phone rang, and she grimaced as the sharp ring cut through her skull.

'Helen Carter.'

She could feel Randall's eyes on her again.

'It's PS Keaton here. Just to let you know, Ted has been phoning the station asking to be put through to you.'

'Ted, as in Ted Fullerton?' She angled herself away to make it harder for Randall to hear.

'How many Teds do you know?'

'Did he leave a message?'

'No, every time he's called I haven't been able to get through to you.'

'Right. Thanks for letting me know. I'll call him.'

Helen hung up the phone and rubbed her forehead. She couldn't face him. Not today.

Randall scoffed.

'Have you got something to say?' Helen regretted asking that as soon as the words slipped out.

'Only that if you weren't so useful in the department you wouldn't have a job.'

In for a penny, in for a pound. 'Sorry, in what way am I useful?' She stood and moved around her desk, perching on the corner of it.

'It's always useful having a woman around for . . .'

'For?'

'Well, for any cases involving woman and children.'

Helen pondered this. 'And how many children do you have?'

'Three.'

'Three.' Helen replied with a chuckle. 'And how many children do I have?'

'None or you wouldn't be here.'

She jabbed a finger at Bell. 'What about you?'

Bell smirked. 'None . . . Well, none that I know about anyway.'

Helen grabbed her jacket. She needed to get out of there.

Randall narrowed his eyes. 'Maybe you shouldn't have come back, you seem—'

'I'm fine.' She could feel all eyes on her.

Randall shrugged. 'I'm just . . . showing my concern.'

Helen stepped forward, clutching her jacket in front of her. 'It would have suited you.' She held a hand up to stop Randall speaking.

The laugh that bellowed from Randall followed her down the corridor.

Helen sucked in a shaky breath.

* * *

This wasn't working. Helen avoided her reflection in the bathroom mirror and splashed the back of her neck with cool water. Her heart thumped in her chest. She closed her eyes until it started to slow. She thought about going home for a while, back to seeing her mum, going anywhere. Ted filled her mind. It was over two weeks ago she left him at the airport. Although he didn't need much persuasion to get on the flight to Spain. He hadn't even looked back once as he crossed the terminal. Hot tears stung her eyes. 'I can't do this now,' she muttered. *Why can't you just let yourself be happy?* Ted had asked her, and she didn't have an answer for him.

Terry McKinley was waiting for her outside the bathroom. Leaning against the wall, he smiled when their eyes met. 'I was worried when you stormed out like that.'

Helen drew a deep breath. 'I'm fine.'

'You don't seem it.'

'I'm just tired, that's all.'

He stepped forward. 'Close your eyes.'

She arched an eyebrow. 'Why? Come on, I just . . . I've got a lot to do.'

'Seriously, I've got a surprise for you.' He stepped forward, keeping a hand behind his back. 'You'll like this. Trust me.'

'Fine.' Helen relented.

'No peeking.'

'I'm not.'

'Hold out your hand.' His soft hand cupped underneath hers. 'Open your eyes now.'

'Ha,' Helen smiled at the Golden Cup chocolate bar in her hand.

'There you go.'

'That's exactly what I need. These are my favourite.'

He gave a thin smile. 'I've been trying to get a list of all the employees at the hospital but most of their records have been destroyed in a fire.'

'Typical. Do you have any names?'

He nodded.

'Maybe they can give us more.'

CHAPTER TEN

'It's not really my type of place.' Craven mumbled as they crossed the road.

They were headed for the Weary Traveller, a crumbling turn-of-the-century watering hole.

'Well, you seemed to know a lot about it,' Helen teased.

'I used to work this patch in my early days on the beat.' Craven said, pulling open the sticky mahogany doors of the pub then motioning for Helen to go through first. A drift of stale smoke and lager wafted towards her. She studied the drinkers in the pub as she made her way to the bar. Only two others, pensioners, sat at a circular table under the dartboard nursing half-drunk pints while skimming through copies of the *Evening News*, an untouched box of darts between them. Helen unbuttoned her jacket. The fire on the left-hand side of the room had been cranked up to its full three bars. The chalkboard above it advertised the pub quiz and cask ales. Craven leaned against the mahogany-panelled bar and traced a glass mark with his finger. The low afternoon sun streamed through the windows behind them.

'Hello,' Helen called out.

She leaned over the bar and could see it led to another room that looked like a private lounge area.

A few moments later, a flustered-looking woman appeared behind the counter. She was wearing a pink frilly apron and had a tea towel draped over her shoulder.

'Can I help you?' She brushed a strand of blonde hair away from her forehead with her arm.

'Yes, you can.' Craven retrieved his warrant card for inspection.

The woman stepped back, her brow furrowing. 'What can I do for you?'

'We understand that Tina French works here.' Craven replied, keeping his voice low.

'Yes, she does. What's this about?'

'When was she last on shift?' Craven carried on.

'Friday night. She's part-time. Thursday, Friday and Saturday nights. She's due in later.'

'And she was in for her last shift?'

'Yes, she was.'

'How was the pub last night?' Helen asked.

'Just a typical night. Busy . . .'

Helen glanced at the side table. The pensioners hadn't looked up from their newspapers.

'I'm the landlady of this pub. So, do you mind telling me what's going on?'

'I'm sorry to tell you this. Tina French was found dead.'

'What?' She grabbed her stomach. Winded. 'No, she can't be . . .' She took one of the clear bottles from the back shelf and poured herself a glass. She downed it in one.

'I've been landlady here for ten years and Tina has been here all this time.'

'How did she seem?' Helen asked.

The landlady pondered this. 'She was a bit distracted. Her son wasn't feeling well. I let her leave a bit early.'

'What about customers?'

'It was busy. It's payday for most people.' She poured herself another glass. 'There was something a bit . . .'

'What?' Helen questioned.

'There was a man. A bit of a weird one.' She pointed to a table behind them. 'He was sat there most of the night. I don't think I'd ever seen him in here before. I thought he was looking at Tina a bit too much and I didn't see him speaking to anyone else either. This is not the kind of pub where we see new faces a lot. He didn't drink much either.'

'Did Tina mention anything about him?'

She seemed to consider this for a moment. 'Not that I can remember. I mean, I'm not really sure.'

'What did he look like?'

'Mid-thirties. Dark hair. It's hard. He just looked normal.'

'Do you think you would recognize him if you saw him again?'

'I'm not sure. Do you think he murdered her?'

'We don't know yet, but we can't rule anything out at this stage.'

'I'll keep an eye out if he comes back in again. I can't believe that anyone would hurt Tina. No one will have a bad word to say about her.'

'What was he wearing, this man?' Craven muttered, as he scribbled in his pocketbook.

'Now you're asking,' she clicked her tongue. 'I think he was dressed smartly. You know, a suit and tie, I'm sure that's what he was wearing. Maybe he was a businessman or something like that. Or one of those travelling salesmen.'

'How about his voice? Any trace of an accent?' Helen put in.

The landlady stared back at her blankly.

'Okay—' Helen placed her card on the table — 'thanks for your time. We'd also like you to come down to the station to help with a composite sketch of the man.'

'I'll do that.'

* * *

Helen was glad of the fresh breeze that cooled her face when she stepped outside. Craven followed behind her. The pub was nestled on the edge of a post-war housing estate. She pointed to two houses on the corner, opposite each other.

'They both have a good view of the pub.'

Randall and McKinley approached from the house on the right-hand side. McKinley was shaking his head.

'We've been up the entire street. Nothing. No one heard or seen anything.'

'Bloody typical,' Craven replied, opening the Granada door. 'That's just what it's like around here.'

CHAPTER ELEVEN

Moira looked up at the lava and ink mottled sky. It was probably pointless doing this but at least it got her out of the flat and into some fresh air. She placed the washing basket on the ground and unfolded one of the towels. It had come out nice with the bleach, she thought, pegging it to the line. A warm breeze caught her off guard, and she smiled. Maybe it was Harold looking down on her, letting her know that he was okay. The thought hit her like a punch in the gut. Harder than even Reggie could hit. It never got any easier. She'd be fine one minute, then drowning in grief the next. She looked up at the window of her flat. Reggie wasn't looking, so she could stay out a little longer.

Moira should've walked past. She shouldn't have gone into the shed. She should have headed straight back up the stairs, but she couldn't resist. The sound of Reggie laughing at the television drifted from the open window.

The door was locked but the padlock at the top hadn't been closed properly. Moira tested it to be sure, giving it a wiggle. It slipped open in her hand. She considered clicking the padlock back in place but *what* was the harm in having a quick look at what was in there?

She pushed the door open and tiptoed in, feeling her heart pounding against her ribs and the palms of her hands growing clammy. A broken lawnmower had been propped up against the wall. Along with bits of wood and bags of what looked like rubbish.

On one other side of the room, there was a wooden box. Lifting the lid Moira furrowed her brow; it was filled with yellowing newspapers. She paused a moment and strained to listen; Reggie was still chuckling at something. The dust from mothballs and mouldy paper tickled the back of her throat as she dug through them. She held up a photograph to catch some of the sunlight. Her stomach tensed. A portrait of a woman in her twenties that she didn't recognize. As she dug deeper, she skipped through some photographs, she didn't know anyone in them. The last bundle of photos caught her attention. *What the fuck?* Some of the faces were scratched out. She squinted at the grainy black-and-white photographs. Her fingers hit something hard in the box. Stuffed down the side of the newspapers was a faded old ring box. She fished it out and opened it to see a thin gold band encrusted with a diagonal line of emeralds, pretty but old-fashioned. She shoved it back in its place. Underneath that, newspaper clippings from old murders. The ink was so faded on some, it was too hard to read. Most of the paper had clumped together from the damp so she gave up on peeling them apart. At the bottom was another jewellery box. Inside it was a small gold brooch shaped like a beetle. She pushed the little box back down the side. A small photograph fluttered to the floor with a name written on the back, Marjorie Lockwood. Moira turned the photograph over. It was a dark-haired woman and Reggie, side by side. The woman was smiling broadly and clutching her handbag in front of her.

The noise from the flat stopped, and the stairwell door opened with a squeak. Moira shoved the lid back onto the box, but it wouldn't fit. Heart pounding, she tried it the other way around and it clicked into place. Footsteps drawing closer. She ran from the shed, shut the door and closed the padlock just as Reggie appeared on the path.

'What have you been doing?' He looked at her accusingly and glanced at the door, then back at her.

She inclined her head towards the shed and gave him her best smile. 'I thought the padlock was broken.'

He didn't return the gesture. Instead, he frowned and looked at the padlocked door. He slipped his hand into his trouser pocket and Moira could hear the jangle of keys.

'I better get upstairs and get a start on dinner.' She brushed past him and headed into the block but saw from the corner of her eye that he was still standing by the door.

'Are you coming?' She flashed her best 'everything's fine' toothy smile again.

'Aye, I'll be up in a minute.'

In the stairwell, Moira had her hand braced on the door, pausing as she heard Reggie unlocking the padlock.

CHAPTER TWELVE

Helen waited for the post-mortem of Tina French. Many members of the public didn't understand why it was necessary to conduct a post-mortem if a victim was obviously murdered. She watched as the pathologist worked quietly and seriously while the photographer's camera clicked continually. The post-mortem suite was a white-tiled room with three metal slabs and brownish linoleum floors with drainage. Tina French had been laid out on the middle slab. Alex Winston carefully unzipped the body bag. The daisy dress was the first thing that Helen saw. Another forensic officer that Helen hadn't seen before helped the pathologist collect the samples. Tina looked peaceful on the slab, her wispy mousy hair draped around her shoulders. The harsh, almost too bright lighting above her made it look silvery. She shuddered, picturing herself on a slab and thinking about how close she came to being laid out like this. Her throat tightened, she swallowed hard. She blinked away her thoughts and forced her mind back to Tina French.

A tiny black-and-purple butterfly tattoo on the victim's left ankle bone caught her attention. The photographer leaned in and captured it from different angles.

The pathologist swabbed her mouth, then took scrapings from under her fingernails. Once complete, he would put all the organs back in and sew the body back together, then compile a report for Helen's team.

* * *

It was a couple of hours later, by the time she got back to the office, most of the officers from the morning shift had finished for the evening. Jack Craven was in his office, it looked like he was skimming through papers, deep in thought. He didn't look up as she passed his window. She clicked off the radio and wiped away the puddle of rainwater that had collected on the window ledge with a tea towel. Randall was in the car park, smoking a cigarette and talking to a uniformed officer. Damn, she had hoped he'd gone for the evening. She stepped away as Randall headed back towards the building. She draped her jacket over her chair and flicked through the new pile of folders that had arrived on her desk. It would be a couple of days before she had the result of the post-mortem back and she tried to push it from her mind. Instead, she was going to speak with Tina's ex-husband. She looked up as the door to the office thudded against the wall. It was Randall, followed by a sheepish-looking Terry McKinley. McKinley crossed over to her desk and waited for Randall to disappear into Jack Craven's office before speaking.

'Do you want to go get some dinner?' He frowned and wiped his forehead with the back of his hand. 'I don't fancy fish and chips again, but—'

'I'm really tired.' She replied, looking back down at her notes.

'Aye, why don't we get food to have in your flat then? I can cook.'

'Another time.'

'It'll be a laugh.'

'I can't.'

'Why not?'

Helen glugged the dregs of her tepid coffee. 'I . . . I'm just not in the mood.'

McKinley made a face. 'I can cook, you know.'

'It's not that.' Helen paused. 'But I have just attended a post-mortem—'

'I'm sorry.'

'I don't need to be babysat all the time either.' Helen clutched the folder, feeling her shoulders tighten. 'Honestly, I'm just back and I'm exhausted,' she shrugged. 'I just want to go home and sleep.'

McKinley's smile faded. He looked like he was thinking of what to say and looked away.

'I'm going to go home and fall asleep in front of the telly,' Helen reiterated, hoping to end this.

'Well,' he scratched the stubble on his chin. 'I'll probably just do the same.'

'Another time?' Helen picked up another folder in front of her and flicked through the photos from the crime scene. 'Now, if you don't mind, I have some work to do.'

'Aye, sure. Of course.' McKinley muttered. He jumped backwards when Craven emerged from his office. Helen shot him a glare. She felt Craven's eyes on her, but she kept her focus on the documents. He grabbed his coffee mug from the top of a filing cabinet, then disappeared back into his office. Half an hour later, Helen slid on her jacket, reaching for her keys in the pocket. Instead, she found Ted's ring box. Her stomach twitched. She had forgotten about that.

* * *

It was just after nine by the time Helen got back to the flat with a few bits and pieces from the shops. She made herself a hot chocolate and a cheese sandwich then curled up on the sofa. An old black-and-white science fiction film had just started on the television; it wasn't something she would normally watch, but she needed to settle herself after her shift today. Tina's face kept coming to the front of her mind.

Helen sighed and put her drink on the table. She couldn't concentrate on the telly, so got up and rummaged through one of her boxes for a paperback to read. One of these days, she would get herself a bookshelf. After a good rifle, she settled on one given to her by her mum, *Rosemary's Baby*. She was only halfway through that one. She jumped when the telephone rang behind her. She slung the book back in the box, knowing exactly who it would be.

'Helen Carter.' She slumped down on the sofa.

'It's Jack,' he sounded groggy. 'We're going to need you back on shift.'

'What's happened? Has there been another murder?'

'Probably.'

'What do you mean by that?'

'You'll see when you get here.'

'Fine,' Helen replied, scooping up her sandwich. 'What's the address?'

CHAPTER THIRTEEN

The net curtains in the bottom flat twitched as Detective Sergeant Helen Carter parked her Mini behind a police car. She reached into the glove box and grabbed a bottle of aspirin, washing a couple of tablets down with the remnants of the warm Cresta she'd left in the footwell. There was something familiar about this block. She'd been here before, but she couldn't remember why. Years ago. It would come back to her, she thought, as she climbed out the car.

The address was a middle flat on the right in a pebble-dashed block of six. The red chipped stairwell door had been propped open with a wooden wedge. The bottom panel of the door was cracked, and it looked like it had been kicked in. A lot of these schemes had developed as part of the slum clearances and to tackle the housing crisis after the war, but Helen wasn't sure of the longevity of these blocks. They were already starting to look well lived-in for their few years.

From the corner of her eye, she spotted various people out on their balconies, huddled together, pointing at the police. She avoided all eye contact with them, not wanting to give them any satisfaction as she passed. The distant echo of a baby crying filled the air; the wind carried the noise, and she couldn't tell where it was coming from. A window slammed shut somewhere and all was silent.

Inside the stairwell there was another door through to the back garden. She could see a couple of red-cheeked uniformed officers were raking through the overgrown bushes.

Helen's foot connected with a mop and rusty bucket that had been left on the side of the steps. It was empty, and the steps were dry. Helen blinked. The hard lights above her head flickered, letting out an electrical hum, plunging her into bright light then darkness. She stepped over some white flaky dog dirt and paused at the first-floor window and peered outside. All she saw were the same dull blocks trailing along the road on both sides. That meant there was a good chance someone had spotted something. The difficulty would be getting anyone to talk to the police; resentment towards the 'polis' had spiralled in these housing schemes along with the unemployment and drugs.

* * *

'Boss.' Helen nodded to Detective Inspector Jack Craven who was standing outside the flat's front door, dragging on a cigarette and blowing the smoke towards the ceiling.

Craven stood up straighter when he noticed her. He always seemed to carry an air of authority. They looked an odd couple. Helen with her hair cut above her shoulder, pinned at the back, and a white blouse tucked into her practical brown trousers.

Craven, on the other hand, looked like he hadn't slept in a week. His tweed jacket was creased and the patches on the elbows had faded. He wore a tan-coloured polo neck that he usually left at the office for when he needed a change of clothes in emergencies.

He had such swagger that when he walked into a room everyone knew he was in charge. It was the way he moved his shoulders, Helen thought.

He must've known what she was thinking because he rubbed the swollen bags that bulged under his hazel eyes. 'I've been on shift for the past twenty-two hours.'

'Is this looking like another one?'

'No, this is different.'

The silhouettes of other people could be seen behind the frosted glass door panel.

Craven took one last drag, then stubbed it out on the wall and flicked the butt over the banister. 'Are you sure you're okay to be back?' He looked genuinely concerned.

'Of course.' She forced a smile.

'What I mean—'

'I'm fine, what's the alternative — sit in the flat and watch the telly feeling sorry for myself? No, there's no point wallowing.'

He rubbed a hand through his dishevelled hair. 'Not many of them thought they would see you back.'

'They thought wrong.'

He shook his head. A hacking cough exploded from his chest, echoing in the stairwell. He looked at her and motioned towards the paint-chipped brown door. 'It's *bloody nasty* in there.' He spluttered, and blood rushed to his face.

'And so is that cough. You've got to give up the fags, Jack.'

'I'll give them up when I'm dead.' He wheezed, cleared his throat and opened the scuffed door to the flat.

'I've been in this stair before, at the flat below this one.'

'Recently?'

'No, must've been when I was a WPC.' She glanced at the door. 'It'll come back to me.'

Helen followed him inside. The metallic smell of fresh blood filled her throat and nostrils. Goosebumps formed on her arms; the flat felt colder than it was in the stairwell.

Two other officers stood in the hallway taking finger-prints. Some of the special powder they used had spilled onto the splintered floorboards.

The bedroom door was open, and a man was sitting on the end of the bed, head in his hands, black hair poking out between his fingers. He was shaking his head.

He would need to wait. She brushed past the officers and entered the lounge, where a women's wool overcoat hung on the door. It had the aroma of rain and stale booze. A tatty black leather handbag lay open beside the chair. Helen could see a brown purse sticking out, and some scrunched-up receipts. She flipped the purse open with the end of a pen — no money in it, just a faded library card and some dry-cleaning stubs.

Craven followed close behind her, his breath tickling the back of her neck.

'This doesn't look good.' She stared at the blue thread-bare carpet, patterned with what she would guess were wine stains and fag burns. A chill ran down her spine when she spotted the coffee table in the centre of the room. A crack ran along it, and a chunk of glass was missing from the corner. Underneath it was a chocolatey looking puddle. Smaller drips trailed along towards the window, red-brown and drier looking. She shivered and looked away.

'What happened in here?' she asked.

'The husband, one Reggie McKenzie, went out for a drink, apparently, and came home to this.'

'Do we know whose blood it is?'

'We think it's his wife's, Moira McKenzie. He's in the bedroom.'

'You think? Is she not in the ambulance?'

'No,' Craven shook his head, 'we've not been able to locate her.' He pointed to the congealed blood. 'He's got no idea where she is now. She's not in the flat or close by.'

She exchanged a glance with him, knowing exactly what he was thinking. *It's always the husband.*

The floorboards creaked as the pathologist, Alex Winston, entered the living room. He rubbed a hand through his slicked-back hair as he did so and was quickly followed by a crime scene photographer.

'Fancy seeing you again so soon, Sergeant.' He brushed past them and knelt in front of the stain. 'What have we got here, then?'

The photographer clicked his camera towards the blood, twisting and turning to carefully capture the thick-looking pool at different angles.

Craven pointed to the blood under the table. 'Will you be able to get much from that?'

Winston clicked his tongue. 'That's a big area, so we will be able to get an analysis,' he said, taking swabs from his examination bag.

'If someone lost this amount of blood, could they still be alive?' Helen took a step towards the gloop.

'If this is Moira McKenzie's blood, based on her physical description and size, she'd need medical help very quickly . . . but potentially,' Winston replied.

'She wouldn't have been able to leave the house alone?' Helen asked Winston.

'It's doubtful, and on the slight chance she did, I'd expect a blood trail.' Winston knelt beside the puddle and slipped on a pair of disposable rubber gloves. They made a snapping noise as he did so.

'There's no sign of disturbance. Though the door was unlocked when the husband arrived home,' Craven added.

'Can you say how old the blood is?' Helen stepped forward.

'The blood has separated into clot and serum. It's very viscous. I can't give you an accurate answer yet.'

'What's the husband been saying about this?' Helen asked.

Craven shrugged. 'Apparently, he came home to this scene. They didnae have a telephone in this dump. So, he used the neighbours' one. He's got no idea where she might be.'

She shot him a glare and a smile twisted his lips.

An empty wine bottle sat on the sideboard next to a packet of Valium. It looked like there were only a few pills left in it.

'Aye,' Craven carried on. 'He got back home at around ten o'clock and called us as soon as he saw this.'

Helen looked at her watch. That was over an hour ago. 'What time did he go out?'

'Half-eight. So that's an hour-and-a-half window.'

'I've got other officers out looking in the back garden and driving round the streets.'

Helen knelt beside the table. The glass looked about an inch thick and would do someone serious damage. The piece left on the corner looked as sharp as a blade. It would've taken some force to smash it.

'Has the bit of glass been found?' Helen pointed to the missing corner edge. She couldn't see any shards on the carpet.

'No.' Craven shook his head.

Helen pulled on a pair of gloves. She hadn't noticed any blood in the hallway or the stairwell on the way up. 'Someone must've seen something.' Helen muttered as she peered through the condensation-coated window. It was minus three outside and set to get even colder through the night. Unless Moira McKenzie had another jacket to wear, she'd die of pneumonia, never mind a head injury.

Helen went over to the side table and picked up the Valium. The label stated that it had been prescribed by a Dr Rushmore a month ago. At the back of the dresser behind a photograph of a young boy at the beach stood a second bottle of yellow pills. She examined the bottle. Half-empty. More Valium to be taken as needed. Prescribed by the same doctor.

'Mother's little helpers, eh?' Craven said over her shoulder.

Helen nodded. 'She's obviously got some kind of disorder, maybe panic or depressive.' Helen put the tablets back down. It was impossible to know with this case, but all too often she found these tablets prescribed by doctors like sweeties, when all the patients really needed was someone to talk to. She'd been offered the same ones by her doctor.

'I'll go through and speak to the husband. Are the search dogs on their way?'

Craven looked at his watch. 'They should be here shortly.'

When Helen entered the bedroom, Reggie McKenzie looked up at her with a tear-stained face, but his blue eyes were dry. He still had his jacket on and a woolly scarf around his neck. The nails on his tobacco-stained hands were bitten short but clean, and he had some older looking scabs on his left knuckles and paper cuts on his fingers. There were no blood stains anywhere on him. The mahogany wardrobe behind him was open and looked full of women's clothing. A suitcase lay on top of it, along with a stack of dusty old newspapers.

'Can you tell me what happened here, Mr McKenzie?' She leaned forward, not smelling any alcohol on his breath; only sweat from his jacket. 'Is anything of Moira's missing?'

'No.' He shook his head and flicked a glance at the wardrobe. 'It wis just a normal night. I went out for a drink. Like I always do every Friday. Moira was in bed when I left.' He spoke softly. 'When I got home there was blood on the floor, and she was gone.'

'Does she have another jacket?'

'No, just the one on the door.'

Helen nodded and gave him a hard stare. 'What happened before you went to the pub?'

He shrugged, 'Nothing out of the ordinary. We had some dinner from the chippy. She was feeling a bit down and took some of her tablets.'

'Which ones?'

'The happy pills.' He swallowed hard. 'I can't remember what they're called.' He waved a hand towards the door. 'They're through in the dresser.'

'What does she take the pills for?'

'Depression, delusions. You name it.' Reggie shrugged. 'I've lost track of what she needs them for. She sees things, sometimes. Hears things that are not there. The pills calm her down, make her more normal.'

'What things did she see?'

66

'I dinnae ken. She was just paranoid. I didnae listen to it most of the time.' Helen followed his eyeline down to his ringless hand.

'You look stone cold sober but the flat reeks of alcohol.'

He looked at her wide-eyed. 'Aye, I'm not a big drinker. Moira had a glass of wine. I'm always begging her not to drink. My wife was an alcoholic. I mean, she is.'

'Has anything ever happened like this before?' There was something about his eyes that was niggling at her. She realized what it was. His pupils were tiny pinpricks.

Reggie McKenzie shook his head.

'Can you think of anyone that would want to hurt Moira?'

'No, of course not.' He paused for thought. 'Well, there's him down the stairs.' He made a face. ''Ave heard he's meant to be a right pervert. There's been a lot of rumours.'

'Who?'

'The young laddie, Billy,' Reggie spat. 'He should be in a freakshow.'

'Would your wife have had a reason to be upset at all? No argument, anything like that?' Helen slipped out her notebook and flicked to a blank page.

'No, what are you trying to imply?' A sneer twisted his thin lip.

Helen stepped closer to him. 'You go to the pub and don't have a drink?'

'No, I didn't fancy it. I had a fresh orange. You gonnae arrest me for that?' He waved his hand dismissively at her. 'You should be out there looking for my wife, not asking me these questions. You *stupid woman*.'

His hands squeezed into fists; she could see the whites of his cut knuckles.

'Mr McKenzie, I just need to ask all of this to do my job.'

'Job?' He shook his head and when he saw her looking, he opened his hands. 'I'm sorry. I just love Moira so much. I can't be without her. I need her back.'

'We're doing everything that we can to get her back.'

'Aye, like accusing me o' things when you should be questioning perverts?'

'I'm not accusing—'

'Excuse me, Sergeant.' Craven's familiar Old Spice tickled her nostrils as he brushed past her. She could feel the warmth of his body. She moved aside as Craven grabbed Reggie McKenzie by his shirt collar, whipped him up and thumped him against the mould-speckled wall. A watercolour of Edinburgh Castle behind McKenzie's head fell onto the floor.

'You don't seem all that upset that your wife's missing.' Craven tutted. 'See, if it was me, I'd be in bits.'

'I am in bits. Get off me!'

'How did someone get in the house when you'd locked the door to go to the pub?'

'The door was open. I told you that already.' He looked pleadingly at Helen. 'If you're trying to pin this on me, you cannae. Plenty of people saw me in the pub.' He struggled to get free, but Craven didn't budge. 'I was there all evening,' he spat. 'Plenty of *witnesses*. I've done nothing wrong here.'

Craven threw him onto the bed, and it groaned under his weight. He stabbed a finger into McKenzie's chest. 'Next time one of my officers asks you a question, you'll answer them without any lip, or I'll give you a fat one. You got that?'

'Aye,' Reggie spluttered and pulled down his scarf which was now wrapped around his face.

Helen exchanged a look with Craven. He rubbed his hands together, walking out of the bedroom.

'You've not been drinking but have you taken anything else?'

'Aye.' He rubbed his forehead. 'Some of Moira's tablets. When I saw all the blood in there, I wanted to take something to help me calm down.'

'Can you think of anywhere she might have gone?'

He shook his head.

'Do you have a recent photograph of Moira that I can have, please?'

He gulped and went over to the drawer. Opening the top drawer, he removed a red leather photo album and slipped a small photo out. He handed it to Helen without looking at it. It was a colour picture of Moira standing outside a hairdresser, 'O'Hara's'.

'Is this where Moira works?'

He nodded.

CHAPTER FOURTEEN

Helen knocked softly on the door of the flat below. The occupants had already spoken to uniform and were expecting a visit from her. The lock turned, and a woman in her late forties with auburn hair wrapped in curlers and wearing a pink dressing down peered out.

'Good evening. I'm DS Carter. You said you had some information about the incident we're investigating upstairs.' Helen held up her warrant card for inspection. 'Are you Anna?'

The woman nodded and sighed. She looked like she was about to move aside and let Helen in but then hesitated. 'Reggie won't know I've been talking to you, will he?'

'No, he won't.'

She considered this for a moment and rubbed her tired-looking eyes.

'We're trying to investigate a very serious crime and you might be able to help.'

'You better come in then.'

The warmth of the central heating engulfed Helen, as she followed the woman through to the brightly lit lounge. The Rolling Stones' 'Angie' was on the record player. Anna pulled the needle up, bringing the record to an abrupt stop, and motioned to a bright orange leather sofa. There was an empty Moses basket next to it and a half-empty baby's bottle on the table.

'Take a seat.'

'Thank you.' Helen sat down and slipped her notebook from her pocket. 'What's your full name, please?'

'Anna Hutchinson.'

Helen noted it down.

Anna sat in the floral armchair opposite and tugged at her dressing gown which had ridden up her thigh. Giving up on that, she slipped a packet of Player's from the pocket and fumbled to open it, eventually placing one to her lips. 'What's happened up there? He's finally done it, hasn't he?'

'Who has finally done what?' Helen asked.

'Him.' Anna pointed to the ceiling. 'He's always shouting and hitting her. I've had to call you lot a couple of times, but you're never interested. When I saw you coming into the stairwell, I thought you might be different, being a woman. You might understand.'

'I can assure you, all my colleagues are taking this incident seriously.'

She didn't look convinced.

'When was the last time you saw Mrs McKenzie?'

'Emm . . . yesterday morning. I saw her going up the stairs to her flat just as I was heading out with the baby.'

'What time was this?'

Anna paused a moment before answering, 'About ten, I reckon.'

'How did she seem?' Helen probed.

'Normal. Maybe a bit flustered, she was in a bit of a rush. She didn't make time to chat which really wasn't like her. She said she had a lot to do in the flat.'

'Can you remember anything she specifically said?' Helen shifted in the seat.

'I told her about Billy not being well as she said I should call the doctor and see if he would come out'

Thanks, this is really helpful.'

'She's not dead, is she?' Anna swallowed hard and put her hands to her mouth. The cigarette fell into her lap. It took her a couple of attempts to snatch it up.

'Right now, we're concerned with Mrs McKenzie's welfare.'

'Moira lives a life of hell up there. She's told me she wants to get away fae him for years. She's always black and blue fae when he's hurting her, and he's always screaming at her.' She shook her head and pointed at the ceiling. 'I'll tell you something for nothing: that man's pure evil.'

'Did you hear any noises from the flat tonight?'

'Some shouting a few hours ago, before Reggie went out.' She shook her head. 'I knew he'd do this, but she wouldn't listen.'

'You saw Reggie leave?'

'Aye.' Anna nodded.

'At what time?'

'About half-eight, I think.' She took a drag. 'There was one other thing. I did hear something, a bang.' She paused for a beat. 'It was loud. It woke my baby. Just this one bang. It was all quiet after that.'

'At what time?'

'Must've been about half-nine.'

Now came the question Helen was dreading. 'You live here with your son, Billy?' Helen remembered why she had been in this flat before. The woman's son had been following girls from his class to their homes.

Anna pursed her lips. 'Look, what Billy has done in the past he didn't mean. He's just not good with people or social situations. When he likes a girl, he goes a bit overboard. But he's just an overgrown child; he wouldnae harm a fly. Ma Billy's got nothing to do with this.'

Helen held her hand up. 'I'm not saying he has.'

'Billy,' Anna called him through then lowered her voice. 'He's a good boy.' The cigarette dangled on the corner of her mouth as she spoke.

A teenage boy with straggly ginger hair down to his shoulders popped his head around the doorframe. The ceiling light reflected on his shiny forehead.

'Mummy.'

'He's mentally handicapped; *backwards*,' she added for emphasis, then turned to him. 'Come and sit down, Billy.' Anna pointed to space beside Helen.

Billy nodded, scuffing his slippers on the carpet as he shuffled towards the chair. He sat down, avoiding eye contact with Helen. He was fidgeting with his hands, and his breaths quickened.

'It's okay, Billy,' Helen said, softly. 'I just want you to help me with a few questions. Can you do that?'

He started picking at a scab on his hand. 'I l-like her. She gives me biscuits and is always nice to me.'

'Who?'

'Moira,' Anna clarified.

Billy nodded. 'I s-saw the police car from my bedroom w-window.' His breath becoming raspier, his chest heaved as he struggled for breath.

'Is he okay?' Helen asked Anna.

'He's got asthma.' She exhaled the smoke through her nostrils and stood up.

'Thank you for speaking with me, Billy,' Helen smiled.

'He'll be okay. Right, son, let's get you back to bed.' Anna helped him to his feet and guided him out of the lounge. He was gulping for air. 'It's all right.' She frowned. 'Let's just get you back to bed.'

Helen listened as the bedroom door clicked shut. She looked around the lounge. The fire was on a bar and the heat warmed her shins. Happy family photographs adorned the mantelpiece next to a little branch of holly. This lounge was a world apart from the one upstairs. It was tastefully decorated with brown and white flock wallpaper and new-looking shag pile carpet, a comfy leather sofa and a television in the corner.

'I know what you're thinking,' Anna stated as she closed the door. She stayed there, her eyes boring into Helen's. 'That he's having that asthma attack because he's done something wrong.'

'No, I'm not,' Helen replied, standing up.

'He's made a few mistakes because he doesn't know how to behave. He's got too friendly with girls he's liked in his class.'

'In what way?'

'Followed them home. Sent them cards. He's been called a pervert by you lot. Slapped about by the teachers.' She took another cigarette out and pointed it at Helen. 'He's been with me all night, though, and we've had the doctor out here for his breathing. Billy was in his bed.'

'Thank you. You've been very helpful.'

Helen stood up and started towards the door. 'Which doctor does Billy see?'

'A doctor at Boswall Medical Practice, Dr Rushmore . . .'

'Thank you, if I need anything else, I'll be in touch.' Helen said, leaving the flat.

* * *

Helen's head pounded. She was going to head back up to the flat, but she needed to get outside for air. She watched the side of Reggie McKenzie's head crack off the door as he was shoved, flailing, and shouting, into the back of a police car. More lights had come on in the street, and people were peering out of the windows of the flats opposite, clearly enjoying the show. She shoved her hands in her pockets for warmth and headed around to the back of the building to an area of overgrown grass with bushes on one side. A couple of officers were searching through it with sticks. From the corner of her eye, she saw Craven approach.

She turned to face him and gave him a nod.

'We'll take McKenzie back to the station and interview him.' Craven retrieved his packet of cigarettes from his pocket.

'Yes, I saw.' Helen replied, and motioned to the uniformed officers. 'Have they found anything?'

'Not yet. What about the downstairs neighbour; anything there?'

'Nah.' Helen shook her head. 'Nothing much. The neighbour corroborated some domestic disputes.'

He nodded. 'Well, we've got uniform out searching the surrounding area. See if she turns up.'

Helen took a breath to steady herself. 'Jack, back there. You didn't need to do that. Don't give me any special treatment.'

'Aye.' He looked sceptically at her. 'I just know what you went through, and I know how hard it is to come back to work.'

'It sounds like you're talking from experience.'

He shrugged, placing a cigarette to his lips. 'I've had my share of dodgy situations in this job.' A smile twitched the corner of his lips. 'Maybe I'll tell you about them sometime.'

'There's nothing to worry about. I'm fine.' Helen shrugged. 'I'm just glad to be back at work.'

Craven nodded towards the uniformed officers. 'I'm going to see how they're getting on.'

CHAPTER FIFTEEN

With Reggie McKenzie en route to the station, Helen headed back up to the flat to get another look around. She found it was always easy to miss things first time around in a crime scene. An officer was examining what looked like the barrel lock on the front door. He shifted aside to let her in and offered a thin smile.

'Any signs of forced entry? Or damage to the lock?' She asked.

'No, nothing,' he shook his head.

Helen headed into the bedroom, but it had already been checked, all the drawers were open, and their contents spilled onto the floor. A stack of newspapers on the wardrobe caught her attention, she lifted them down and dropped them onto the bed. They were all yellowed and over ten years old. She flicked through them, some of them were multiple copies of the same paper and on the front page of every single one was the hit and run of Harold McKenzie. Sad. Helen skim-read them, most of the pages showing pictures of the young boy, smiling broadly in his school uniform. Big eyes full of hope and life.

'Found anything?'

Helen glanced over her shoulder. Craven was standing in the doorway, hands in his pockets.

'Nothing yet.' She gathered up the papers and placed them back where she found them. The wardrobe doors were ajar, she pulled them open. Two creased dresses hung from the pole. The smell of damp and mothballs filled Helen's nostrils and she placed her finger to her nose to stifle a sneeze.

'What a dump, eh?' Craven muttered.

Helen shrugged. 'I just hope we can find the poor woman alive, but that doesn't look likely.'

Craven shrugged and headed towards the lounge. Helen followed him.

He crossed over to the window and pulled back the net. 'Tragedy seems to follow this family.'

'What do you mean?' Helen avoided looking at the blood stain.

'Well, not only did Moira McKenzie's son die in a hit and run but her sister was hit by a car outside in the street there.'

'Did she—'

'No, she's still alive but needs full-time hospital care.'

Helen sighed. 'They don't seem to have much luck, do they?'

What do you think of the husband?' Craven questioned.

'We'll need to check out his alibi then go from there.'

CHAPTER SIXTEEN

Outside the block, Helen's teeth ached from the chill in the air. She ran her tongue over them, then shoved her hands in her pockets and looked up at the stars. A full moon lit the sky and Orion's Belt twinkled as a plane rumbled overhead. A bush rustled in the garden next to her. She stepped back as a tabby cat darted out of a gap in the fence, a squirming mouse in its mouth. It ran under the nearest car. Helen shivered at the sight.

'Excuse me. Excuse me, miss!'

Helen turned around to where the voice had come from.

A woman with a floral scarf over her head and a cream duffle coat that looked at least a size too big for her stepped forward. 'Here, Mrs,' the woman hissed, 'are you wi' the police?'

'Yes, can I help you?' Helen walked towards her.

'I was watching from my window.' The woman pointed to a flat directly opposite the McKenzies'.

'I just wanted to tell you that there was a car outside here earlier. It was parked about two hours ago where you were standing. I saw it when I was coming back home from work.'

Helen took her notebook from her pocket. 'What kind of car?'

'I dunno. It was a dark one. Dark brown, I think. I havnae seen it around here before.' The woman shrugged. There are no' many cars around this area.

'Was it a big car or small one?' Helen prompted.

'I'm not sure. Is everything all right in there?' she asked, craning past Helen.

'Did it look like a new car?' Helen replied, taking a step sideways to block the woman's view.

'Aye. I think it might have been a Cortina or Viva. It was like one I saw in a telly advert.' She opened her eyes wide, remembering something new. 'It had a black vinyl roof.'

Helen took a moment to jot this down. 'Okay. What about the licence plate?'

'I think it might have ended in FXB, but I could be wrong.' She bit her lip. 'I'm sorry, I hope that helps.'

'It might, thank you. Can I get your name and address, please?'

* * *

After speaking with the woman, Helen walked around to the back of the flats. The frosty air stung her face and stole the feeling from her finger ends. Shivering, she thrust her hands deep in her pockets. The old railway line — removed in the sixties — had since been repurposed as a cycle path. A web of lost stations spiralled around the north of the city and beyond. This line cut a twisty path through overgrown bushes and nettles, and a wooded area the size of a football field. Helen watched uniform and volunteer members of the public sifting through the undergrowth, their torches flashing as they inched forward. Helen blinked away spots that peppered her vision. A photographer aimed his camera at the searchers. Trembling in the wind, she turned up the collar of her jacket and trudged towards him. She strained to read the time on her watch. Moira had been missing for just over three hours now. The newspapers seemed to be quicker off the mark than the police at times. A twig snapped under her boot, alerting the photographer to her proximity. He lowered his camera, and disappeared into the shadows behind the trees. Helen stopped and swore under her breath.

* * *

Detective Constable McKinley waved and cut across the grass towards her. 'It's not looking promising,' he called out as he approached. His face was red, and his damp blond hair stuck to his cheeks. The bottoms of his trousers and boots were caked in mud. He pointed towards the estate. 'I've been all around the back. There's nothing.' His words escaped his mouth in a plume of frosty smoke.

'No.' Helen shook her head slowly. She could see the McKenzies' flat from where she was standing. Moira wouldn't have been able to get far with a head injury and no jacket.

'You still up for the pictures tomorrow . . .' he glanced at his watch, 'or should I say, this evening?'

'I think it's a bit early to make a decision on that, don't you?' She gave him a small smile. 'It's going to be a long day.'

McKinley shifted his weight. 'Maybe you're right. Wishful thinking, eh?'

'It's not that, it's just . . .' Helen took a step back when she noticed Craven approaching.

'I'm going back to the station. Head home, get a few hours' sleep, and I'll see you in the office when it's light.'

McKinley turned to Helen once Craven had left. 'Do you want me to walk you to your car?'

'I'm all right being alone, you know.'

'I know; it's just—'

'I'll catch you later,' she replied and headed towards her car.

She just managed to get into the Mini as thick blobs of rainwater splatted on the windscreen, slowly at first, until a thick blanket of water covered the glass.

She flicked the windscreen wipers to the highest setting and sat forward, straining to see a few feet in front. Every time she closed her eyes, the pool of blood in the living room was all she saw.

CHAPTER SEVENTEEN

It was just after lunchtime when Helen and Craven headed to the White Horse, Reggie McKenzie's local. One of those old pre-war boozers with a crumbling facade and rickety sign swaying in the wind, it was flanked on both sides by modern blocks of grey flats with 'for sale' signs in the windows. Two boys that looked about ten sat on the kerb, sharing a Wagon Wheel biscuit and a bottle of Tizer. Helen stepped past them and pulled open the scuffed black door.

The landlord, a man in his late sixties with a receding oily black hairline, looked up from the bar, his eyes narrowing, as he wrung the cloth he had been using to wipe the counter. Helen squinted trying to adjust to the dim lights, and heard Craven sigh as they approached the mahogany-panelled bar. The walls were nicotine-yellow from the fag smoke that drifted around them, and spilled beer and fag ash made the floor sticky. Helen produced her warrant card from her pocket. The barman nodded and looked around to check that no one noticed the police presence. Only a couple of pale regulars sat at a nearby table, but they were too entranced by their pints to notice what was going on around them.

'What do you want?'

The barman stared at Craven with a look that told Helen they had history.

'We want to ask you a few questions about Reggie McKenzie. I understand he's a regular,' Helen replied.

The barman glanced at the punters, avoiding any eye contact with Helen. 'Aye, what do you want to know?' He tried to keep his voice low.

'Was Reggie in the pub last night?' she asked.

He took a moment to think, then nodded. 'Aye, he was. What's this about?'

'All this chatting is making me thirsty. I'll take a whisky.' Craven sat down on the bar stool and rubbed his hands together. 'Are you wanting anything?'

'No,' Helen shook her head.

The barman furrowed his brow in surprise then poured a glass. 'Is that all you want?' he asked Craven as he slid the glass across the counter.

'What time was Reggie in until?' Helen carried on, ignoring his question.

'He was here until about half-nine. Maybe ten.'

'Are you sure?

'Why? What's he meant to have done?'

'We're trying to trace the whereabouts of Reggie's wife.'

The barman nodded. 'Lads—' he waved at the regulars — 'Reggie was in last night till about half-nine, eh?'

They both nodded in unison.

'Did he leave the pub during that time? Even for a short period?' Helen prompted.

The barman shrugged. 'If he did, I never noticed.'

'Do you remember what he had to drink?' Helen carried on.

The barman looked at Craven then back at her. 'Does it matter?'

'I was just wondering.' Helen smiled. 'You never know what might be relevant.'

'I think he had a half-pint. Nothing much.'

Helen slipped her notebook into her jacket pocket. 'If there's anything else we'll be in touch.'

Craven drained his glass and slid it towards the barman.

The barman shrugged. 'If there's anything else, I'll let you know.'

Helen exchanged a look with Craven.

'That's 30p for that.'

'What?'

'The drink. Coppers or not, you need to pay.'

Craven looked as though he was thinking about it for a moment, then replied, 'Nah. I get the polis discount.'

Helen rummaged in her pocket for some coins and dropped them onto the counter, then headed towards the door. She could see from the corner of her eye that Craven kept staring at the barman.

Outside, Helen sucked in cool fresh air. She could still taste the stale smoke in her mouth, and her lips felt dry. Craven appeared in the doorway with a tobacco pouch in his hand. She was about to say something when a cigarette-stained finger poking out of a fingerless glove tapped her on the arm.

'Hen.' The man hissed, rubbing his runny nose with his sleeve. He must've been in his late fifties, with a leathery face. 'Ah hiv information.'

Helen stepped away, finding it hard not to stare at the one tooth jutting from his gums. 'Can I help you?'

'You were asking questions aboot Reggie?' He nodded to the pub. 'Ah heard ye in there.'

'Right, what is it?' Craven stepped between the man and Helen.

'Information,' the old man offered.

'Get on wi' it, then,' Craven ordered, putting a roll-up to his mouth.

'It's no' free, though, officer. Am skint.' The old man made a show of patting his pockets.

Craven pulled out his wallet and held out a pound note. 'Talk. And this better be worth it.'

'That's it?'

'Aye, police cutbacks. Do you want it or not?'

'Aye, 'mon then.' The old man snatched the note and stuffed it into his pocket. 'Reggie wis in the pub last night but he wisnae alone. He's got a girlfriend the wife doesnae ken aboot.' He smiled and licked his lips. 'He's always got a bird on the go. Good-looking lassies tae, like. Kind o' bird ah like.' He looked Helen up and down.

'This *bird* got a name?' Craven asked.

'Maureen or something like that; dinnae ken her last name. I heard him boasting about it in the pub, and I've heard him talk about how he wanted to dae away wi' his wife.'

'That's a big help. There can't be too many Maureens in Edinburgh,' Craven replied.

'Actually, the lassie's name might be Morag.'

Craven snorted.

'Or Marj, maybe Marjorie.'

'When did you hear him say that about his wife?' Helen asked.

'A few months back.'

'What exactly did he say?'

'That it would be convenient if she had an accident or fell doon the stairs.'

* * *

'What do you think of that, then?' Craven asked when they were both back in the car.

Helen shrugged, fumbling with her seatbelt. 'Moira is more than likely dead. Reggie has an alibi, but that doesn't mean he didn't have a hand in it.'

Craven frowned. 'Aye, that's what I was thinking.'

'And if he has a new girlfriend maybe she wanted the wife out of the way.'

'Are you thinking of a woman scorned?'

'Maybe.' Craven turned on the ignition and pulled out into the traffic.

They drove most of the way to the station in silence —
broken by crackles of radio static and the rhythmic swish
of the windscreen wipers. She would need to get someone
to look at that radio when they were back at the station . .
. A gust of wind rocked the car and Helen felt her stomach
clench. Maybe it was just the weather — the radios were
always poor in the rain.

It had started to rain for a couple of minutes before
Craven seemed to notice and flick on the wipers.

Helen sighed, and fixed her gaze outside. Her ribs
throbbed, she shifted in her seat, but it didn't seem to make
a difference. If the pain carried on, she'd need to get back to
the doctors and get it checked out, not something that she
looked forward to.

CHAPTER EIGHTEEN

Helen had put this off long enough. That evening, she took a breath to steady herself, feeling her stomach constrict and her chest rise. After a moment, she knocked sharply on the door. A bitter wind was blowing, yet she could see the upstairs windows were open. She shoved her hands in her pockets and bobbed on the spot in a vain attempt to keep some warmth in her body. Coming here was a mistake. She took a step back, ready to turn and leave, when the door opened. He raised a bushy eyebrow. His normally neat hair looked windswept, and salt-and-pepper stubble sprouted from his jaw.

'I didn't expect you.' He shook his head.

'I know,' she replied, rubbing her damp nose with the back of her hand. What a state she must look after a twelve-hour shift and no sleep. 'I thought I should give you this back.' She fumbled in her pocket and shakily produced the ring box. 'I know you said I could keep it, but that just feels wrong.' She held it out, but he made no move to take it.

Instead, he gave her a suspicious look. 'I don't need it.' He sighed and opened the door wide. 'Come in, we need to talk.'

'I don't have much time.'

'There's no point doing this out on the doorstep, is there?'

'Right.' Helen hesitated then entered the house. The smell of fresh gloss stung her nose. She stepped over the dust sheets that were laid out to protect the tiles. Even in the hall, she felt the warm glow of the fire.

'This looks . . .'

He cut her off. 'Watch yourself on the walls; they're wet.'

'You've done a lot of work.' Helen glanced into the front room as they passed it. It had been painted a light green and was still empty.

'I'm selling,' he retorted. 'Well, I've nothing keeping me here now, have I?'

She didn't know what to say as she followed him through to the kitchen. Her gaze fell to the empty wine rack. 'I don't drink anymore.' He gave her an uncomfortable half-smile as he held the kettle under the sink. 'That's what you were looking at, weren't you? I stopped two months ago. Tea?'

'If you don't mind.'

'I wouldn't ask if I minded.'

'You're looking well,' Helen said, taking a seat at the kitchen table. 'One of my colleagues is in the car so I can't stay long . . .'

He nodded and put the kettle on the Aga. Smoke trailed from a fag that rested on a tea plate. He stubbed out the cigarette.

She looked out the kitchen window and could see that the conservatory was full of cardboard boxes. She heard him swallow and remembered their last conversation when he was sitting at the table in there, drunk. Out in the garden, the solitary apple tree she had planted had shed all its leaves. The skinny trunk swayed in the wind, its branches splayed, pointing in all directions like accusing fingers. She was going to plant a few more but never got around to it. It seemed like yesterday that she used to sit out there when it was in full bloom with a coffee in hand, doodling in her sketchbook.

'I'm going to get rid of it,' he said as if he knew what she was thinking. 'The new owners won't want it, and I've got most of my stuff ready to go. You're lucky to catch me, in fact. I'm away in a few days.' He narrowed his eyes, as he rummaged through a box of kitchenware, then produced a tea tin and a cup that were both wrapped in newspaper. 'I didn't expect to see you before I went . . .'

'No, I didn't either.' Her words hung in the air. She looked down at the yellowed newspaper on the worktop. It was an article about an unsolved murder along with the picture of the victim, smiling. It felt wrong that the poor woman's face was being used to wrap kitchen utensils. That murder was before Helen's time in CID, but she remembered it from the papers well. The woman was found battered and bloody in some wasteland near the docks in Leith.

'Do you mind if I take that?' Helen nodded to the newspaper.

'If you want.'

The kettle whistled and blew steam, filling the silence. He went to fill a cup with hot water and dropped a tea bag into it.

'Thanks,' she said, taking her cup. She cradled it in her hands, savouring the heat that soaked into them.

He sat down opposite her with a glass of water.

'Where are you going?'

'London, like we'd planned.' He slumped back in his seat and looked like he was thinking of what to say. He eventually added, 'You didn't give me a real reason.' He stared hard at her. 'You were keen to go at the hospital, then you ended things completely.'

'I just couldn't leave the police.' She placed the ring box on the table between them. 'It was never going to work. We both want different things.'

'Even after everything you went through?'

She slid her cup away and made a move to get up.

'Please, just tell me!' He furrowed his brow. 'I want to know.'

'My Dad was bent, all right . . .' She rubbed her face with the heel of her hand, not daring to look at him. 'I found out he took backhanders from criminals. I want to keep working and make that right.'

He rolled his eyes. 'That's not your fault, though.'

'I know.'

'Is there no way back for us?'

'It's not a good idea.'

'Can you come back when you have more time?' Please?'

'Ted, I don't know. I put a lot on the line for you, for us. The times I was late to work and the mornings I spent trying to sober you up?'

'I have changed.'

Helen zipped up her jacket. 'I'll leave you to get on with your packing.' Without looking back, she walked out.

As she was climbing back into her car, she heaved a sigh to try to control the tears that wanted to escape from her eyes. She slipped a glance at the house. He was still standing in the doorway. She gave him a half-hearted wave then pulled out.

Detective Constable Terry McKinley was in the passenger scat. He looked up from the *Evening News* on his lap. 'Everything okay?' he asked.

CHAPTER NINETEEN

Helen awoke and sat bolt upright on the sofa, knocking her cushion to the floor. Unsure of what it was that had woken her, she listened for any noise. Nothing. She shivered, rubbing the sleep from the corners of her eyes. Chances were it was one of the neighbours or a car rumbling past. The windows in these old buildings let every little noise in. The curtains were half-drawn, and a light from the lamppost leaked through the gap. The lamp she'd left on in the corner cast a faint glow over the room. Her eyes finally adjusted so that she could read the time on the art-deco clock on the wall. Was that five-thirty? She clambered up and opened the curtains as a car rumbled past. Plenty of time for a shower and coffee before work, she thought, as she peeled her T-shirt from her stomach.

Standing in the shower, she closed her eyes as the hot water trailed down her neck and shoulders. She stretched and rolled her neck until the joints stopped clicking. Sleeping on the hard sofa was doing her back no good, and she hadn't been on a jog for ages either. She would need to sort out what she was going to do soon. Maybe rent somewhere else and put this flat up for sale, but it would need a lot of work to get it ready. Her gaze fell to the faded, cracked tiles above the sink. She rubbed the bar of soap over her shoulder and grimaced. The bruise was long gone but a dull ache in her shoulder joint still lingered. When she stretched her arm out in front, the joint clicked a couple of times in a vain attempt to ease the stiffness.

As she was drying her hair, the bottle of Valium on the medicine cabinet stood out among the other bottles. She picked it up. Had the tablets really been helping her? She wasn't sure. Mostly, they made her tired and forgetful, so as soon as she had gone back to work, she stopped taking them. Determined not to be tempted, she shoved them out of sight behind a pot of moisturizer. Ted's Brylcreem and toothbrush still sat on the shelf above the sink. In one swift motion, she swiped them into the little bin. He wouldn't want them back, and there was no point keeping them.

After a cup of coffee and a slice of toast, Helen headed for the car. It was only half-six, and there weren't many cars on the road as she drove towards Princes Street. The blood and the cracked coffee table in the McKenzies' flat swarmed her mind. She kept a tight grip on the steering wheel. Frost glistened on the roads, and she felt the car wobble a couple times as it moved over the cobbles in Stockbridge.

As Helen entered CID, Randall stood beside the case board, a cup of tea in one hand, pinning an image of a brown-haired woman onto the board with the other. The smell of bacon rolls hung heavy in the air, and her eyes were watering from the warm air and tobacco smoke. She blinked hard as she draped her jacket over her chair. Randall's top lip curled into a sneer when they made eye contact. *Arsehole.*

'Morning,' she muttered as she turned away from him and dropped her bag onto the desk.

'Is it?' Randall scratched the bald patch on the top of his head. She felt his glare on her as she sat down.

Randall's moods would change depending on whoever was in the office. Alone, he could be pleasant enough. With his group of pals though he was a bully.

McKinley cradled his head in both hands, and his elbows were propped on his desk. He was reading a paper, reminding Helen of a bored schoolboy. She slipped a glance over to Craven's office, behind a glass partition at the far end of the room. It looked like he was in, orange lamplight spilled out from a gap in the blinds. She went over, took a deep breath and knocked on the door.

Craven was on the phone when she entered, a fag dangling from his lips. He looked up at her, the receiver was balanced between his ear and shoulder and he was scribbling something into his notebook. He waved her in. In front of him sat a tea plate with crumbs on it and a half-drunk mug of greasy looking coffee.

He slammed the receiver back down. 'Moira McKenzie is still missing. The dogs have been out and found nothing.' He sat back in his chair and took a long drag on his cigarette.

'What about the car?' Helen asked.

'Nothing's come up with the partial licence plate you were given. Terry's gone through the list of known criminals' vehicles, and nothing fits so far.' He stifled a cough, then grimaced. 'The new DCI will be making an appearance this afternoon as well.' Craven didn't look pleased. He had applied for the promotion but was turned down.

'Try these.' Helen put a half-pound bag of Liquorice Allsorts onto Craven's desk. He looked up from the reports he was skimming through and raised an eyebrow. 'What's this?'

'I got them from the sweet shop. If you're giving up the fags these will help.'

He weighed the paper bag in his hand. 'It sounds like you're talking from experience.'

Helen shrugged. When she was nearly out of the office, she turned her head to face him. 'You should know I've eaten the pink ones.'

'Oh, you're in.' McKinley gave her a half-smile as she emerged from Craven's office.

'Did you not see me walk past your desk ten minutes ago?' Helen arched an eyebrow.

'Nah.' He shook his head. 'I've been busy.'

'Aye?' Helen stepped towards him.

He yawned and rubbed his eyes with the heel of his hand. 'I think I need glasses. My eyes keep going blurry.'

'What have you been busy with?'

Standing up, he waved a folder at Helen. 'I've checked the missing persons register. Moira has been reported missing twice previously.'

'What?'

'Aye.' McKinley nodded.

'By who?' Helen crossed the room and took the files from McKinley's hands.

'Reggie McKenzie,' McKinley stated.

She shook her head. 'He told me Moira hasn't gone missing before.'

Helen skim-read the information. 'Three years ago, Moira went missing for two days and was found in Glasgow at a boarding house. Then, six months later, she didn't come home from the pub. Reggie reported her missing but apparently she turned up half a day later.' Often someone going missing like this could be a good indication that they'd return home safe again, but the blood in the flat made it more than likely that Moira was dead.

'Check that boarding house in Glasgow.' Helen handed him the folder back.

'I have,' McKinley replied. 'No one matching Moira's description has been found there.' McKinley rummaged under more folders and retrieved a slip of paper. 'I've got a few more calls to make.'

His main job as an 'aide' in the CID department was to collate all the information from cases, and although he complained about it a lot, he was good at it.

Helen nodded. She had somewhere else she needed to be. 'I'll see you back here later, and we can then go through what we have.'

'There's one more thing — and you're not going to like this.' He made a face. 'PC Rafferty had also been to a domestic disturbance at the property six weeks ago, only he hasn't filed much information in the reports.'

'Oh, god. Not that man,' Helen replied.

'Want me to—'

'No, I'll speak to him. I'm a glutton for punishment.'

CHAPTER TWENTY

Helen waited until a group of teenage lads had passed before she opened the door of the Granada. They had parked in one of the doctors-only spaces in front of the medical centre. Helen rubbed her shoulder where the seatbelt had rested and looked over to the centre — a modern flat-roofed building. It looked to serve the new scheme of prefab high-rise flats and maisonettes that sprung up in the cornfields in the fifties. Some of the construction work was still going on. These flats were meant to be an escape from the crumbling one-bed tenements with outdoor toilets. Unfortunately, with a lot of people in this area becoming unemployed due to the closure of the nearby docks, plus the influx of heroin, this scheme was in danger of becoming hell.

It was on the same street as the graffiti-stained wreck of a picture house which cast a shadow over them. Thankfully, that was now in the process of being demolished. There were two metal skips out on the street filled with debris, wood and broken chairs. A man in his twenties was picking some of the old cinema posters out of the wreckage. She shuddered and looked away.

'That will be gone soon.' Craven knew exactly what she was thinking. 'Think they're building a supermarket on it.'

'Can't come quick enough,' Helen replied as they walked down the path towards the entrance of the surgery. She pulled the dented red door open for both of them.

Craven stopped at the brass nameplate at the side of the door, his face darkening.

'What is it?' she asked.

'Nothing.'

As they passed through a second set of double doors, warm radiator heat hit them, along with the sickly smell of cleaning fluid and stale alcohol.

A couple of people looked up, but most kept their gaze on the tiled floor.

'It's *Night of the Living Dead*,' Craven said, making no attempt to whisper.

The waiting area in the middle of the surgery was full of people hunched on chairs, yellow-faced. Some looked old well before their time with haunted faces. Helen shuddered. There was the quiet murmur of restless conversation. Two men with skeletal bodies and puffy faces sat under posters about balanced diets and notices that said *Help your doctor to help you*.

An old woman stood waiting by the receptionist's desk. She moved aside as Craven spoke but just enough so that she could hear everything that they were saying.

The receptionist, a hard-faced woman in her fifties with her greying hair scraped back, stared at them. 'Have you got an appointment?' she asked with an air of exasperation.

Helen could hardly see her over the patients' folders that were stacked on the counter — no doubt in place for the doctor to take when they called a patient in. *God, there must've been a hundred.*

'I don't need an appointment.' Craven held up his warrant card for inspection. 'Is the doctor in?'

'Oh.' She peered over her national health glasses. 'Which doctor? There's five, you know,' the receptionist replied.

Craven looked at Helen.

'Dr Rushmore?' Helen smiled.

'Yes, he is but—'

Before the receptionist could finish Craven started down the narrow corridor of closed teak doors.

'Third door from the bottom,' the woman said to Helen.

Helen nodded. 'Thanks.' She followed him, feeling the eyes of the patients in the waiting room on her.

Craven knocked hard on the open door marked with a silver nameplate saying, 'Dr Rushmore'.

Helen took one glance at the man who looked up from the desk and knew what Craven would think of him. The man was in his forties. Handsome, with a strong jaw and big brown eyes. He was wearing a badly fitting light green tweed jacket that looked like it belonged to a much bigger man, but he looked fairly muscular, so maybe he'd lost weight.

He was signing a stack of prescription slips with a tobacco-stained hand. 'I'm not seeing patients. Wait outside.' Before they could respond he returned his focus to the slips on his desk. Annoyance creased the lines on his forehead when they remained standing in the open door.

'Dr Rushmore, we're police officers.' Helen flashed her warrant card.

'Oh.' He looked up wide-eyed and placed his pen in front of him. 'Come in, take a seat.'

The doctor motioned to the two red plastic chairs squashed up in front of his desk.

The room was barely big enough for the desk and an examination bed. The small window was open a crack, and they could hear the traffic outside.

Craven flicked a glance down the corridor before closing the door. 'Are you the only doctor here?'

'No, Dr Nairn is taking patients.' He spoke with a soft Morningside accent. 'I don't see what that's got—'

'It's about a patient of yours, Moira McKenzie,' Craven said.

'Who?' Dr Rushmore asked, appearing confused.

'You've prescribed some medication to her, Valium tablets.' Helen stepped forward. 'You prescribed these last week, on the twenty-eighth.'

He looked at her blankly. 'We have over two thousand patients in this practice between five doctors. I don't know everyone's names. I'm dealing with more and more patients with drug problems, drink problems.' He sighed and shook his head. 'It's becoming an epidemic.'

Helen approached the desk and sat down in the chair opposite him. 'I didn't say that she had a drink or drugs problem.'

He furrowed his brow. 'I just assumed from . . . To be honest, that's a fairly common prescription.'

'Would you be able to get her records and tell us why she was prescribed these tablets? Her whereabouts are unknown and we're very worried for her welfare.' Craven stepped forward and made a show of looking around the room.

The doctor looked like he was considering this for a moment then finally stood up. 'They're kept in another room. If you want to follow me, but I don't think there's much I can help you with.'

'We'll be the judge of that.'

'Thank you, Doctor.' Helen added.

Dr Rushmore took his glasses from his shirt pocket, and they followed him along the narrow corridor behind the reception area and then through to a side room with rows of shelves stuffed with manila folders. He brushed a finger over the folders on the bottom shelf and muttered 'McKenzie' several times as he searched. Some of the sleeves had faded in colour and others looked damp around the edges.

The doctor pulled out a thick brown folder. He dropped it onto an empty table at the other side of the room and flicked through it. 'Ah, I remember her now,' he said, nodding as he turned the pages over. 'What is it you're after?'

Furrowing his brow, he looked back down at the folder. 'She's been prescribed Valium for psychotic episodes. She has schizophrenia. She's suffered it for the past five or so years. As well as sleeping problems, paranoid delusions.' He shrugged. 'It's quite standard treatment, officers. Sadly, I'm now seeing a lot more patients with these kinds of problems.'

'Was the twenty-eighth the last time you saw her?' Helen asked.

'No, I didn't actually see her. I just signed her repeat prescription that day.' He puffed out his cheeks and looked back at the folder. 'Last time I saw her for an appointment was in October. Actually no.' There was a pause as he flicked through more papers in the folder. 'Last week, actually.' His glasses slipped down the bridge of his nose. 'Yes, on Thursday. It was a house visit — she wasn't feeling very well, with headaches. I told her to rest and I re-evaluated her medicines. That medication can make the patient feel drowsy, all perfectly normal.' He skim-read. 'Told her to keep the stress down; all the usual stuff.'

'Thank you, doctor,' Helen replied. She took a note of the dates in her notebook. 'Has she ever had bruises on her? Things she couldn't explain?'

'I don't know. There's nothing I can see in the file, but it's not something I would examine for routinely. She was a very quiet woman, reluctant to get treatment. It was her husband who sought it for her and would bring her to the practice.'

Helen noted how he used the word *was* to describe Moira.

'What's happened to her?' His voice softened.

'She's missing from home, and we found some evidence to suggest that she might have been hurt.'

'Oh dear. Well, I'm terribly sorry to hear that.' He shoved the folder back into the slot. 'Sadly, I only have records from when she moved to this area two years ago.'

'If there is anything else you can think of, let us know. Thank you.'

Dr Rushmore looked up at the big clock above their heads. 'I'm really sorry but I have to go now. I'm going to be late for my morning house appointments.'

'Just one more thing, did you visit a patient last night? William Hutchinson?'

'Yes — I did. He was in quite a bad way. I left his property about nine.'

'Thank you for your help doctor.'

* * *

'Wait.' A male voice called behind them as they headed back to the car.

Helen noticed Craven's shoulders tense, but he carried on towards the car.

'Jack! Jack!'

Helen turned to see a thin man in a black suit who broke into a jog to catch up with them.

'Didn't know you worked here.' Craven slotted his keys into the Granada. 'Thought you were in some posh practice.'

'No, I enjoy being on the frontline so to speak, with the salt of the earth.' The man smiled at Helen.

'Anyway, nice chat, we've got to go.' Craven pulled open the door.

'I'm so glad I caught you. I wanted to speak with you anyway.'

Craven turned to Helen with a smile on his face. 'This is the lovely man who married my ex-wife.'

The man chortled, then introduced himself. 'I'm Milton.'

'I won't take up much of your time.' Milton had his hands in his pockets and bobbed on the spot. 'I know you're planning on seeing the twins at the weekend.'

'Not planning, I am.' Craven motioned to Helen to get in the car.

'Thing is, we've managed to get a small weekend away. Down in the Cotswolds and I hardly ever get time off you see . . .'

Craven fished in his pockets for his cigarettes then placed one to his lips. 'I don't fancy going to the Cotswolds.'

'I wasn't, I meant . . . We're wanting to take the twins. Get a bit of R&R.'

'Go another weekend.'

'We've mentioned it to the twins, and they're really looking forward to it. We're going horse riding . . . No offence, Jack, but you've cancelled that many times before, sometimes we've just got to plan things.'

'I've no' got time for this. I'll speak to Liz.' Craven started the car and pulled out into traffic.

'I'm still trying to get my seatbelt on', Helen said, as he pressed down on the accelerator, his gaze fixed ahead. They got a few streets away before he spoke.

'That Dr Rushmore was a bit of a tosser, there's just something about him that doesn't sit right with me.' Craven took a few drags of his cigarette in quick succession.

Helen waved smoke away and grimaced. 'What's in that cheap tobacco?'

Craven shrugged.

'Anyway, I thought you had stopped.'

'I've cut down.' Craven coughed a couple of times as they pulled into a side street. He wrenched the handbrake. 'I'm starving,' Craven said, nodding towards the little greasy spoon across the road. 'Looks all right in there.'

'That'll do,' Helen said, grabbing her handbag from the footwell. It had been a while since she'd eaten too. The mid-morning sun had cleared away the rain, and white clouds streaked with pink sat low in the sky as Helen got out of the car.

Helen stepped forward and shielded her eyes from the sunlight reflecting on the surface of a big puddle.

'C'mon, let's grab a cup of tea.'

They chose the table by the window, and Helen returned with two mugs of pale tea that felt slimy in her hand. Craven looked at his cup, then back out of the window.

The only other people in the café, a bored-looking couple, sat near the counter. Helen brushed away some toast crumbs from the last person who had sat in the chair and plonked herself down. She took a sip and watched people pass by outside. A shivering couple were huddled in the bus shelter and looked deep in conversation about something. Something serious.

Craven grabbed a copy of the *Evening News* from another table.

A few minutes later, a fat old woman with a pink apron around her waist and a cigarette dangling from her lips slapped down two plates of yellow-looking scrambled egg lying in the middle of a puddle of liquid. The toast from Helen's plate slid off onto the rubber tablecloth.

'Cheers,' Helen said as she put the toast back on the plate. The woman mumbled something that Helen couldn't hear, then wandered back behind the counter.

'Well, this looks nice,' Helen muttered.

'Ach, it's no' that bad.'

'What are you going to do about the weekend?'

Craven tutted. 'Once a month I get to see my kids. That's if he's not whisking them away somewhere. 'It was Costa something a few months ago, then skiing before that. If he's promised them horse riding, they're hardly going to want to kick a ball up the park with me, are they?'

'You're still their dad. No one else can replace that.'

'Milton's doing a good job of that. Must be hard being back in this area,' Craven said, as he scooped some scrambled egg up with a fork. He swallowed a mouthful, made a face then carried on.

Helen thought for a moment. 'Seeing the cinema reminds me of what happened.' She took another sip of her tea, and this time it didn't taste so bad. It would take a long time for her to forget what happened. The damp and dust that burned her throat. The rope around her wrist. Throbbing. She swallowed hard. Thinking about it wasn't going to do her any good.

Helen turned her attention back to the window. From what she had heard from the gossips at the station, Craven's wife left him after a couple of years of marriage for a childhood friend.

A woman with bleached hair carrying a couple of shopping bags caught her eye. It couldn't be her, could it? The woman was wearing a purple velvet coat and knee-high black boots. The same outfit Helen had seen at the station before. She stopped at the bus stop and pulled a small mirror and lipstick from her pocket. From that angle Helen finally got a good look at her face. Craven must've noticed her staring because he shifted so he could see what she was looking at. They watched as she freshened her lipstick and gave a look of approval then picked up her bags and carried on down the street.

'Oh god, Sally.' He sneered.

'I thought she was in London.' Sally was a typist in the station. A bottle blonde with a tendency to wear too much make-up. Helen couldn't work out why Craven was sneering as he was always friendly with Sally — too friendly. Sally disappeared around the corner once she had lit her cigarette.

'She's like a bloody boomerang that one. You can't get rid of her.' Craven remarked.

Helen shrugged and turned her attention back to her meal.

'If she's back on the scene, Terry will lose all interest in you then.'

'Terry has no interest in me.'

'Aye right.' Craven chucked. 'I'm not blind.'

'How's your food?' Helen asked.

'They go way back.' Craven heaved himself up from his chair. 'I need a slash.' He gave a small sigh and headed towards the back of the café.

He was probably right, though. Helen slid her untouched plate away. She made a move to pick up her handbag and noticed a slip of paper next to his chair. His tweed jacket was draped over the back, so it must've fallen out of a pocket. She picked it up, the NHS logo visible on the corner of the thick paper and unfolded it: an appointment for a lung clinic, tomorrow afternoon. She shouldn't have opened it. It was none of her business. She put the paper down beside his teacup. When Craven returned, he looked down at the letter and slipped it into his pocket.

CHAPTER TWENTY-ONE

For the best part of three hours had Helen been sifting through folders at her desk. She blinked back tiredness and took a couple of paracetamols to ease her headache. The couple who lived opposite Moira and Reggie McKenzie hadn't heard anything that night. They kept themselves to themselves, apparently. 'Looked pleasant enough.' Moira sometimes had a visitor in the mornings, a dark-haired woman. They'd sometimes be seen leaving the stairwell, chatting, or with a pile of books from the library. *She seemed a nice woman.* That's what everyone kept saying. Reggie, though, wouldn't stop to say hello. Kept his head down, and always seemed in a rush.

Moira didn't have many living relatives in Scotland, only a niece and brother-in-law. A few relatives were in Australia, it seemed, but so far, they hadn't been able to track those down. The brother-in-law spoke positively about Reggie and seemed to be devastated. One dead end after another.

Helen skimmed through the report of Moira's sister Agnes's accident. At the time, Agnes stepped out onto the road and was struck by an oncoming car. Since then, she struggled with memory loss and required continual care. Reggie had been the one to get her medical attention.

Moira's colleagues at the hairdressers were shocked and full of grief. None of them had met Reggie, but Moira hadn't mentioned any problems either. They echoed what the neighbours had said — she kept herself to herself.

The owner of the salon, Molly O'Hara, who spoke with a soft hint of a Belfast accent, ushered them through into little room separated from the rest of the salon by a dye-stained curtain. Her hair looked perfectly coiffed, with not a strand out of place, and her thick blue eye shadow had started to smudge. Helen had her own hair cut shorter as she struggled to keep it neat. A biscuit tin and coffee jar stood on a shelf, and a small table and chairs filled the space, for staff to sit at while on breaks.

Molly slumped down in the seat with her head in her hands. 'I can't believe this.'

'Are you close to Moira?' Helen asked.

'Aye.' Molly looked up, her lip quivering. 'We were just out a couple of nights ago.'

'Where did you go?'

'A pub, The World's End. We go there a lot.'

The smell of hair dye made Helen's head tingle. She stepped forward. 'I know this is hard, but I need to ask some questions that may help us find Moira.'

Molly nodded.

'Did Moira drink often?'

Molly crinkled her nose. 'A wee bit, but it didn't affect her job.'

'Was she anxious?'

'Things did get a wee bit on top of her from time to time, but nothing bad.'

Helen flicked to an empty page on her notebook. A solitary dusty lamp on the shelf provided the only light in this part of the building.

'Moira's worked here for a couple of years, and she does a good job. I wouldn't have said she was an alcoholic or that. I know her husband says that, but that's just to control her. Make her feel like rubbish.' Molly pulled a face that looked like she wanted to spit at the mention of his name.

Helen nodded. She believed the woman. 'Has she talked about going on holiday? Talked about going to any foreign places?'

'Not really. I dunno.'

'When would Moira have got paid?'

'Wednesday.'

'Did she collect her wages?'

Molly put her hands to her lips. 'Yes, she did.'

'How much does she get paid?

'£24, I think. She's part-time,' Molly added, as she reached up for a black folder on the shelf and skimmed through it. 'Aye, 24.'

'Was she working on Wednesday morning?'

'No.'

'Does she often come in specially to collect her wages?'

'Not normally. She collected her National Insurance card too.'

A ginger-haired girl popped her head around the curtain. 'Molly, your 11 a.m. is waiting, and she's no' happy.'

'I'm really sorry,' Molly said to Helen, as she wiped a tear away with the back of her hand. 'I better go. Mrs Anderson doesn't like to be kept waiting.'

CHAPTER TWENTY-TWO

Helen slipped a glance to the staff sergeant, Robert Keaton on the front desk. He had his head down, leafing through reports. He had been in CID before her, but his drinking problem sent him back to uniform. That was one of the rea sons she was resented in the department — most of them in there thought she had taken his job.

She headed round to the constables' room, but the officer she needed to speak to wasn't there. A biscuit tin on a desk caught her attention; a black-and-white photo of a constable was taped to it. The words 'funeral collection for Tim Morrison' were scribbled on a small card beside it. Helen reached into her bag and slipped out a fiver from her purse. She didn't know him, but judging from the photo, he had been in his mid-twenties.

An officer she didn't know mumbled his thanks as she slipped the note into the tin. 'It's for his wife and son,' he added.

Helen nodded. 'Have you seen Alan Rafferty?'

The officer looked like he was considering this for a moment then shook his head. 'I'll let him know you're looking for him. I know he's in the station somewhere.'

Helen had made it most of the way back up to the CID office when PC Rafferty called after her from the bottom of the stairs.

'You were wanting to speak to me,' Rafferty shouted from the bottom step, not hiding the exasperation in his voice.

'Aye,' she said rubbing her forehead as she waited for him to catch up. That headache still hadn't let off.

Rafferty was younger than her by a few years, with short ginger hair and freckles. He scowled at her. 'I've got to get back downstairs in a minute, so you'll need to be quick.'

'This won't take long.'

Rafferty slapped his hands to his sides, sighed and followed.

She headed into the office and sat down at her desk. 'You attended a domestic dispute in June at the McKenzies' residence.'

He rolled his eyes. 'You'll need to do better than that, darling. I've been to a few of them.'

'I've got all the information here. Well, I say information . . .'

'Can we just get this over with?'

The CID room was quiet but the upcoming visit from Strathclyde and the new DCI was making everyone tense. McKinley was going through a folder and didn't bother to look up. Randall had his phone balanced between his ear and shoulder and his feet up on his desk. She noticed that Rafferty was trying to make eye contact with Randall, but Randall kept his gaze down.

The file on the domestic dispute was at the top of her papers. Helen picked it up and handed it to Rafferty. 'You attended a domestic incident with two alcoholics. There's not much information on this report, and the female, Moira McKenzie, has now gone missing.'

'Aye, well, if that's what it says,' he shrugged, 'that's what happened.'

'Well, that's the only information on here. What *happened*? I need to know more than that. It looks like this woman has come to some serious harm.'

'Fine.' He tapped his foot impatiently while flicking through his notebook.

Now it was Helen's turn to roll her eyes. 'You do have the information, Constable?'

His face reddened as he flicked back and forth through the pages. 'Aye, just give me a minute.'

'Take your time.' Helen sat back in her chair.

'Found it.'

'And?'

Nothing much happened,' Rafferty replied flippantly.

'I'd like more information than that,' Helen countered.

He shook his head. 'It had all calmed down by the time we arrived. The husband was apologetic, and I gave him a stern warning to behave himself, the usual. We asked the female if she wanted to press charges. She said no. End of.' He snapped his notebook shut.

Helen shook her head. This wasn't finished, not by a long shot. 'Was there any sign of violence?'

'I don't think so.'

'You don't *think* so?' Helen sighed and shook her head. 'So, again, what happened?' She made no attempt at hiding the annoyance in her voice.

'I listened to them.' He offered her a smile. 'I'm a good listener.'

Helen glared at him. His attitude annoyed her. 'What exactly did you listen to?'

'Just the usual excuses for having too much to drink.' He paused for a second and furrowed his brow. 'It was really nothing out of the ordinary. Do you actually know how many of these domestics I attend in a week?'

She knew and also knew that a lot of people thought police shouldn't get involved in domestic incidents that happened in the privacy of their own home. Helen couldn't understand that approach, but many officers also agreed with it.

'On that night, you were on duty with PC Tulloch?'

'He's left Lothian and Borders now.' Rafferty handed Helen the recording sheet back.

'You shouldn't fail to pass on information because you think it's trivial. It may help us do our job. What you write in your notebook is often used for reports and statements. There are procedures to follow.'

He nodded, his jaw stiffening. 'Will that be everything, *Sergeant*?'

'For now.' She began to sort through the folders on her desk.

Rafferty slammed the CID door on the way out.

'He's going to go far, that one.' Randall chimed in.

CHAPTER TWENTY-THREE

McKinley stood up from his desk with a slip of paper in his hand, 'A second search of the McKenzies' residence found no cash or passports. Reggie McKenzie had said she does have one, but had no idea where it would be now.' He crossed around his desk.

'Is he sure about that?' Helen asked.

McKinley shrugged. 'One of the neighbours has also got in touch to say that Reggie has a shed out back. As part of the communal block.'

'We asked him if he had any access to buildings like that and he said no.'

McKinley looked back down at the paper. 'He may not officially own it, but he rents it from the neighbour. The neighbour is elderly and didn't want it.'

'We'll need to look at that.' Helen sighed and looked at the case board. She moved over to the tea station and made herself a tea, then stirred it with one of the lesser-stained spoons. Uniform had been out throughout the night, and no one fitting Moira's description had appeared at any of the hospitals. The crucial hours were ticking away, and so far she had nothing to show for them except bloodshot eyes and a feeling of dread in her stomach.

She sat down at her desk, clearing some space among the papers for her chipped mug. Randall hung up his phone and started battering his typewriter while he dragged on a cigarette, the noise drowning out the disco tunes that filtered through from the radio.

The board, which took up most of the left-hand wall, was plastered with images and mugshots from various cases. Helen's attention fell to the composite drawing of a man responsible for a spate of house burglaries. A creepy, almost alien-like thin face and eyes that were almost comically too close together.

McKinley pulled open the filing cabinets. He was wearing a crumpled brown shirt, and it looked like he needed a new blade on his razor. Retrieving another folder, he walked over to her desk, stared at her tea, and made a face. 'Don't you want milk in that?' He dropped the folder on her desk and spilled some of the tea from the mug onto Helen's notebook.

'This happens to be how I like my tea.'

'Sorry about that.' Blushing, he mopped it up with his shirt sleeve.

'You're looking rough,' he carried on.

'Thanks,' she smiled.

'No, I just mean it looks like you've not had much sleep.'

'I haven't.'

'Here's the medical report,' he said, flicking through a couple of pages in the loose-leaf folder. 'The blood type found in the McKenzies' flat is AB negative.'

'That's extremely rare and it matches Moira's, according to her doctor's report. Still doesn't mean it's hers definitively though.' She moved the backlog stack of house robbery reports already on her desk to the side to give herself some room. Her back felt tight, and she rolled her neck from side to side until it cracked.

McKinley made another face.

'Sorry.' Helen grimaced and straightened in her seat. 'This old chair is horrible.'

She grabbed an A4-size road atlas of Edinburgh from the shelves and flicked to the right street. Bending the spine of the book, she placed it between her and McKinley. He slid a chair around and sat down, banging his knee on the edge of the desk as he did so. Swearing under his breath, he splayed his spindly legs out. She picked up a scrap piece of paper and began scribbling. Some of the ink had smudged from being brushed by her left hand as she wrote. She squinted to read it. 'So, Reggie was in the pub until nine thirty.'

'He's in there most nights, apparently. Neighbours backed this up, too.'

Helen's team had circulated Moira's details to the hospital, bus station and newspapers but it was looking increasingly unlikely that they would find her alive.

She slipped out the newspaper article from Ted's house from her pocket. 'Can you also get me all the reports for this murder?'

McKinley took and unfolded it. 'I'll see what I can do.'

'Are you still up for the flicks tonight?' Helen motioned to the *Evening News* on the shelf. She wanted to ask him about Sally but thought better of it.

'Aye, if we find the time.' McKinley replied.

'I just thought you might've had plans.'

'I don't but—'

They both looked up as the CID door thumped against the filing cabinet. A man in his late forties, wearing an expensive-looking tailored brown suit, stood in the doorway. Helen caught the glimmer of a silver watch peeking out from under the cuff of his jacket. He took his time and made eye contact with everyone in the room before stepping over the threshold. The chatter in the office stopped abruptly and Randall turned off the radio.

After a few moments of silence, he spoke with a thick Glaswegian accent. 'I'm DCI Tam Murphy. Some o' you I've worked wi' before. Get results! Do as you're told, and you'll find ah'm fair. Ah'm fae Strathclyde and ma team's gonnae be helping with the unsolved murders and getting this department into shape.'

Murphy made a show of looking Helen up and down. His blue eyes looked like they were boring into her. Daring her to say something. She could tell from his face that he didn't recognize her.

She took a shaky breath and glared back at him. She wasn't going to be the one to look away first. She'd heard Murphy had taken over from their last DCI, and a lot of the officers had been dreading the change, but this was their first face-to-face meeting.

'Bloody hell. All I need is one of the foreigners and then we'll have the full set.' He opened his question out to the rest of the room. 'Where's the wee one-legged one?' He chuckled and rubbed his hands together. A pathetic comedian laughing at his own jokes.

The pencil snapped in Helen's hand. *Little man syndrome at its finest.*

Tam Murphy swaggered into the centre of the room, enjoying the moment. He tilted his head, looking under Helen's desk. 'You could've put a skirt on, love. Nae point in having you in my department if you dress like a man.' His top lip curled into a sneer.

McKinley shifted in his seat, as Randall snorted.

'Is Jack in his office?' He pointed towards the closed mahogany door.

'No, he's no',' Randall answered. 'He should be back soon, sir.'

'What a shit,' McKinley mumbled.

Helen watched him grinning as he walked into Craven's office.

'Well, at least we won't need to work with him if we're on this case.'

Heart pounding in her chest, the trill sound of the telephone cut through the office like a knife.

Helen snatched up the phone. 'Helen Carter.'

'We've got someone in the interview room for you and he's confessed to murdering Tina French.'

CHAPTER TWENTY-FOUR

'Tell me again what you've told my colleagues.' Helen asked, sitting down opposite the suspect. He looked to be in his late forties with thinning brown hair and was missing his front left tooth. He was wearing a green shirt that was stained. Craven remained at the door, arms crossed.

'I killed her.' The man tore off a nail and spat it onto the floor. 'What else do you need to know?'

'Quite a lot more,' Helen rebuked.

'What? You not going to arrest me, copper?' He looked at her with what looked like genuine confusion to Helen.

'We're not in a rush, are we? If you have killed someone, it's not like you're going to go anywhere?' Helen smiled. 'We have all the time in the world.'

'Fine. What do you want to know?'

'Why don't you start with telling me why you killed her?' Helen looked down at her own notes.

He groaned. 'Do I really need to go through this again?' I already told that fat polis officer at the desk everything.'

Helen could see Craven step forward from the corner of her eye. 'This is a serious confession.' Helen replied. 'I need to hear it myself. I can't arrest you unless I have all the facts.

'It's like what the papers say.' He leaned back in his seat and made a show of looking her up and down, slowly. 'Exactly like the papers say, don't you read them, darling?'

'Well, I want to hear it from the horse's mouth.' Helen looked back down at her notebook, flicking to the page that detailed Helen's last movements.

'I'm evil. Stabbed her, didn't I?'

'Did you?'

'Aye, of course.' He rolled his eyes. 'You can't do that and not be evil.'

'What did you do with the knife?'

'Took it with me.'

'So, you took it with you, then what?'

'I just . . . I went home.'

'Where is it now?'

'What?'

'The knife.'

'I got rid of it.'

'Oh! That's convenient,' Craven interjected.

'Why come to the police now then?' Helen asked.

'I hear voices,' he tapped the side of his head. 'They told me to do it.'

'And why did they tell you to do it?'

He shrugged. 'You got any fags? And I want a cup of tea. And a sandwich too, cheese. Actually, corn beef.' He licked his lips. 'Nice thick bits.'

'What do you think this is? A greasy spoon?' Craven shook his head. 'The only thing you'll be chewing on in a minute is my boot.'

'Right, *these voices*,' Helen carried on.

'They told me to kill her and the others.'

'What others?'

'Tina French and others. I don't know all their names. They said they were evil and I needed to get rid of them . . . for the greater good.'

'I killed Moira McKenzie too.'

116

'I've not got time for this,' Craven muttered.

'How did you kill Moira?'

'I broke into her house. She begged me not to. Then I did it.'

'I was wondering why you painted a circle on the wall. After you left her on the sofa?'

'I was . . . I was compelled too.'

Craven shoved passed Helen and knocked the man and his chair to the floor. He grabbed him by his shirt collar and shook him. 'You're a dirty little liar. There's a real killer out there and you're wasting our time.'

'I am not.' Flailing, his eyes darted between Helen and Craven like a wild animal. 'I'm telling the truth!' He spat.

'Right, you killed all these women?' Craven asked the man.

'Aye.'

'No, you didn't.' Helen shook her head.

'You were in prison for being a grubby little thief, when the other two were murdered. What, you just fancied another little spell behind bars?'

Craven shoved a knee into his side, and he squealed. 'Please, it was me. You have to believe me!' He looked up at Helen, pleadingly.

'You didn't do this,' Helen replied. 'It's not possible.'

'I did. I know I did,' he sobbed. 'I remember doing it, I need to be punished.'

Outside the interview room, one of the officers who had done the initial interview approached. 'We're being overrun by nutters; the phone line is blocked with them too. All wanting their fifteen minutes of fame. Why would someone do this? I don't get it.'

Helen looked back at the door. 'He's maybe got some deep-seated guilt about something and wants to be punished for that.' She could see from the glass partition that the man had his head in his hands and was wailing. 'Who knows, with years of drug and alcohol abuse he might have even convinced himself that he did do it.'

CHAPTER TWENTY-FIVE

After a night in the cells, Reggie spoke in a low voice to Helen and McKinley in Interview Room One. He looked different to the night before — all bravado gone. Grey-faced, eyes swollen, and lips cracked. Last night's veneer of arrogance washed away when faced with the insides of a police interview room.

'You've not found Moira, have you?' He blinked hard and stared ahead, glassy-eyed.

'No, we haven't,' Helen replied. 'But we are doing everything in our power to do so.'

'You all think I've done something to her, but I haven't.' He rubbed his nose with his shirt sleeve and sniffed. 'I know what you're like. Blame the husband.'

'We're trying to find out what happened, to do our best to find Moira.'

'Sure, you are.'

'Can you take us through the day again?'

'I've already told you all this.'

'You said you had a good relationship with Moira?'

'Aye.'

'But you've hurt Moira previously.'

'What?'

'Well, you've assaulted her,' Helen stated. 'The police had attended your address two times previously due to domestic disturbance.'

A look of distress twisted his features. 'I . . . know. I mean things would get heated from time to time but nothing serious. A wee slap now and again. Nothing bad.'

'I would call that bad.' Helen countered.

Reggie looked down at the table. All couples argue. I never claimed that we got on well all the time. We've been married for twenty years!'

'Maybe things got out of hand this time.'

'What do you mean by that?'

'Well, maybe an argument got a bit physical and she fell?'

'No, that's not what happened.'

'So, what did happen then?'

'I left her in the house, she was fine, then I came back to all that blood.'

'And there was nothing else out of the ordinary?'

He seemed to be considering what she said and took a moment to answer. 'It's what I've already told you.' He sighed shakily. 'I wouldn't bloody murder her, all right? I've not laid a hand on her. She was fine when I left her. You shouldn't be wasting your time with me.'

'We had plans,' Reggie blurted out. 'We were going to visit Harold's grave tomorrow.'

The door opened, letting the sound of the busy corridor into the room. Craven popped his head round the door and motioned to the corridor. Helen followed him outside. He walked a few steps until he was out of sight of the interview room, then leaned against the wall. 'I've just heard back from the hospital that had treated Moira.' He made a twisting motion with his finger beside his temple.

Helen let out an exasperated sigh. 'What?'

'She's had electroshock treatment.'

'Moira? Recently? That GP didn't mention it to us.'

'There's a lot Reggie's not told us. Their son died from a hit and run in 1970, and Moira has been severely depressed ever since.'

'That's not surprising.' She thought back to the silver photo frame with the picture of the smiling boy on their mantelpiece and the newspapers. 'When did she have the ECT?'

'About six weeks ago.'

'It can cause memory problems.' She knew a little about the treatment, though it wasn't something she had covered much in her psychology degree, as it was still a controversial issue. 'It can take a few months for side effects like that to subside. You can also get symptoms like dizziness. Uniform found anything yet?'

Craven sucked air through his teeth. 'The DCI wants us to scale back this investigation if nothing's found shortly, and there's another thing you should know. I've managed to track down Reggie's girlfriend. Her name's Marjorie Lockwood. Works in Safeway's, with an address in Morningside.'

After Helen had finished speaking with Craven, she closed the interview room door and stared at Reggie McKenzie. He held his head in his hands.

Reggie McKenzie looked up with a quivering lip when she sat down opposite him. 'Have you found Moira?'

'Not yet. Why didn't you tell us Moira had undergone electroshock treatment?'

'Because I wanted you to take this seriously.' He shook his head. 'You wouldn't have if you knew, would you? You'd just think she's a nutter.'

'In these crucial hours, Mr McKenzie, we need to know everything.' She sat back down behind the table. 'There were some old blood spots in the lounge. How did those happen?'

'I don't know. We both used to drink a lot. Things got out of hand. I stopped drinking. I haven't done anything to Moira. You have to believe me.' A sob escaped his body.

'Why did you stop drinking?'

Reggie looked down at the carpet tiles. 'If I hadn't been drunk, maybe my son wouldn't have been knocked over by that car. I would've been there.' His body rocked back and forth, and he blinked back tears. 'I'd still have him here.'

Helen took a deep breath to steady herself. The thought of her own brothers drowning when she was a child came to her mind. Her parents' grief. The fear of water her mother had instilled in her. She rubbed a hand across her forehead and blinked away the image of him smiling in her mind's eye.

'I thought your new girlfriend might've had something to do with why you don't drink?'

'What? I don't have a girlfriend. What are you talking about?'

'I assume Moira didn't know about her?'

'I've got no idea what you are talking about.'

'Marjorie Lockwood?'

'Oh, her. We're just friends. If I run into her, I have a quick chat, that's it. I'd hardly call that a girlfriend.'

'So, when we speak to her will she say the same?'

'She's not my girlfriend. We just have a laugh at the pub. That's all. I've nothing to do with Moira's disappearance. I was at the pub. You know that.' He thumped his fists down onto the table. 'I've made mistakes, but I haven't touched her.'

'I'll need Marjorie Lockwood's address.'

'She's nothing to do with this.'

'We'll be the judge of that, Mr McKenzie.'

As soon as Helen got back to her desk, she reached into her pedestal and slipped out the photograph of her brother from the back pages of her police manual. A portrait shot for his first birthday. She rubbed her thumb across it. The picture was curled at the edges and yellowed from cigarette smoke, but it was the only thing she had of her brother. The only proof that he existed. A lump expanded in her chest and her breath quickened. She looked up to the ceiling and blinked back tears.

'Are you all right?' McKinley stood in the doorway with a folder in his hand, his brows furrowed.

She nodded and rubbed her nose. 'I didn't hear you come in.'

'Sorry.'

She grabbed her jacket from the back of her chair. 'I'm going to speak with Dr Rushmore again, and with Marjorie Lockwood.'

'I'll come.'

CHAPTER TWENTY-SIX

'That's her over there.' A teenage shop assistant pointed to a woman in red overalls who was unpacking tins of baked beans from a pallet onto a shelf. The woman looked up as Helen approached.

'Can I help you?' the woman smiled.

'Marjorie Lockwood?'

The smile faded. 'Who wants to know?'

Helen retrieved her warrant card. 'I'm DS Carter and this is DC McKinley.'

Marjorie sighed. She was quite a bit younger than Reggie, maybe mid-thirties, Helen guessed. Pretty with shoulder-length auburn curls, partially clipped at the sides.

She glanced over Helen's shoulder, 'Can we talk in the staff room? I don't want to get in trouble with my boss. He might get the wrong idea.'

'Of course,' Helen said, slipping her card back into her pocket.

They followed Marjorie through a set of double doors at the back of the supermarket then through a narrow brick hallway, manoeuvring past pallets of toilet paper. Marjorie spoke. 'It's just through here.' She led them into a small room that was barely big enough for a battered wooden table and four chairs.

'I can't afford to lose this job,' she added.

'I do understand,' Helen replied, taking a seat. She motioned for Marjorie to do the same, which she reluctantly did. 'We'll try and make this quick.'

'What's this about?'

'We'd like to ask you some questions regarding your relationship with Reggie McKenzie.'

'Why are you asking me about that?' her eyes darted between Helen and McKinley. 'I don't understand. I thought you were here to talk about what happened in the shop?'

'What happened?' McKinley shifted in his seat, struggling to get his gangly legs under the table.

'A couple of boys raided the till. I spoke to officers about it at the time.'

Helen looked down at her notes as Marjorie sighed, and shook her head.

'I will check that,' Helen replied. 'But we would like to ask you about your relationship with Reggie McKenzie. I understand you were with him in the pub?'

'I wasn't the only one there.'

'What time was this?'

'I don't know. I stayed for a few hours. I think I was there until nine.'

'How long have you known Reggie?'

'A couple of years.' She tugged at a loose thread on her overall. 'Why are you asking this?'

'We are trying to trace the whereabouts of Reggie's wife.'

'I've never met her.'

'How would you describe your relationship with Reggie?'

Marjorie's eyes flickered. 'Not in the way you're thinking.'

'Did Reggie ever mention anything about his relationship with his wife?'

'Not really, I know that she's not well and requires a lot of care. I think it takes a toll on him.' She exhaled a sigh. 'I've got to be back on the shop floor . . .'

McKinley leaned forward. 'We won't take up much more of your time.'

'How was Reggie when you met him in the pub?'

'The usual.' She ran a hand through her curls. 'Have you got a cigarette on you?'

McKinley fished in his pockets and slipped a packet of Silk Cut towards her.

She put one shakily to her lips. 'Reggie was Reggie,' she explained. 'We had a laugh, he played darts. It was just a normal night. Thanks,' she replied when McKinley handed her his lighter. She took a long drag on the fag and savoured the smoke. 'I wish I could tell you more.'

'How would you describe your relationship with Reggie?' Helen pressed.

'We're friends.'

'Have you ever been anything more than friends?'

Marjorie flicked the ash onto the linoleum. 'No, we're just good friends. Not that it matters.'

'Do you think that Reggie wants to be more than friends?' Helen asked.

'He's never said . . . What's happened to his wife?'

'We are trying to trace her and have reason to believe she may be hurt.'

That's so sad . . . I'm very sorry to hear that,' she stood up and handed McKinley his packet back. 'I don't know anything else. But I do hope that you find her safe and well.'

* * *

'Reggie's punching above his weight with her, is he not?' McKinley asked, as they headed back towards the Mini. Helen couldn't get a spot close to the entrance and now drizzle dampened her head. She slid her hands in her pockets for warmth.

'Clearly there must be a side to Reggie that we're not seeing,' Helen admitted. 'When I questioned him it looked like it was taking all his effort not to knock my block off.'

'Maybe that's just you.' Smiling, he nudged her elbow.

'Aye, thanks.' Helen replied, stepping over a puddle. They managed to get back to the car just before the heavy downpour started. Rain battered the windscreen as the wipers squealed in vain, drowning out the radio. The supermarket was on the northwest side of town about five miles from the medical centre, Helen guessed. It shouldn't take too long to get back to the station, but Edinburgh seemed to be in a constant state of flux with new housing estates sprouting up around the city. They had got up to Queensferry Road when again, they ground to a stop as a cement mixer pulled out from a building site. Helen slipped the car down to first and peered out the window. Another soulless block of flats.

Helen pulled up outside the medical centre just as a thin man with black hair was locking the door. He turned around as they approached with a look of annoyance etched on his thin features.

'Can I help you?'

Helen held out her warrant card for Milton Nairn to see. 'We briefly met before. I am DS Carter, and this is my colleague DC McKinley.'

'Oh, yes, with Jack, I remember. Please make this quick. I've an appointment this evening.' The doctor scooped up his scuffed medical case and started to walk past them.

'Is Dr Rushmore around, we'd like to speak to him?'

'His mother died this morning. He's in Dundee to be with this family.'

'I'm very sorry to hear that.' Helen exchanged a glance with McKinley.

The doctor nodded. 'I know. Terribly sad.'

They followed Dr Nairn towards his car.

'We're investigating the disappearance of—'

'Moira McKenzie,' he interrupted. 'I know.'

'We weren't told she has had electroshock treatment or that her son died from a hit and run. This should all be in her medical records.'

The doctor sighed as he opened the door of his Escort and chucked his medical case in. 'We're relying on paper records, my dear, it's not all updated straight away. I'm sure

Dr Rushmore gave you all the information he had. Now, you will need to excuse me.'

* * *

Dusk was settling when they got back to the car. Helen sighed and leaned back into the driver's seat and released the handbrake.

'So that's who's married to Jack's ex-wife?'

'Aye, that's him,' Helen replied, pulling out into traffic.

'He's a bit different to the inspector.'

'Is he?'

McKinley arched an eyebrow. 'Jack came from the army, didn't he?'

'Aye.'

'Well, that doctor looks like a gust of wind would snap him in half.'

'Maybe there is more to him than meets the eye,' Helen mused.

The cemetery was only about a quarter of a mile away from the medical centre, and Helen wanted to check something out. She drove up the gravel path and stopped near the bins that were overflowing with decaying wreaths. An elderly man was emptying a withered bouquet into them. He looked up as they parked the car.

'We don't even know where he's buried.'

Helen wrenched up the handbrake. 'Doesn't matter. I need to stretch my legs anyway and get some fresh air'

McKinley sighed, then climbed out of the car. Helen paused a moment, not wanting to leave the warmth. As soon as she opened the door a gust of icy wind prickled her cheeks, taking her breath away. She zipped up her parka and followed McKinley who had his hands in his pockets, his thin oversized jacket whipping back and forth. They carried on up the path. Helen glanced around. Grey headstones stretched as far as the eye could see, like crooked teeth jutting from the ground.

'There's so many but these look old.' McKinley motioned to a row of damp, faded headstones. Helen took a quick scan of the dates, all over seventy years ago. Passing a row of bushes, Helen caught sight of a field mouse scurrying into them. She shivered as they trudged side by side through the damp grass. The hems of Helen's trouser legs were getting soggier with each step. At least the rain had stopped.

Helen slipped a sideways glance towards McKinley. He'd been a help recently, a friend even, spending time with her after she had left Ted, even putting up the kitchen tiles that Ted had picked out, keeping her mind off things. He gave her a smile and his arm bumped off hers.

'It's going to be too dark soon, and we won't find it then.'

'I know. Let's just try up there.' Helen motioned to some newer-looking stones beside the wall.

'All right.' McKinley nodded, his blond hair flopping onto his forehead.

'There.' Helen pointed to a small angel-shaped headstone.

Harold McKenzie

The little black pot next to it had been stuffed with fresh lilies.

'What were you expecting? For Moira to be here?'

Helen shook her head and motioned to the white flowers. 'I don't know what I was expecting. But Reggie McKenzie said they were going to put down flowers today and someone already has.'

'Anyone could've put them here, though.'

McKinley placed his hand on the small of her back and guided her back towards the path. 'I really hate being here,' he said. 'Let's go and get a drink to warm us up.'

The Cask and Barrel, a small pub a few minutes from the station, was where most officers would stop for a few drinks between shifts. A sticky, smoky, old-fashioned place decked out in mahogany panels with a few tables and a dartboard in the corner.

The pub was already crammed with drinkers getting an early start by the time they arrived. Most were perched at the bar and, judging by the glasses in front of them, they weren't on their first pint either.

'Who's that talking to Craven?' McKinley asked Helen as they approached the bar.

She shrugged and slipped a glance at Craven who was sitting with a dark-haired woman at a table in the corner. 'No idea.' They both seemed deep in conversation, yet uncomfortable in each other's company.

'There's a table over there.' McKinley pointed to a beer barrel table and stools.

'Fine. Get me some cheese sandwiches, too. I'm starving.'

He nodded and slipped a five-pound note from his wallet.

Helen sat down at the table and tore at the edges of a beer mat while she waited. Smoke from a nearby couple tickled the back of her throat. If Craven had noticed her, he hadn't bothered to acknowledge it. The woman he was with was tearing at a nail while shaking her head at whatever Craven was saying.

It was most likely his ex-wife, she imagined.

McKinley approached with a pint in one hand, a Babycham in the other, and was holding the corner of a packet of crisps between his teeth.

Helen took a sip of her drink and tried to push the thoughts of Moira from her mind. Her gut feeling wasn't good.

'I think I've seen her in the office,' he said, pulling Helen from her thoughts. He opened the crisps and placed the packet in the centre of the table.

'I've not,' Helen countered.

'It might've been when you were in hospital, actually.' He licked lager foam from his lips, then sprinkled the salt sachet over the crisps.

Helen traced the rim of the glass with her finger. 'Have you heard from Sally since she moved to London?'

'Only that she's going to give acting another chance.' McKinley scratched his jaw.

'Sorry, Terry.' Sally had been Terry's on-off girlfriend for the past year, but they always seemed miserable together. 'You don't seem all that upset about it, though.'

'I'm not really.' He shrugged. 'I kind of expected it, to be honest. She threatened it often enough.'

'Well, it was always her dream to be an actress, wasn't it? Do you think she'll make it this time?' She looked up from her glass and felt Craven's glare on her.

She thought about telling McKinley she'd seen Sally but thought better of it. Sally was the type of woman that would let her presence be felt if she wanted to.

'Do you know whereabouts she is in London?' Helen asked.

Crack.

She jumped. Laughter and claps erupted from the bar. A dropped glass had smashed and scattered all over the floor. The barmaid, holding a dishcloth in her hand, looked red-faced.

Bang.

Helen closed her eyes and she was back there again. The cold draught brushing against her cheeks and the smell of damp plaster and mould. The thick darkness she had endured for hours. Stanley pulling against the ropes, the screwdriver slowly pressing further into the skin of her arm. The pressure. 'Don't, please.' It twisted.

A cool, soft hand squeezed hers. She opened her eyes and took a shaky breath.

'Are you okay?' McKinley's brow furrowed.

'I'm fine.' She took a gulp of her drink. It tickled her throat. 'It's just difficult to forget the things that happened to me.'

'Listen, I'm not good with this stuff but if you want to talk . . .' He leaned in closer. 'It might help.'

'Talk?' Helen sat back in the chair. 'It won't help.'

'What happened to you in that house?' He looked down at her blouse sleeve where he knew the scars were.

130

Helen pulled her trembling hand away and slipped it under the table. 'I'm just tired.'

McKinley's mouth tightened, and he gave a small shrug.

Helen watched as the barmaid swept up the pieces of glass with a dustpan and brush. 'I just want to keep working. It's all I've got. You know this job takes its toll on you. No sleep. No evidence. No leads. It's all normal.'

The barman with a tea towel draped over his shoulder plonked a plate of curled-up-looking cheese sandwiches down in front of them. They picked at them in silence. Once she'd eaten enough to kill her hunger, she guzzled the last of her drink.

She didn't fancy going home. 'I think the cinema is a good idea,' she said, rising from her chair. 'Will I meet you at your flat later?'

'Meet me about half seven?'

'I'll see you then.'

* * *

Reggie could still taste blood in his mouth from where he had bit his lip so hard in that station. He could still hear her whiny voice in his skull, see her sneering face as she sat opposite him in that interview room probing him with her stupid questions. Carter, that was the bitch's name. Helen bloody Carter. He slotted the key into the front door and it made a clicking sound. Blood intermixed with chemical cleaner lingered in the air. He slipped off his jacket and hung it on the corner of the bathroom door. The boom of music leaked from one of the flats, it wasn't loud enough to pick out the song.

The bedroom door was ajar, he could see the drawers in the dresser had been pulled open. Moira's hairbrush was on the floor and the mattress had been ripped from the bed. He shook his head, maybe he could get Marjorie to come over and put the place back together, that was a woman's job. The lounge hadn't fared any better. He stood in the doorway;

the bloodstain, although lighter from bleach, was still visible. She'd ruined the carpet — that would need to be replaced. Picking up his Marlboros from the sideboard, he placed one to his lips, then pulled back the curtains and opened the window a crack. Condensation dripped down the window, he wiped it away with his shirt sleeve. From this window, he got a good view of the road. Her from downstairs and her mongrel of a son were heading towards the block pulling a shopping bag. He looked away as soon as they noticed him and took a long drag on his fag, exhaling the smoke slowly.

At least the kitchen was tidy. He sifted through the cupboards for something he could cobble together for dinner. He pulled out a tin of Spam and the container of Smash instant potato. Jackpot, there was a can of Tartan on the kitchen table. A few moments later, he slumped down at the table with his meal and pulled open the lager. He gulped the warm lager as his attention fell to the copies of the *Evening News* in front of him. He flicked through the first couple of pages about a murder in an old picture house. His jaw stiffened when he noticed a picture on the bottom of the page. A grainy black-and-white photograph of Carter on the steps of the picture house with Inspector Craven. He folded the page back and traced the outline of her face with his index finger. There was a prettiness to her, although she'd look nicer with longer hair and if she dressed more like a woman. She was staring off to the side and he wondered what she was looking at.

He stabbed a slice of Spam with his fork and chewed slowly, not taking his eyes off the photograph. The caption underneath said, *Police officers at the scene.* After his meal, he took the picture over to the worktop, then took a pen and scissors from the drawer underneath. He cut around her silhouette then carefully coloured in her face with blue ink. 'You're not so talkative now, are you?' he said, holding it up to the light.

CHAPTER TWENTY-SEVEN

He knew he would find her here. That was one of the reasons he liked her so much, her predictability. Reggie blew on his hands for warmth as he crossed the grassy mound towards Marjorie, a smile tugging at his lips. She was sitting on a bench next to the pond, tearing bits off a loaf and making a shit job of throwing them towards the murky looking water. Three quacking ducks scrambled towards her. Marjorie's hair was covered with a peach-and-brown headscarf, and the wind had blown some of her auburn curls loose. She was wearing a long brown jacket that went to her knees, and her trademark scuffed knee-high black boots. She was so different from the others. Homely.

She gave a thin smile when her eyes met his. 'Reggie, I didn't expect to see you.'

'They had to let me go.' He slumped down next to her and felt in his jacket pockets for a cigarette. They must have taken them all at the station — he was meant to be a criminal.

'It was in the papers this morning about Moira. I do hope she is okay.'

Was that a look of pity on her face? The familiar sting stabbed at him.

'I haven't seen them,' Reggie explained.

'I thought I'd come here to clear my mind.' Her voice was barely a whisper.

'Aye, and has it helped?'

Marjorie tore off a hunk of bread and passed it over. He threw a bit of the crust into the water.

Movement on the other side of the pond caught his attention. A little boy was dipping a fishing rod into the other side of the pond. He looked about the same age as Harold had been when . . .

Dampness from the bench seeped through Reggie's cord trousers. He slipped a glance at Marjorie. Her jacket looked waterproof, so she probably didn't feel it.

Marjorie offered him another forced smile. Her eyes looked puffy, as though she had been crying.

'Sorry.' She shakily sighed and he followed her eyeline over to the little boy.

'Your son would have been nearly the same age too?' he asked.

'A little older,' she replied.

It was one of the things that united them. She knew the pain he had suffered. He looked up at the morning sunlight, enjoying the warmth on his face. Moira never liked going out like this. Not the way Marjorie did. Moira would never do anything unless it involved having a drink in her hand.

The little boy lifted his fishing rod out of the water with a look of disappointment on his chubby face. Reggie smiled. When Harold was young, they used to live for the weekends, watching him develop, play football. What he wouldn't give for another minute standing on the sidelines of that soggy pitch on a Saturday morning. Moira was never the same afterwards. She died inside on that day, too. The years since then had been just an existence. After it happened, people avoided them, not sure of what to say. The kids Harold's age developed into teenagers, and all they had was that fucking picture in a silver frame.

He took a deep breath to hold back the tears that were threatening to break through.

Marjorie stopped tearing the bread. 'Do you think she's dead, Reggie?'

He stared into the distance. They could see Edinburgh Castle from here. The words nearly choked him, more than he would expect. 'I don't know. I don't think so. You have enough to worry about, Marjorie.'

'Do the police have any ideas?'

He shook his head and reached out for her hand. She flinched but let him take it, soft and warm. He squeezed it gently.

'It wasn't me.' He couldn't bear to look at her. 'Don't believe what any of the papers say.'

'I didn't think that, Reggie. I could never think something so horrible of you. It's just-'

'Everyone else will, though.'

'They are not blaming you. They're saying she's missing.' Marjorie clarified.

'That's a surprise.'

'They'll find her soon and this will all blow over.' Her head rested on his shoulder.

'You're probably right.'

'The police came to my work yesterday too.'

'What did they want?'

'They just wanted to know about our relationship.'

'Did you tell them anything?'

Marjorie took a pause like she was thinking about what to say.

'Marjorie, you need to tell me what you said.'

'I was terrified about getting you in trouble.' She moved her head and created some distance between them. 'Why does it matter, anyway? You're innocent — you said so yourself.'

'You think that will matter to them? Was it that woman officer, Carter?'

'I think so.'

'I want to know for certain.'

'Anyway, you don't need to worry about me. I can take care of myself.' She wriggled her hand free.

'I never said you couldn't.' Reggie countered.

'I think her name was Carter and a young man, Constable McKinley.'

'I can't stand that woman. She thinks she's better than me.' Reggie's hands were tightly clenched in his lap now. 'You should have seen the way she questioned me.' The familiar feeling of rage warmed the pit of his stomach.

Marjorie frowned. 'Try not to think about it.'

'This wasn't why I wanted to speak with you.'

'I'm listening, Reggie.'

He heard her suck in a breath.

'We need to stop seeing each other.'

'Why? What have I done wrong?' She twisted her body towards him, her mouth twitching and her eyes searching for answers.

'Nothing.'

'Then why can't we be together? There's no harm in—'

'Just until there's some answer with Moira.'

'I don't see why it would matter.'

'It'll give people the wrong impression. Especially the police.'

'Surely, with you being in the pub you're in the clear? They must understand you were practically the woman's carer, not her husband.'

Reggie could see her reasoning, but he had to protect himself. It wouldn't look good to the family and those bloody papers if he was carrying on with a relationship when no one knew what happened to Moira. 'No, we can't see each other for a while. For a few months, until this blows over.' He was surprised at his own determination. 'It will all work itself out.'

'What about people at the pub? Lots of people have seen us together.'

Reggie dragged the palm of his hand down his face. 'No one's going to tell the police anything. They all know I need to keep things quiet with you.'

'You promised me, Reggie. You promised we would be together.'

'I'll keep that promise. Just give me some time. If I don't, it will look bad for us both.'

'If we play our cards right, this could work out well for us,' Reggie explained.

'What do you mean?'

'There'll be no one left to come between us.'

'Reggie, promise me you had nothing to do with whatever happened with Moira. You've threatened to hurt her often enough.'

'Aye, I promise. C'mon. You know I say things when I get angry. That's why I need you to keep me on the straight and narrow.'

CHAPTER TWENTY-EIGHT

Helen parked a few streets away, fancying the short walk to clear her mind. Her headache had softened, but every so often it would give her a nudge to let her know it was still there. Buttoning up her jacket, she passed an old Morris Minor missing its two back wheels and propped up with bricks. That was the only other car parked. Relishing the quiet for a few moments, Helen sighed as the evening sun hung low in the sky, and the wind had died down. She missed this — pounding the pavements, the jogging and the long walks that she used to do. She had got addicted to jogging from spending time in the states on holiday with Ted. Terry's flat was on Leith Walk on the north side of town, a wide long straight road lined on both sides by shops and houses, in a Victorian block not that dissimilar to her own. She stopped to look in a clothes shop window as a bus sloshed by, spraying up muck from the road, narrowly missing her boots and trousers.

His flat was above a small sweet shop that had now closed for the evening. A couple burst out of the pub on the corner, smiling, laughing, carrying a jug of ale. She stepped aside to let them by.

The light was on in the living room, and the floral pattered curtains drawn. As she approached the stairwell door, a couple of young boys rushed past hauling a rusted shopping trolley full of sticks and bricks, taking no notice of her.

Helen pushed open the scuffed door and headed up the winding concrete staircase, manoeuvring past an empty baby's pram. A cooking smell that reminded Helen of mince and potatoes drifted out from the flat opposite McKinley's.

After she rattled on the door and waited a few moments, she had almost given up hope of McKinley answering and had turned to walk away when the lock unclicked, and he popped his head around. His hair was ruffled, and the top two buttons of his shirt were open. His eyes widened when they locked with hers.

'Sorry,' Helen smiled. 'Did I catch you at a bad time?'

'Not really, I . . . I was going to go in the shower.'

'The film's on in half an hour.'

'Right, it slipped my mind.'

'Who is it?' A female voice called behind him sweetly. Helen recognized the voice and noticed McKinley's cheeks reddened. It was his on-off girlfriend, Sally.

Sally opened the door wide, a smile spreading across her glossy lips. She was wearing a tight, almost dangerously low-cut purple dress that jutted out at the hips emphasizing her tiny waist. London life obviously suited her.

'Helen, hi. This is unexpected.' She glanced between Helen and McKinley. 'Is everything okay? You look really . . .' She looked like she was considering what to say. 'Tired.'

'It's nice to see you too, Sally.'

'Helen was just . . .'

'You're being so rude, Terry, invite her in.' Sally scolded.

'No need,' Helen replied. 'I've got to get back to the station.'

Sally flicked a blonde curl from her face and smiled. 'You look like you've eaten but come in. I've just made some dinner. I'm sure there'll be enough.' She made a show of looking Helen up and down. Helen noticed McKinley look at Sally wearily.

'You can't talk in the stair; you'll get a reputation with the neighbours.'

'Aye, come in Helen. Have a drink. Sally just dropped by about an hour ago, I didn't even know she was in Edinburgh.' McKinley added.

'I've ruined your little evening, haven't I?' Sally pursed her lips. 'We completely lost track of time catching up.'

Helen smiled. 'It's nice to see you back. Terry, I'll see you at work tomorrow. You both enjoy your evening.'

'And you, it was *so nice* to see you again,' Sally muttered as she slammed the door shut.

Helen slumped back into the driver's seat and slipped her keys in the ignition just as McKinley climbed into the passenger's seat, looking out of breath.

'Sorry, it's not what you are thinking.'

Helen shrugged her shoulders. 'Terry, I'm not thinking anything.'

'She's back for a few days,' McKinley muttered. 'She thought it would be a good idea to talk.' He brushed his blond hair from his forehead and leaned his head back against the seat. 'You know what she's like, it can be hard to say no.'

Helen gave him a look. 'You better run back home then. She'll be wondering where you've gone.'

'Can we talk tomorrow?'

'Yes, I've got some work to do anyway. I'll see you later.'

After McKinley clambered out the car, Helen flicked the radio on and settled on the news as she drifted through the mid-evening traffic. A mass suicide has left nine hundred dead, the news reported announced. That put Helen's problems into perspective. She flicked the channel over to one blasting out disco tunes. The air felt warmer than usual, so she rolled the window down a crack. A few minutes later, she was cruising along Ferry Road and took a deep breath to steady herself. She hadn't really fancied the cinema anyway and wasn't sure why she had said yes. The flat had seemed so big and hollow now that she was alone.

Rush hour traffic should've died down by now, but the roads were still busy and she could see no obvious cause. She slowed at the traffic lights. There were school grounds on the left and a group of boys were playing rugby. She could've carried on straight ahead to get home but instead she took the left turn towards the station. The thought of going home filled her with dread, sitting there alone with her thoughts, remembering what happened in that house. The feeling of thinking she was going to die. Sleep didn't come easy these days. Her heart pounded as she pulled into a parking space. Her ribs still ached; they hadn't completely healed yet.

The CID room still teemed with life when she opened the door. DCI Murphy was in Craven's office. The blinds were up and she could see that he wasn't happy about something. Craven looked equally unimpressed.

Helen sifted through the files from downstairs and lifted out the ones related to Tina French's murder. There weren't any leads to go on, except for a poor quality black-and-white sketch of a nondescript man with big glasses who was seen loitering around the pub and had left at the same time as her. The sketch had no distinguishable features and could've easily been anyone. There were a couple more sketches of the crime scene, the positioning of the body, and the locations of items in relation to the body.

Tina's family had reported that the silver cross necklace that she had always worn was missing from her when she was found. Helen sighed, looking at the picture of the poor woman who was only a year older than Helen and had left a young son. Helen squinted at the drawing again. So far, no witnesses had come forward either.

'Thought you had gone home.'

Helen looked up as Craven moved around her desk.

'I had, but I can't sleep, so I thought I'd go through this lot.'

'I've got the post-mortem report through too.' He placed the report on top of the one she was looking at.

'Take a look at it.' He motioned to the file.

She flicked it open. 'What am I looking at?'

He tapped the notes section at the bottom. Helen skim-read it. A lock of hair at the back of her head was missing. Ear-piercing marks on her ears but no earrings.

'I checked with Tina's aunt and she normally wore a pair of gold hoops,' Craven added.

'She had no money in her purse, too.'

Craven nodded. 'But her aunt was unable to confirm if she would've had any money in her purse or not.'

'I don't think this killing was motivated by robbery. It's also quite a risky thing for the perpetrator, she was abducted from a fairly populated area and she would have needed to have been transported to the area where we found her body.'

'Or she knew her attacker,' Craven countered, 'and got in his vehicle willingly.'

'Potentially. But I think her attacker targeted her specifically, and had been watching her movements, learned her routine, and that's why he was so confident in striking in the way that he did.'

'The missing lock of her hair suggests that he's taking a trophy of his killing. Something to remember Tina French by.'

'That's what I was thinking.'

'Have you come across anything like this before?'

'I might have.' DC Randall piped up. 'But it was a long time ago, I'm talking ten-fifteen years. The woman wasn't murdered though, if I am remembering correctly, but I remember that she reported a hunk of her hair was carved off with a knife, but her attacker ran off when she was startled.'

'Right,' Craven replied, 'I want you to pull out everything you can about it before the briefing in the morning. I want to speak to this woman.'

'I'm going to go through files for the past ten or so years too and see if I can find anything else. I also have a few contacts in Strathclyde, I'll see if they have had anything similar.'

'Oh, of course you do,' Randall shrugged. 'I think Robert Keaton will remember it too.' Randall clambered up from his desk. 'I'll go see what I can find.'

Helen nodded. 'I'll come with you.'

'If you must.' Randall sighed.

CHAPTER TWENTY-NINE

The records room was a windowless storage facility that seemed to stretch on for miles, with four aisles separated by metal shelves that were stacked high with cardboard evidence boxes and folders. Randall held open the door for her, then turned on his heels and headed down the middle aisle. Goosebumps peppered Helen's arms as she followed, breaking into a jog to keep up with him.

'I am capable of going through these. I was doing this job while you were still in nappies.'

'I know, but it will be quicker if we're both looking.'

'Whatever you say, Sergeant.'

Randall grabbed a pile of manila folders and took a seat at the table opposite.

Helen grabbed the next pile, the ticking of the clock above their heads sounding like a boom in the silence. It was over an hour later before Randall spoke again.

'I'm not angry, I know you're just taking advantage of a situation, and I would probably do the same.'

Helen closed the folder. 'What are you talking about?'

'You think if your dad wasn't a DCI that they'd promote some overzealous WPC?'

'I've worked hard.'

He scoffed and looked back at his notes.

'I'm still the sergeant in the department.'

'*Acting* sergeant.'

'It wasn't my fault you didn't get the promotion.'

'We all know your dad was bent, and what's that old saying? The apple doesn't fall far from the tree.'

Helen's heart pounded, and her stomach twisted.

'Tell me,' he carried on. 'Who paid for your education? That fancy university degree you enjoy rubbing in people's faces.'

Helen's heart felt like it was in a vice, being squeezed slowly. The same anger she felt before surged in her. She wanted to tell him to take a running jump. Not that it would do any good. That she only did her university course to please her father, and even then, that didn't work.

'I don't . . .'

'All paid with backhanders, and he was good friends with DCI Whyte.'

'My dad paid for my education, that's true, but I've given everything that I can to do a good job, and I'm nothing like my father.'

'I'll believe that when I see it.'

'I nearly died on the job last month, and all I want is to find out what happened to Moira McKenzie and get justice for Tina French.'

He dragged a hand across his stubble. 'Fine, I'm nearly through this lot.'

* * *

Craven headed towards his car, downing a couple of pills as he did so. His temples throbbed, and his jaw was stiff. He rubbed it and the pain spread. The icy pain trickled down his arms as though cold water was spreading through his veins. He slumped in the driver's seat of the Granada. Gasping for breath, he massaged his chest and closed his eyes. A knock on the window startled him, and he looked over to see a uniformed officer peering in.

Craven wound the window down a crack.

'What is it, son?' he asked.

'Sorry, I just wanted to check you were all right?'

'I'm fine.'

'It's just you looked . . .'

Craven turned the key in the ignition and the engine purred into life. The officer stepped back, as Craven reversed out of the parking space. There was somewhere else he needed to be.

* * *

'I knew I would find it.' Randall slid the folder across the table. Helen looked down at the yellowed sheet. Eleanor Aldridge had been walking home and was just yards away from her house when she was attacked by a man who grabbed at her hair and sliced off a chunk of it with a blade. He was disturbed by a neighbour of the woman's, Paul Shipley, and fled the scene. There were no suspects. Helen flicked the page and looked at the composite sketch, it looked like it had been sketched by a child and had massive inhuman eyes and swollen hamster cheeks.

She held the picture up. 'Well, that's not very helpful!'

'That's what it was like in them days, sometimes. It's not like it was the crime of the century.'

'Still.'

'It was hard in them days. We were coping with low staffing numbers and we didn't have radios or anything.'

Helen carried on reading. 16 August 1967. The notes described a woman of low intelligence who gave conflicting information. Helen gritted her teeth. She couldn't even find a statement from the neighbour and apart from a couple of cuts and bruises the woman wasn't badly hurt. The hunk of hair missing from her head was at the back of her head, in a similar position to Tina French. She was also a brunette like Tina French, with hair roughly the same length.

'Why would he want hair?' Randall asked, making a face.

'For a souvenir, it helps keep the memory of the murder alive longer in their minds.' She slid the photo away. 'It's also something far more personal than taking a purse or bit of jewellery, this is something that actually comes from the victim.'

Randall considered this. 'I mean, I can't remember much about it. This could just be a coincidence.'

'Some coincidence,' Helen replied, standing up. 'Get her address and we'll visit her in the morning.'

CHAPTER TWENTY-NINE

'What the hell have we got here?' Helen wrenched up the handbrake behind a police van. Randall clambered out the car and headed over to the wreckage. The smouldering shell of a Morris Minor lay on a grass verge. The fuel tank had exploded in the fire, charring the grass around it and throwing molten plastic and shards of glass onto the road and pavement.

A fire engine was parked opposite. One of the firefighters was in the process of clearing the hose away. The ground around the car was wet. Enough of the licence plate remained to get a positive identification.

The smell brought her back to the last year during bonfire night when groups of teens had set random cars on fire. It was something the police and fire services were dealing with more and more in Edinburgh. Several cars on housing estates in the north of the city were gutted, with windows being smashed and cars ablaze. Some of the firemen dealing with the carnage were even being punched and kicked as they battled the flames, and officers were pelted with fireworks. Not something that you would commonly associate with Edinburgh. She shook the thoughts from her mind.

A police van had cordoned off the scene with rope, and a couple of firemen were getting back into their vehicle preparing to leave.

'What's happened?' Randall shouted over to a uniformed PC who was walking towards them.

The officer had a white handkerchief covering his mouth. 'I didn't realize CID had been called?'

'We weren't, we were due to visit a house over there.' Helen motioned to a row of houses on the other side of the green. 'Any witnesses?' The thick fumes of plastic and petrol hung in the air like a smog, burning Helen's throat as she spoke.

'Aye,' the officer replied. 'A couple of laddies from the scheme down the road set fire to it — both only twelve.'

'Great.' Helen suppressed a cough.

'We've got them in custody as they were seen running away from the scene with petrol on their hands, and they admitted to it right away.'

The officer mopped a bead of sweat from his brow and waved a thumb towards a house opposite. 'The couple in that house, they saw the car go up in flames.'

'We'll leave it with you.' Randall patted the officer on the back and started towards the house.

Helen heard the television blast out an Open University programme. Mathematics, it sounded like. The window was open, and she could see an overweight man in his fifties sitting in an armchair beside the window supping on a can of lager.

'At least we know they're in.' Randall motioned to the man.

Helen pressed the buzzer, and a moment later the man appeared at the door, eyeing them both suspiciously. She retrieved her warrant card and held it up for inspection.

'I'm DS Carter and this is DC Randall, we'd like to speak to Eleanor Aldridge?'

'Right, she's through here. Can I get you a drink? Tea or coffee?' The old man belched then rubbed his hands on his ketchup-stained white vest.

'No, you're all right.' Randall crinkled his nose.

The house smelled of cheap cooking fat and wet dog.

They followed the man through to a small garden where a woman was kneeling tending to some weeds. Her brown hair was pinned up in a high bun and she was wearing a brown smock dress.

'Elle, police want to speak to you.'

The woman looked around in surprise. 'What for?'

'We want to ask you about when you were attacked in 1967, when you were on your way home from the dance hall,' Helen prompted.

Eleanor clambered up to her feet and brushed dirt from her hands onto her skirt. 'No one was interested at the time.'

'Are you able to tell us what happened?'

'It all happened really quick, this man grabbed me from behind and bashed me on the top of my head.' She put her hand to her head, and Helen could see tears welling in her eyes.

'I can understand how hard this must be to think about this again.'

The woman nodded. 'He pulled on my hair and I could just feel him hacking at the back of it. I was trying to fight him off and ended up with these.' She held her hands out, palms up, showing a couple of silvery scars that ran across them.

'Did you get a good look at the man?' Randall asked, retrieving his notebook from his pockets.

'No, I didn't. It was my neighbour Paul who did. I got a quick glimpse, but I was just so scared, I can't remember. I was sure I was going to die.'

'Does Paul still live around here?' Randall carried on.

'No, he died last year in a car accident.' She rubbed her nose with her sleeve. 'That man spoke into my ear though. I remember his voice.'

'What did he sound like?' Helen asked.

'Horrible,' she muttered. 'He said that I laughed at him, but I wasn't going to be laughing long.'

Randall copied this down into his notes.

'And that's all he said?' Helen asked.

'That was it. He had this horrible voice; it was almost like a snarl. Animal-like. I'll never forget it. It was just so full of hate.' She closed her eyes, as if she was reliving the moment.

'Did you spend any time in the dance hall with anyone that might have heard him say that?' Helen questioned.

Eleanor shook her head.

'Can you think of anything else?'

'This *man* wanted to dance,' she paused, blinking back tears. 'I didn't want to. That's the only thing I can think of.'

'Do you remember what he looked like?'

'Not really . . . he had dark hair. He didn't stick in my mind.'

'You were on your way home from the dance hall? When the attack happened?' Randall interjected.

'Yes. I can show you where I was if that helps?'

'Thank you,' Helen replied. 'That would be useful.'

'Did you see anyone unusual that night?' Randall probed.

'I couldn't remember. I had drunk too much. It was my friend's birthday, so there were lots of people around.'

'Right,' Randall rolled his eyes.

They followed Eleanor around the side of the building. This part of the garden resembled Steptoe's yard. Helen stepped over a rusty car wheel, then narrowly missed tripping over some wilted strawberries in a plant pot, grazing her shin on the terracotta pot instead. She gritted her teeth as pain shot through the bone.

'I used to go to that dance hall every week and had never had a problem before,' Eleanor explained.

'Who did you go to the dancehall with?' Randall asked. Randall and Eleanor walked together as Helen put the upturned plant pot back to its original position.

'A girl called Abi Foster, but she moved away a long time ago.'

Helen looked around the street. Rows and rows of similar style properties and three-storey blocks of flats enclosed them from both sides and spread back as far as the eye could see. A woman walking a Scottish Terrier eyed them suspiciously.

'It's just along here,' Eleanor explained. The woman stopped to see where she was pointing.

Eleanor took them to a grassy verge with a swing in the middle of it and a winding path along the side.

'It was just here on this path.' She pointed to the house opposite. 'That was where Paul lived.'

Helen surveyed the area; it was open and came with a high risk for the perpetrator. Maybe that was what gave him some of the thrill.

'There is something else though . . . It's probably nothing.'

'What is it? Anything may help us, no matter how small,' Helen replied.

'I didn't go to the police as I didn't think I'd be believed like last time.'

* * *

They both waited in the kitchen as Eleanor retrieved a shoe box from a side table. She placed it on the table and peeled back the lid.

'This was sent to me. Maybe about a year after the attack.' She retrieved a card and opened it for Helen to see.

Scribbled in smudged black ink, it said, '*To the one that got away, I think about you every day.*'

'And there's no one else that may have sent that, maybe at the end of a relationship?'

Eleanor shook her head.

On the other side of the wall was a watercolour painting of some flowers with gold writing saying 'With Sympathy' across the top.

'Is this the only one you've been sent?' Helen leaned forward to get a better look.

'Yes, there's been nothing else. I was really scared for a long time, I thought he was going to come back and finish the job.'

'Will it be all right for us to take this?' Randall asked.

* * *

Helen sighed as she clipped her seatbelt then slipped a glance at the burning wreckage. 'It is possible that this was our killer's first attempt at murder.'

'It fits.' Randall adjusted the rear-view mirror then pulled out into the road.

'Rejection seems to fuel his desire. He's organized in some ways but disorganized in others.' She looked out at the scene as they drove out. 'This was extremely risky; there was a high chance he could've been caught. Same with Tina French.'

'What about Moira McKenzie? All that blood could've easily been caused by a mallet,' Randall remarked.

CHAPTER THIRTY

Opening the door to the flat, Helen slipped off her shoes as she patted the wall for the light switch. She dropped her keys into the bowl on the shelf and headed through to the lounge, slipping off her jacket. Maybe she'd have some toast, then a hot shower. A gust from the window stopped her in her tracks. The net billowed against the wall. Her heart thudded and she placed her hand on the door handle to steady herself. Her eyes darted around the room, ears straining for any sound that would tell her if someone else was in the flat. She hadn't left the window open. She wouldn't have left the window open. Her legs felt like lead, as she moved to the window, then pulled it shut. A lump rose in her throat when she noticed the photograph of her brother had been placed back in its upright position when she knew she had left the frame face down on the shelf. She leaned against the window ledge scrambling to catch her breath. The room swirled around her. *Get a grip.* Maybe Terry had moved the photograph when he stayed that night. No, she definitely would have noticed that before now. A thud from the kitchen told her that she was not alone in the flat. She tiptoed around to the other end of the sofa and retrieved the vase from the box of stuff she hadn't got around to sorting. Thud. Adrenaline surged across her chest. She stepped over the creaky floorboard in the hall. The vase felt slippery in her grip. The kitchen door was ajar, but she couldn't see anything. She pushed it open with her foot.

'What are you doing here?'

Ted looked up at her wide-eyed. He was wearing a big pair of headphones and ripped them off when he noticed her. 'Sorry, I—'

'You gave me a fright.' Helen dragged a hand down her face. 'Bloody hell, Ted!'

He placed the headphones on the worktop. 'Sorry, I didn't hear you come in. I was listening to the radio.' He gave a half-smile and motioned to the radio watch around his wrist.

'Why are you here?'

'I still had your keys and I was going to give them back to you.'

'You should've just put them through the letter box, and you look like an idiot with those giant things on.'

'I know, I just . . . I didn't want to go home.'

'That's not my problem, Ted. You need to go.' Helen put the vase down on the table.

'I've been tidying up for you.'

'That's not the point.'

He shook his head. 'I can't do anything right, I'm sorry. I just didn't want to be alone and I've got nowhere else to go . . . no friends.'

Helen shrugged. 'That's not my problem.'

'I know. I know it's not. My brother died.'

'No, he couldn't have.'

'He had a heart attack this morning.' He shakily sighed. 'He's gone.'

'I'm sorry.' Helen looked away. He was just a few years older than Ted, so was only in his early fifties at most. No age at all. Helen had only met him once, last Christmas. His children were still only teenagers too.

'I didn't know where to go, then I found the keys in one of my jacket pockets. I've been trying not to think about it.'

'I'll make you some tea.'

He nodded and sat down at the table, wiping a tear from his eye.

Opening the cupboard to see what random ingredients were left over, Helen found a jar of jam that she had probably owned for the past decade, and a tub of cocoa powder that was empty, although she couldn't remember finishing it. Why the hell that was still in the cupboard she had no idea. The loaf of bread at the back passed the sniff test, so she grabbed the rest of the cheddar from the fridge and compiled a plate of sandwiches. 'Are you hungry?' she asked.

'Not really.'

'I'll make you some anyway,' she replied as she poured water into the kettle. 'Its nothing fancy, I've not been to the shops.'

'I wouldn't expect anything else.'

He smiled as she placed the plate in front of him. 'Thanks for this, I really do appreciate it.'

'Do you know when the funeral is?' Helen sat down opposite him and tore a piece of crust off her bread.

'Not yet but I'm going to go back to Cardiff tomorrow.'

CHAPTER THIRTY-ONE

The next morning Station Sergeant Robert Keaton stood at the reception desk, keeping an eye on a woman who was outside, shaking her head. She was on her third fag at least, he guessed. She smoked them quickly too, her hand trembling as she put them to her mouth. He looked away as soon as she faced him, not wanting to make eye contact. *Beautiful.* Still, he wouldn't have a chance with her. Probably waiting for the release of her old man. A stunner like that wouldn't be interested in some dumpy old bastard with nothing to show for his life. His ex-wife would remind him of that often enough. He sighed and went back to his work.

When the main door opened, he looked up from the endless amounts of reports he was processing. The woman was click-clacking towards him, a look of determination pursing her lips. The sweet aroma of fruity perfume intermixed with smoke reached him first.

Her black hair hung loosely around her shoulders, coiffed out. It bounced as she walked. She was skinny and wearing a long, green hippy dress with a big belt that emphasized her tiny waist. She didn't have any make-up on, and as she stood opposite him, he could see she'd been crying and her cheeks were swollen.

'Right,' she swallowed hard as she got to the counter, 'I . . . need to speak to a DS Carter.'

'What's it about?'

'A case . . . I was talking to her before.'

'I can help, love,' he replied. He was a better copper any day of the week than that fashion piece upstairs anyway.

'No, I want to speak to her . . .' Her clasped hands rested on the counter, she stared at the floor tiles.

'Give me a minute,' he replied and flicked through the phone sheets that were pinned to the wall beside him.

'Please be quick. I don't have much time,' she said, her voice sounding raspy.

He flicked to the last page and found a couple of numbers to try.

'I've found her number,' he said. 'What do you want to speak to her about?'

She sighed and looked like she was thinking of the right answer. 'It's to do wi' a case. Moira McKenzie. I've got some new information.' She pointed to the row of empty plastic chairs. 'I'll wait here. She'll want to talk to me.'

She sat there, head bowed, hands on her lap.

'Do you want a cup of tea?'

She looked at him with big brown eyes then shook her head.

He made the call to the CID suite. Hopefully, this time one of them would pick up. They were all standoffish up there now. Thinking they're better than everyone else. Always busy. Always with an attitude. He dialled the second number on the list, and this time someone answered after the third ring.

* * *

By the time they'd got a message to Helen, Molly had left the station and was walking down the hill towards Comely Bank. Helen chased after her, her chest burning as her feet pounded the pavement. She'd missed the feeling, but with Molly wearing stilettos, it wasn't hard to catch up with her.

'Molly!'

Molly turned around with a look of surprise on her face.

'Sorry, Molly. I was in a meeting.'

The hairdresser nodded but didn't say anything. She dragged hard on a fag.

'I've got to get back to work soon.'

'Shall we go for a tea and have a chat? There's a nice wee café just around the corner. It won't take long.'

* * *

Molly kept her gaze down, tracing a finger along a scratch in the table, her teapot and cup untouched in front of her.

'Why didn't you tell me this before, Molly?' Helen asked as she jotted some of the new information in her notebook.

Molly furrowed her brow. 'I hoped Moira would be found, then . . .' She looked around the café. 'It didn't feel right to drag all of this out for no reason.'

'I understand the desire to want to protect your friend, but we need to know everything. Every detail could help us at this stage.' Helen spoke in a low voice. Fortunately, the café was quiet in the lull between lunch and dinner. There was only the woman behind the counter, and she was scrubbing a big pot and was half-deaf, anyway.

'Fine,' an exasperated sigh escaped Molly. 'I just didn't want her to be angry with me when she turned back up and I didn't want you lot to tell Reggie.'

'We aren't going to tell Reggie.'

Like a petulant child, Helen thought. She resisted the urge to lecture her on how vital having this information was.

Molly chewed on a nail. 'Fine. I don't know his name.' Her eyes opened wide. 'Do you promise that Reggie won't find out about this?'

'No, he won't.' Helen assured her. 'How long has Moira been seeing this man?'

'I'm not sure exactly but at least a few months. I never met him.'

'What did Moira say about him?'

Molly took a moment to think. 'That she wanted to leave Reggie but didn't have the money to do so. This man was going to look after her. It's been a long time since I'd seen her this happy.'

'Do you know where they met?'

Molly shrugged and poured some tea from the pot into her cup. 'I don't know anything about the man, other than that he exists. I was happy for her. She was miserable with Reggie and deserves better.'

Helen nodded.

'I know he gave her books to read or was recommending her books to read.' Molly's forehead crinkled as she tried to think. 'Can't remember the names of them though.'

Helen couldn't remember seeing any books in the flat.

'He also gave her a pair of earrings. Little gold hoops.' Molly gestured to her own ears.

'How did she explain that away to Reggie?'

'I dunno. I think she said they were her sister's. She used to wear a lot of cheap-looking big ones until he gave her those. I've no' seen her take them off since.'

* * *

The front door rattled just as Helen sat slumped down on the sofa. She was tempted to ignore it, but whoever it was knocked again.

'Am coming. Am coming.' She clicked off the television and headed to the door. Terry McKinley was standing in front of her with two chippy meals wrapped in newspaper.

'I hope you haven't eaten?' He gave her a half-smile.

'I'm not hungry, Terry.'

'Well, I'll just eat mine then.' He shrugged. 'Now, you going to let me in or not?'

'I'm tired. I just want an early night.'

'It's getting cold!'

Helen sighed and slipped off the security chain. She opened the door wide, then headed through to the kitchen.

He followed behind her, bringing the smell of chips with him.

'Mine better be fish,' Helen said, as she took two pint glasses from the cupboard and filled them with orange juice from the fridge.

'Aye.' He slung her packet onto the worktop. 'And I got salt on it.'

He had mud on the hem of his grey suit trousers, and she could smell the faint aroma of cigarette smoke.

He rubbed a hand across his stubble. 'It's been a long day.'

'That bad?'

'Something like that.'

'Are you back on shift after this?'

'No that's me done for the night.'

Helen swallowed a mouthful of orange. 'What are you doing here, Terry?'

'We didn't have a chance to talk earlier.' McKinley smiled. 'C'mon, at least have some chips.' He sat down at the kitchen table. 'There's no point wasting it.'

Helen sat opposite him, struggling to find her appetite. She tore a bit of batter off the fish.

'I haven't eaten all day, you know, I'm really looking forward to this.'

Helen wiped grease from her fingers. 'Look, you don't need to keep checking up on me, I'm fine.'

'I'm not checking up on you. I've been enjoying our dinners. It's just . . .'

Just get to the point. 'Just what?' She could see he was thinking of which words to use. Her stomach tightened, and she suddenly became aware of her heart beating in her chest.

'The thing with Sally.' McKinley frowned. 'I don't want you to think.'

'It's none of my business.' Helen interrupted. 'I don't need to know.'

'I didn't expect her to come back. She was clear about things being over before. She just turned up.'

'Is she staying?' Helen chewed on a chip. It was too soggy for her liking.

'I don't know.'

'She's short of money. She didn't get any acting work in London.' McKinley explained.

'That's hardly surprising.' Helen slid the chips away. 'Acting work is hard to come by, I expect.'

'She's thinking about coming back to work at the station.'

'That's good.'

'I'm not even sure it is.' McKinley furrowed his brow. 'It didn't exactly go well last time.'

Helen shrugged, standing up and heading to the sink. 'Are there vacancies?' Yesterday's dishes sat in a pool of murky water. She began to wipe the plates.

'I think so.' He paused.

'I know she enjoys winding you up.'

'I think she likes to do that to everyone.' A lump settled in Helen's throat. She tried to swallow it away.

'Do you want me to stay a while?'

'I'm really tired. I just want to be alone.'

CHAPTER THIRTY-TWO

It had been years since Helen had set foot in a building like this. She flicked through some of the new releases while waiting for the librarian to fetch the books she had requested. Another member of staff was hovering nearby, stacking a freestanding shelf with paperbacks from a trolley. She gave a small smile when she noticed Helen. Helen returned the gesture as she slotted a hardback on golf back into its place on the shelf. Five years ago — that would've been the last time she had been in a library. It would've been the one at the policing college. Helen wandered over to the cookery section and brushed a finger along the titles. She glanced over her shoulder. A couple of girls were sitting around a nearby table, reading copies of *Jackie*. A smile tugged at Helen's lips when she noticed a group of young children sitting in a carpeted area entranced in a game of snakes and ladders.

'Right.' The librarian tapped Helen on the shoulder. Her cheeks were flushed with pink and sweat glistened on her forehead. 'Sorry it took me so long,' she explained. 'People keep putting the books back in the wrong place.'

'I'm in no rush.' Helen replied, glancing down at the books the librarian was clutching.

'Okay,' the librarian blew out a sigh. 'So these are the titles that were borrowed on that account.' She held up a white hardback with a red rose in the centre of the dust jacket. *The Missing Piece* was written in gold lettering along the bottom of it.

Helen took it and skimmed through the first couple of yellowed pages. It was about a woman who disappeared. Her husband had gone to work in the morning as normal, and when he came home, she had vanished. The other one was a modern diet book, *The Egg and Wine Diet*. Helen scoffed and handed that one back to the librarian.

'I should say, that's not the actual book that was borrowed.' The librarian nodded to the title in Helen's hand.

'What do you mean?' Helen asked, flicking to the next chapter.

'We had two copies of this book. The other copy is still out on loan with Moira.'

Helen nodded as she looked at the loan ticket for this one. It hadn't been borrowed once in the past two years. She hadn't heard of the author either.

'Would it be okay for me to borrow this one?'

'Of course, but you'll need to join the library first.'

Back in the car, Helen read through more of the book, it was old, published in 1953. The wife went missing, the husband served twenty years in jail. Helen slung the book onto the passenger seat and headed back to the station.

* * *

Helen managed to grab herself a mug of coffee before the briefing. She had the book under her arm. Craven sat at the table but didn't look up from the notes he was reading. DC Randall was next to him, looking bored. She could feel McKinley's gaze on her as she shuffled around the table to an empty chair. A moment later, DCI Murphy entered the room, a folder in his hand and a bottle of single malt in the other. 'Right, I've read the papers this morning and I'm not happy.'

'You two,' he pointed to Randall and McKinley, 'I want you to carry on with the door-to-door enquiries.'

Randall grunted. 'Aye, sir,'

'My focus in on Reggie McKenzie,' Murphy thumped the bottle down on the table. 'I don't like the look of him.'

Helen met eyes with Craven.

'I'm not so sure,' Helen said, looking down at the novel in front of her.

'What?' Murphy scoffed, he looked taken aback. 'I don't understand.'

Helen blinked. She could feel all eyes in the room centre on her. 'Moira took her wages from her job the day before she went missing.'

'Oh aye, woman takes money, that's a first. She probably spent it in a shop. That's what you lot are good at. Just ask my wife.' Murphy told her.

Randall shifted in his seat and sucked in his cheeks like he was trying not to smile.

'There's also this.' Helen took a breath. She could hear her heart pounding.

Murphy lifted his eyebrows. 'A book?' He motioned for her to hand it to him.

'As you can see, it's about a woman who went missing.'

Murphy flicked through the opening pages. 'My wife reads books — all these romantic sagas. Do you think I need to worry?'

'No, sir but—'

'This is it? A bloody book?' DCI Murphy seethed and threw the book back down onto the desk.

'Sir, Reggie McKenzie was in the pub at the time of Moira's disappearance.' Helen reminded him.

'No, you think Reggie was at the pub. Was he there all night? Could he have slipped out? Paid someone to do it? He's got motive and he's got form.'

'That book,' Helen carried on, 'is about a woman who disappeared and was never found again. It's told from the husband's point of view.'

'So, it's a bloody work of fiction.' Murphy muttered.

'Yes, but it could mean something, sir.'

'It doesn't mean anything.'

'I just think it's a bit of a coincidence.'

'So, maybe Reggie read it and got some ideas.'

'No, what doesn't add up is that we have had a violent alcoholic downstairs, and you don't think he should be charged.' A sneer curled his lip. 'Reggie has had more bother with the police than I've had hot dinners.'

Helen cleared her throat. 'Sir, I—'

Craven sighed as he slid a composite drawing across the desk. 'This is a sketch of a man that was seen showing an interest in Tina French before she was murdered.'

Murphy snatched it up.

'We're going to circulate this to the press. So far we haven't found anyone that's been able to say a bad word about her.'

'What about her ex-partner?' Murphy asked.

'He has an alibi. He was on holiday at a Pontin's in Wales with his new family.'

* * *

'Helen, are we okay?' McKinley had waited around until the briefing was over.

'We're fine, Terry.' Helen bundled the book under her arm. 'Why wouldn't we be?' She tried to move past him, but he stepped in her way.

'Sally, Sally just likes to cause trouble, that's what she does.'

'Why are you telling me this?'

'I don't know.' He looked away. 'I don't want you to think bad of me.'

165

She put the book back on the table and sat down, motioning for him to do the same. 'I don't think bad of you.' He reached out and placed his hand on top of hers.

As the door opened, Helen whipped her hand away, knocking the book onto the floor.

Craven looked between the pair of them.

'The DCI wants to have a word with you in his office.'

'Right, thanks.' Helen replied, picking up the book.

The briefing room was on the floor below CID suite. She followed Craven along the corridor, then up the stairs.

'I'm going to head to the care hospital this afternoon and see if I can speak to Agnes.'

'I'll come with you,' he replied.

CHAPTER THIRTY-THREE

Reggie arrived in the car park of the sanatorium. A couple of the inhabitants were sitting in the conservatory, playing what looked like dominoes. He picked up the bunch of flowers and headed inside. A winding staircase took him to her room on the third floor. The cleaning fluid aroma tickled the back of his throat. As he approached, he saw the door was ajar. She sat in an oversized armchair by the window, a paperback novel in her hand, and looked up as he knocked on the door.

'Hello, she smiled. 'Do I know you?'

'I could ask you the same question,' he replied, forcing a smile. 'Have you been here long?' The hospital smell was stronger in here.

The frail-looking woman nodded. 'I wasn't expecting anyone,' she muttered and put her book down next to a plastic cup with a straw.

'I think I've got the wrong room. Sorry about that.'

Back down at the reception area, Reggie gritted his teeth, waiting for the nurse to find the right file. 'If she was being moved, I should've been told.' He crushed the stems of the flowers in his hand.

'We normally do,' she replied, 'but I can't find the folder.'

'This is ridiculous, what do you expect me to do? Just wander around all the rooms?'

'No, we don't normally move people unless . . .'

'Unless what?'

The nurse pulled out another pile of folders, flicking through them, not finding Agnes's name.

'If this is how you look after your files, I dread to think how you look after the patients.'

'Sorry', her cheeks flushed with pink. 'I just started yesterday; I don't know all the patients' names yet.'

'Aga, Aga!' The woman shouted towards a side room.

'What is it?' A girl with a mop in her hand appeared, her eyes darting between the nurse and Reggie.

'Agnes Smith? Do you know what room she is in? I can't find it on the chart. I can't find her folder either . . .'

'Aggie was moved about three months ago.'

Reggie tutted. 'No, she wasn't.'

'She was, I helped with it.'

'I don't think we're talking about the same person here.' Reggie slammed the flowers on the counter, petals spraying to the floor. 'Agnes Smith, she's about this high.' He motioned with his hand to his shoulder height. 'Brown hair. Epileptic, and suffers with severe memory loss.'

'Yes, I know Aggie well.' The girl with the mop stepped forward. 'She's moved on.'

'I need to see her; I need to tell her about my dear wife.'

'I understand, I saw it in the papers this morning.'

Reggie sighed, dragging a hand down his face.

'Agnes is definitely not here. I helped her pack myself.'

'Where did she go?'

'I don't know,' the girl shrugged.

'How can you not know this?'

'We were simply told that she was moving to a new facility.'

'So, any stranger could've walked in off the street?' Reggie clenched his fists, feeling his nails dig into his palms.

'No, Moira, your wife. She was the one that instructed it.'

'No, she didn't, she wouldn't.'

'All I know is that she said you were both moving away from the area and that you wanted her to be somewhere closer.'

'Oh, are we now?' Reggie muttered and headed for the exit. 'I'll see about that.' He had someone else to ask.

* * *

Reggie pulled open the door to the café. The coffin dodgers were ensconced in the window seat, the old man was working his way through some toast and the old lady nursed a cup of tea. They looked up as he approached and sat down opposite the old man. A Rod Stewart song played from the radio on the counter. He tried to wave to the waitress, but she had her head down, putting cakes onto a tray.

'Thanks for agreeing to meet me.' Reggie smiled. 'I can only imagine how hard this must be for you.'

'Aye,' the old man slid his plate away. 'We just want her found, back home safe.'

'That's all I want too,' Reggie agreed. 'I love Moira.'

The old woman produced a bundled-up newspaper from her handbag. 'The papers are saying that she might've been murdered. Murdered like the woman who disappeared a few days before her.'

'What? No, that's impossible.' He took the paper from her bony hand and skim-read. 'No,' he leaned forward and stared hard into her green eyes. 'You shouldn't be reading nonsense like this.' He took a breath then shoved the paper into his pocket. 'Did you know that Agnes has been moved to another care facility?'

The old man shook his head. 'We were going to visit Agnes, but Moira said she is not able to have visitors at the moment.'

'So, you have no idea where she would be?' Reggie clenched his fist.

'No, we don't.' The old woman shrugged.

'Well, have a think.' Reggie said, rising to his feet, 'and if you have any ideas, let me know. It's especially important that I speak to Agnes.'

'Do you think the police will find her, Reggie?' the old woman asked.

'No, I think it will be up to me to get all the answers.'

CHAPTER THIRTY-FOUR

Taking a breath, Craven rattled on the brass knocker that he had fitted a long time ago now. Although the name plate he'd installed at the same time had been removed and only the screw marks remained.

'What are you doing here, Jack?' Liz shook her head, opening the door just as far as the security chain would allow. 'I'm just about to go out.' She had her jacket on and her blonde hair scraped back into a bun, but no make-up, which was unusual for her.

'I just want to talk to you.'

'I'm busy, Jack.'

'It's important.' He dragged the heel of his hand down his face. 'I wouldn't be here otherwise.'

'There's nothing else to say.'

'I ran into Milton.'

'He said.'

'I just want to see the twins. That's it.' He replied, stepping forward. 'I thought we had an agreement?'

'We did, but you don't turn up and we're the ones left picking up the pieces.'

'The last time was an emergency at work.' He cleared his throat. 'It was a big case.'

'But there's always going to be a big case.'

'Can I not just see them now then?'

'They're not here.'

Craven's stomach lurched. 'Where are they?'

'They're away at Milton's mother's.'

'What are they doing there?'

'They enjoy it. She has a swimming pool.'

'How the other half do live, eh?' He shoved his hands in his pockets for warmth.

'It's all different to when we were growing up.'

She furrowed her brow. 'It breaks their heart when they think they are going to see you and then you don't turn up.'

'I know.'

'Milton won't be happy with this.' She unlatched the chain. 'Come in and we can talk. I don't want the neighbours gossiping.'

He flicked a glance to the house next door. 'Does old Mrs Walters still live there?'

'Yes, she does.'

Mrs Walters or 'curtain twitcher' as he liked to call her. The only good thing about living next door to her was that your house wouldn't be burgled, as she was always watching it for you.

He followed Liz through to the front room. 'I can't be long though,' she said, 'I have an appointment uptown . . . Do you want a tea? Coffee?'

'No, I had one at the station.'

Craven looked around the lounge. Hardly anything in the room had changed from when he called it home. Surprising as he assumed Milton would've wanted to put his stamp on the place.

'Well.' She shrugged her shoulders and slumped down on the sofa, picking up one of the scatter cushions and hugging it tightly.

'I won't let them down again.'

'It's not that.'

'Then what is it?'

She looked across to the photographs that adorned the mantlepiece. 'Milton promised the twins a holiday.'

'Go another time. Go next week or . . .'

'We can't . . .'

'When can I see them then?'

'It's hard. Milton's having a lot of stress at work and he just wants to get away for a while.'

'I haven't seen them since their birthday party, that was what, at least six weeks ago.'

He sat down in the armchair opposite and held his head in his hands. 'I know I wasn't the best husband.'

Liz laughed, 'That's an understatement.'

'I am sorry.'

'For what exactly? For carrying on with all those women?' she pursed her lips. 'It doesn't matter now.'

'I'm sorry for it all. It was the worst mistake of my life.'

'I don't want to get into all this again.'

His eyes fell to the doll house in front of the bay window, and the Holly Hobbie doll next to it.

'She plays with that all the time.' Liz motioned to the doll.

'I'm glad.'

She reached into her handbag and pulled out a packet of Players Number Six. She offered one to Craven, he shook his head.

'Milton is a good man,' she muttered, placing one to her lips. 'He just gets protective. He thinks of the children as his own now.' The words hung heavy in the silence.

Craven clenched his fists and tried to think of the right words that wouldn't make this worse. 'They're not his though and they never will be.'

'Maybe not, but he is there for them.'

He bit his lip. He never seemed to get anything right. 'I'm not saying that he isn't,' he countered. 'But I'm their father.'

Sighing, she lit her cigarette and took a long drag.

The smoke drifted towards him and lingered in the air. 'I thought Milton didn't like you smoking in the house.'

'What he doesn't know won't hurt him,' she replied. Her blue eyes met his. 'I only smoke when I'm stressed.' She stood up and straightened out her pink dress. Craven was sure it was one of the ones he had bought her.

'You never used to let me smoke in the house.'

'Don't start,' she groaned, then turned on her heels and headed towards the kitchen. 'I'm going to have a cup of tea, do you want one?'

'Aye,' Craven replied, following her.

'Take a seat if you want.' She motioned to the bar at the bottom of the room. It looked like a cocktail bar with glass shelves lined with bottles of alcohol and a fruit bowl stacked with lemons and limes.

'This is new.' Craven perched on the end of one of the stools, admiring an expensive-looking bottle of whisky.

'It's Milton's idea.' Liz reached into a cupboard and took out two cups and saucers, the cigarette dangling precariously on her lips as she spoke.

'There's no milk. I've not been shopping,' she said, dropping a tea bag in each cup.

His gaze fell to the pile of letters stacked beside the fruit bowl. The top one stamped with 'Final Demand'.

Liz handed him the cup then picked up the letters. He watched her shove them in one of the drawers.

'There's something else that I wanted to tell you.'

'What?'

He fished in his pocket for the letter, then handed it to her.

'When did you get this?'

'Last week.'

'I'm so sorry Jack. Are there treatments? What are they going to do?'

'Aye, I mean, modern medicine, there's lots they can do.'

She stubbed out her cigarette. 'Oh god, Jack,' she muttered, 'I can't believe this.'

Craven swallowed the lump in his throat.

'Do you want me to ask Milton? See what he thinks.'

'No, I don't want anyone else to know. You're the only one I've told, and I want it to stay that way.'

'This is hard, Jack. We're not just looking at a holiday. Milton also has a potential job offer down there, so we're going to be looking at houses.'

'Do you not think this is something I should know about?'

'It's early days, the twins don't even know.'

CHAPTER THIRTY-FIVE

It had started to rain lightly as Randall parked up outside the McKenzie residence. Helen glanced at the flat. All the lights were out. The car came to a juddering stop behind a rusted Reliant Regal.

'Think I ran over a nail or something,' Randall muttered, wrenching up the handbrake. 'And the bloody roads are full of potholes.'

'Let's look at the damage then,' Helen replied, opening her door.

Randall sucked air through his teeth as he knelt next to the front driver's tyre. 'It looks a bit flat.' He clambered up and kicked it with his boot. 'But I can't see anything in the tread.'

'It looks fine to me.'

'Know all about tyres, do you?' Randall grumbled.

'Okay, you stay here and deal with that — I'm going to have a look at Mr McKenzie's shed.'

'What, alone?' Randall asked dryly.

'I won't be alone.'

'If you're sure.'

'I can shout you if there's a problem.'

'You do that.'

'I'll see you in a bit.'

The stairwell door was wedged open, so Helen was able to walk straight through the back garden area to a small concrete block of flat-roofed sheds. McKenzie's was the last one on the right. The only one that looked locked and was also bolted with a padlock. She gave it a tug, but the padlock didn't budge.

'What do you want?' The voice came from behind.

She twisted around to see Reggie McKenzie behind her. Fists bunched, he stepped forward. 'What do you want with my shed?'

'Nothing in particular.' Helen backed away from the door. 'And besides, I didn't know this was *your* shed. You told our officers that you don't even own one.'

'I don't. I rent it from one of the neighbours. There's nothing here for you to find, Moira. Yet you want to have a look around the junk I keep in a shed?' He stabbed a finger at her.

'Would you mind?'

A sneer twisted his lips. 'What?'

'Can I have a look in there?' She tilted her head towards the door. 'I'd just like a quick look.'

'You're so eager to put the blame on me, aren't you?' Reggie snarled.

'No, I only want to get to the truth.'

'Truth?' he scoffed. 'You lot wouldn't know the meaning of the word . . . Did you come alone?'

'What would that have to do with anything? And we are doing everything that we can to find your wife.'

'Aye?' He scratched his stubble. 'Then where is she? I had hoped you had come here with some answers.' His eyes bore into hers.

'I'll have some soon.'

'You are sharp one, aren't you?'

Helen stepped back and tried to slip a glance over her shoulder, feeling her throat tighten.

'I'm not alone. I'm with a colleague.'

He made a show of looking over his shoulder. 'I don't see anyone.'

'He's just out front.' Helen sidestepped. There wasn't enough room to get past him. 'Are you going to let us have a look in your shed.'

He shrugged. 'If you really want to, then who am I to argue?'

'Thank you.'

She took a deep breath when Randall emerged from the stairwell. 'You're just in time,' Helen told Randall. 'Mr McKenzie is about to open his shed for us.'

'Aye.' Randall nodded.

Reggie pulled open the door. 'Here you go, have a look.' He motioned for Helen to go first.

'It's empty.'

'Well, I had a few old garden tools but dumped them, a while back. Go on, take a closer look if you want.' He asked Randall, 'Do you want to have a look too?'

'That's fine.' Helen replied. 'We've seen all we need to see.'

CHAPTER THIRTY-SIX

Helen's heart still pounded as she shoved open the door to the CID room. Randall followed in close behind her. She shrugged off her jacket and sighed as her telephone rang. She could've done with a moment to get herself together. The confrontation with Reggie swirled in her mind and the danger that she could've put herself in again. She took a deep breath, then snatched up the phone.

'Helen Carter.' She twirled the chord around her finger.

'You've got a visitor waiting for you down in reception.' She recognized the voice as the staff sergeant Robert Keaton.

'Can't it wait?' she asked, matching his annoyed tone.

'He says it's important.'

'Who's 'he'?'

'Ted.'

She sighed and dragged her hand across her forehead. 'I'll be right down.' She hung up the phone and grabbed her coat from the chair.

* * *

'What are you doing here?' Helen asked, casting a glance around the entrance foyer to make sure no one was listening.

She had had enough of the gossips in this station to last a lifetime. She moved towards the door.

Ted followed looking sheepish; he had his hands in his pockets of his jeans and he was wearing a navy-blue shirt with an open collar. A more casual look than she had seen from him before. 'I'm really sorry to bother you at work.' He shook his head and looked like he was struggling for what to say.

'I've just been really busy,' Helen replied, folding her arms. 'You know what it's like.'

'I'm sorry.'

Helen softened her voice. 'How are you doing?'

He sucked in a breath.

Helen met his eyes. 'I know what you're going through.'

Ted nodded. 'Got my bags packed. I'm going to drive down in the next few hours . . . I still can't believe he is gone.'

'I know. I can't either.' She had only met him once but knew he was into fitness and didn't drink much.

'Anyway,' he bobbed on the spot. 'I don't want to take up your time.'

Helen nodded. 'I don't have long, I'm right in the middle of a case.'

'This is important, and I wanted to speak to you in person.'

'Okay, let's go down to the canteen and get a coffee.'

'Are you sure?'

'It should be quiet at this time.'

Relief was apparent on his face. 'I'd really love that actually. I haven't had one all day.'

* * *

Helen grabbed a seat near the window facing out onto the fields. On the far side of the grass an officer was out training an Alsatian. The afternoon sun streamed through the gaps in the blinds. Ted smiled again, as he approached the table with two cups of coffee and scones on a tray. He placed it between them. 'I thought you might be hungry. I know you never eat properly when you're stressed.'

'Thanks.' Helen took the tea plate with the fruit scone and sliced it in half.

Ted took a sip of his coffee and looked out to the fields. His blue eyes looked clear; Helen leaned forward trying to smell if there was any alcohol on his breath but all she could smell was the sweet aroma of his aftershave.

'What did you want to talk to me about?' Helen asked, between mouthfuls of scone. She was hungrier than she thought. She picked a raisin from her teeth.

'Well, a few things . . . I'm sorry, my head's all over the place.'

'Right.'

He exhaled a breath. Helen noticed his expression change, obviously thinking about what to say.

'You're starting to worry me now,' Helen replied, sliding the plate away.

'I came here to tell you something important,' he blurted. 'This is really difficult for me. I don't know what to do.'

She made eye contact with a couple of uniformed officers clutching trays, debating where to sit. 'I've got to get back soon.'

He shook his head and rubbed a hand across his forehead. 'I really wanted you to come with me.'

Lowering her voice, she slipped another glance at the officers who were now smirking. 'I can't. I mean, we've been through this. I would if I could.'

'I understand, but it's not going to stop me hoping though, is it?' He shrugged and took another sip of coffee.

Helen put her piece of scone back on her plate, losing her appetite.

'Your mum also called my house yesterday,' he explained. 'She didn't know that we had split up or that you had moved out of my flat.' He brushed some crumbs from the table. 'It did give me some hope that we could sort this out.'

Helen considered this. 'No, I don't think we can. I mean both our heads are all over the place now.'

'I know I was rubbish . . . inconsiderate . . . selfish, but I've changed.'

'It's not been working for a long time and I know you felt that too. This is just the grief talking.'

'That's not true.' He slid his plate away and leaned forward. 'Remember when we stayed in that little cottage up the Highlands?'

Nodding, she looked back outside. It was one of the best weeks of her life, holed up in that little cabin with an open fire. The long country walks, and not a care in the world, but that was a long time ago now.

'I keep thinking about that, I want that back again.'

'I loved it too,' she agreed.

'Why didn't you tell your mum, then?'

Helen considered this for a moment. 'I just didn't want to disappointed her or have her worry about me. She's been planning our wedding ever since I brought you home for the first time.'

He took a deep breath. 'I thought maybe, it was . . .'

Helen shook her head. 'I'm sorry. I really am.'

'I know things got a bit rough towards the end, but I honestly thought we could've achieved so much together and been really happy.'

'I know.'

'I have stopped drinking.'

'Good, you needed to.'

'I was so stupid to come here,' he muttered, rising to his feet. 'You need to call your mum, anyway.'

'I will.'

'I didn't tell her what happened. I think it's better coming from you.' He drained the last of his coffee.

'I'll be thinking about you.'

Ted nodded. 'There was something else.' He retrieved a brown envelope from his pocket. 'I was given this for you when you were in hospital.'

Helen took it. 'Why didn't you tell me this before? What is it?'

'I guess I was being selfish. Why break a habit of a lifetime, eh?'

'You should have given this to me.'

'I didn't want you to have any more upset.'

Helen slipped the envelope into her pocket. She'd open it when she was back in the CID room.

CHAPTER THIRTY-SEVEN

McKinley looked up from his paperwork and offered her an awkward smile. She looked away and headed to her own desk. There was a moment of silence as Helen shoved the envelope into the drawer underneath her police manuals. She couldn't face that right now.

McKinley stood up, clutching a folder. 'I tried to speak to the sanatorium about Moira McKenzie's sister, Agnes, but she's been moved.'

'Moved where?' Helen draped her jacket over her chair.

'I don't know, but she was taken from the sanatorium three months ago and they don't know where she was taken to.'

'Have you—'

'Yes, I've checked with other hospitals in Edinburgh and Glasgow. She's not a patient in any of them.'

'Do they know who moved her?'

He looked down at his notes. 'Moira McKenzie.'

'Well, that's strange.'

'Aye.'

'I'm going to keep checking other institutions. She'll have to be in one of them . . .'

'I think maybe it's time to have another little word with Reggie.' Helen moved around her desk, picking up her mug;

only the dregs of coffee remained in the bottom of the cup. She swirled them.

Nodding, McKinley flicked to another page in his folder. 'On a cheerier note, I also have the autopsy report for Tina French. Alex Winston reckons her cause of death was the choking, but she was badly hurt before by what he reckons was a wooden mallet.'

Helen grimaced at the thought and exhaled a breath at the senselessness of it all.

'I'm also working with DC Randall to see if we can find any similar cases with other divisions.'

'Good,' Helen shifted in her seat. 'I also want to speak to that Dr Rushmore again. Can you find out when he is back in the surgery?' Her throat was dry, and she needed to get some water. She slipped a glance over at Craven's office. He was on the telephone and had a cigarette dangling from his lips. He didn't look happy with whoever he was talking to, and was waving his arms.

A few minutes later, Craven emerged from his office with his jacket on. 'Marjorie Lockwood was seen at the McKenzie's address the day before Moira disappeared.'

'How did you find that out?' Helen asked.

One of the neighbours has come forward during door-to-door enquiries and gave a positive identification. 'I've had Marjorie picked up and she is down in Interview Room One now. I want you in on this one.'

'I'll be down in a minute,' Helen said, picking up her jacket.

A few minutes later, Helen and Craven found themselves sitting across from a nervous-looking Marjorie Lockwood in Interview Room One, a stuffy windowless room that reeked of bleach and sweat, barely big enough for the table and four chairs.

Marjorie shakily sighed as Helen flicked open the manila folder. Puffy bags hung heavy under her bloodshot eyes; she had a half-drunk mug of tea in front of her.

Marjorie cleared her throat. 'I . . . I don't understand why I am here; I haven't done anything wrong.' She looked pleadingly at Helen.

Helen slid a picture of Moira McKenzie across the scratched mahogany table. 'Do you recognize the woman in this photograph?'

Shaking her head, Marjorie looked like she was blinking back tears. 'No, I've never seen her before.'

'Take another look,' Helen prompted.

Marjorie made no move to look at the photograph again. 'I . . . I mean I know who this is, it's Moira McKenzie.'

'And how do you know this?'

'I saw her picture in the newspaper.'

'You've never met her in person.'

'No, I haven't. I didn't recognize her at first. She looked a bit older in that one.' She turned it over and slid the photograph back towards Helen.

'So, you've definitely never spoken to her before?' Helen clarified.

'No.'

'Have a think,' Craven prompted. 'Maybe it has slipped your mind.'

Marjorie shook her head. 'No.'

'Marjorie, a woman may be dead right now, and we're trying to find out what happened to her.' Helen leaned forward and placed her hands on the table.

'I understand that . . . I do.'

'What if we told you that you were seen arguing with Moira in the street.'

'No, we weren't.'

Craven made a clicking sound, 'The day before Moira's disappearance. A woman bearing a striking resemblance to yourself was seen arguing with Moira McKenzie. Do you have a twin sister, Marjorie?'

'I don't. It's not like that.' Marjorie's hands were shaking, she reached into her pockets and put a cigarette to her lips.

Craven retrieved his lighter and handed it to her.

'Thanks,' she lit the cigarette and took a long drag exhaling the smoke slowly. 'I spoke to her, but I haven't hurt her.'

Craven looked down at his notes. 'Why don't you tell us what this conversation was about?'

Marjorie exchanged a look with Helen, and she wiped away a tear that trailed down her cheek with the back of her hand. 'I was fed up. Reggie had told me they were over, but I wanted to see for myself.'

'And what exactly did you see?' Craven asked.

'He made all these promises about us being together, but nothing ever seemed to happen.'

'So, you and Reggie were an item.'

Marjorie nodded. 'We were. Reggie didn't want me to tell you in case you got the wrong idea . . .'

'How long have you been together?'

'About eighteen months . . . give or take.'

'What did he say about Moira?'

'He said she was this mad alcoholic and I wanted to see for myself.'

'What happened when you confronted her?' Craven asked.

'I didn't *confront* her,' she countered, 'I told her that Reggie and I were together and that she needed to let him go.'

'And how did she take this news?' Helen asked.

'She didn't believe me at first, then she got angry. Really angry. It was the way she looked at me, I thought she was going to hit me. I told her that I loved Reggie and he loved me and that we were going to be together.'

'Then what happened?'

'She screamed at me, called me some . . . unpleasant names, then stormed off into her stairwell. That's the last I saw of her. I don't think she must've told Reggie either because he hasn't mentioned it.'

'How do you know?' Helen asked.

'I saw him . . . yesterday, and he was his usual self.' Marjorie let out a long breath.

'I was terrified that he'd blame me for what happened, but she mustn't have told him. Anyway, it's all backfired on me because now he wants to call things off.'

'It was a waste of time going to speak to Moira then.' Craven flicked over the page in his notebook.

Marjorie shifted in her seat. 'He doesn't want to give you lot the wrong idea.'

CHAPTER THIRTY-EIGHT

'At every turn, that woman's lied to us.' Craven shook his head, as they approached the stairwell. 'I wouldn't trust her as far as I could throw her.'

Helen considered this for a moment. 'I know, I'm going to go and speak to Reggie McKenzie again shortly.'

'Good idea.'

Now was as good a time as any. 'What's your history with DCI Murphy?'

'Typical woman, eh?' Craven started up the stairs.

'You were going to tell me before . . . You know what the gossips are like around here, so if you don't tell me someone else will.'

He shrugged. 'This better not get back to him.'

Helen crossed herself, 'I promise.'

He looked around to make sure no one else was on the staircase and lowered his voice. 'I can't stand him.' He stepped closer. 'We were at the policing college together, he's a rubbish copper, always has been.'

'But there's more to it than that?'

Craven nodded and motioned for her to follow him down the corridor. He opened the meeting room door on the left. It was empty, so she followed him inside. He perched on the edge of the desk. Arms crossed.

'We worked together a long time ago on an undercover sting to bring down "Wee Bob Harvey". Have you heard of him?'

Helen knew the name — he was a notorious Glaswegian organized-crime boss, a big force in the sixties.

'We had been watching Bob for months, and he was so careful, but we had him. He was planning a set of heists on a couple of banks. We had all the surveillance ready; everything was in place.'

'The day of the heists, he disappeared off to Spain and we never saw him again. He's disappeared off the face of the Earth completely.'

'You think someone from the team fed him information?'

'I'm sure of it.'

'And you think it was Tam Murphy?'

Craven scratched his stubble. 'I can't prove it.'

'No,' Helen sat down in one of the chairs. 'What made you suspect him?'

'A lot of us were really poor in them days. My salary barely covered my rent and food, but Tam, well, he managed to do well for himself. Holidays, a nice place to live. Flash suits . . .'

Helen considered this. Corruption was rife in the force at all levels, that was something she knew well herself. She looked across to the empty evidence board. Even her own father was guilty of taking backhanders, and that hadn't stopped him having a long and decorated career in the force.

'You know it might not have just been him.' Helen had heard of whole teams at all levels being in on it.

'I know, and like I say, I can't prove it.'

* * *

Craven slipped his hands behind his head and looked up at the ceiling tiles. The building was only a few years old, and already there were water marks in the far corner of the room above his filing cabinet. He chewed on the last of a Marathon bar. He clicked off his lamp and closed his eyes. Faint orange light from the main office leaked through the blinds. He couldn't remember the last time he'd had a full night's sleep. The desk phone rang, he thought about not answering it but relented.

'Jack Craven.'

'Hi, Jack, it's me.'

'Liz, is everything all right?' He slipped his feet from the desk sending his notes flying to the floor. She never called unless . . .

'Fine. Listen, I spoke with Milton.'

'And?' He shifted in his seat. He could hear her draw breath. 'Just spit it out, Liz.'

'He's been offered the job.'

'For fuck's sake,' he scratched his stubble and sighed. 'I thought you loved living in Edinburgh, you'll be away from all your friends and family.'

'I know and I do . . .'

'Then tell him to stuff it.'

'Milton is not in a position to turn down jobs now.'

'That's a load of rubbish. He's loaded, he's quick enough to rub it in my face often enough.'

'You should see the pictures of the house he wants to get. He can offer the twins such a good life, you know.'

'Are you still going away this weekend?'

'No, Milton is going to go and get things sorted but we'll stay here.'

'Great,' he dragged a hand down his face.

'The twins have been asking for you a lot.'

That was something at least. 'I'll come by on Saturday then, maybe we can go to the park or something.'

'I'm sure they'll enjoy that but please come.'

'I'll be over about eleven then.'

* * *

Once McKinley left to go down to records, Helen sat back in her chair and retrieved the envelope from the pedestal. Her mouth felt dry and she could feel her heart pounding in her chest. She recognized the handwriting on the front. The loop of the 'e' in Helen. The flick of the 'n'. She traced it with her finger. It was her father's handwriting. She carefully peeled open the lip of the envelope and slipped out the letter.

Dear Helen,

My darling — I'm so proud of everything you have done and will no doubt achieve in the future.

I hope you find happiness in whatever you do in life. Don't waste a minute of it! I've had a little gift for you that I wanted Ted to give you once the tenancy ended.

I have a little house in the country that now belongs to you! My gift to you.

You can sell it if you wish, the money will free you up from having to work. If not, rent it out or live in it as your home, it is a lovely little place. Beautiful during the summer.

I spent many a happy year there. Whatever you decide to do, look after your mother, she's not as self-sufficient as she leads you to believe.

With all the love in the world,

Dad

Helen turned over the letter, it had an address in the Scottish borders scribbled on the back of it. Helen felt in the envelope and found a bronze key in the bottom of it. She slipped both into her pocket and took a deep breath before heading out. Helen's head swirled, she never knew her dad had a house in the country, but then it seemed like she was finding out new things about him all the time now. She never really knew him at all.

* * *

Craven flicked his cigarette onto the ground and crushed it with his boot. A piece of paper on the door was scribbled with '*come around to the garden*'. Craven sighed and followed the stone steps around the side of the house. He could see Liz sitting in the conservatory with a paperback book in her hand. She offered a thin smile and waved. The twins were over by the pond, kicking a football back and forth. They looked up and cheered, 'Dad!' as soon as they noticed him. They came pounding over and wrapped their arms around his waist, knocking him backwards. 'We missed you, Dad.'

'You never came to our show.'

'I missed you both too.'

'We thought you didn't want to see us anymore.'

'I'm so sorry.' He knelt down so he was level with them both. 'I really did want to come but I had an emergency.'

'It went really well, Dad.'

'Milton came to see it and he took us to Wimpy afterwards.'

'That must've been nice.'

'It was yummy.'

'He's taking us on holiday too.'

'Aye, your mum told me.'

'We're going to go horse riding!'

Craven retrieved a paper bag of Midget Gems from his pocket. 'Here, split these between you both and no fighting, I need to go and speak to your mother for a minute.'

'Thanks, Dad!'

'Can we go to the park after?'

'Aye, we'll go shortly.'

'I'm glad you could come.' Liz smoothed down a crease from her floral-pattern dress and dropped her book onto the wicker chair.

'Of course, I said I would.' He sat down in the cane chair opposite. The place smelled of that polish that she liked to use. It was oddly comforting.

'I'm sure you can understand why I might have doubted you.'

'Don't.' Craven dragged a hand down his face. 'I try my best.'

She nodded, sighing. 'What have the doctors said?'

'Not much really . . .' He forced a smile. 'They aren't that worried.'

'I can still smell smoke on you.' Liz frowned, as though she was searching for the words that would put everything right.

'Aye, well, I've cut down.' He looked down at his nails, tinged with purple. He shoved his hands in his pockets.

'You need to stop.'

'I will.'

She sighed again. 'And how many times have you promised that?'

'What about you?' he snapped back.

'This isn't about me, Jack. I'm not the one that's ill.'

'Oh, come on, Liz, don't be like that.'

'You don't look well, Jack, and Milton was saying that too. He can be prone to exaggeration, but . . .'

'I'm fine, I'm just a bit tired, that's all.' He looked out at the garden. The twins were sitting cross-legged on the grass, sharing out the sweets.

'Milton doesn't like them having too much sugar.'

'I didn't think it was going to last when you started going out with him.'

'Why? Because he's a milksop?'

'No . . . I didn't mean.'

'The twins told me that's what you called him.'

'Sorry.' Craven swallowed hard. 'If you want to move, I'm not going to get in your way.'

Liz nodded.

'I just hope this makes you happy.' He made a move to stand. 'I want what's best for you even if that means you have to move to the other side of Britain.'

'I am happy.'

Craven shrugged. 'You never look it.'

'I could do with a drink, but I'll need make to with some tea. Do you want some? She rose to her feet and he followed her through the double doors back into the kitchen.

'Aye.' He took a seat while Liz lifted the pot from the Aga. She opened the cupboard and pulled out two identical red mugs from the shelf.

'Do you want something to eat?'

'No, I don't want to put you out.'

'I don't mind.' She retrieved a *Teatime* box of biscuits from the top shelf.

He looked around the kitchen. 'It's strange to be back in here again so soon.'

Liz placed a mug of tea in front of him and a plate of Custard Creams.

Morning sun beamed down on them from the skylight above. Craven took a sip of his tea.

She slumped down across from him, cradling her cup. 'Remember when we were teenagers and we were going to do that big road trip across America.'

'We got as far as Blackpool.'

'Jack,' she paused and shook her head. 'There is a reason that Milton wants a fresh start.'

CHAPTER THIRTY-NINE

Helen flicked through the *A-Z* on her desk, a small red book with *Edinburgh and Lothian 1965* emblazoned on the front in gold lettering. She toyed with the idea of driving to the address scribbled on the back of the letter. If traffic was good, she could do it in forty minutes. Her neck and shoulders felt stiff from slouching at her desk. She stretched out her neck until it gave a satisfying click. Randall, who was sitting opposite, flashed her a disgusted look at the noise, which she returned with a smile. She took a sip from her cold mug of coffee, which did nothing to ease the dryness in her throat. Randall's cigarettes were getting into the back of her throat too. Giving up, she shoved the map book onto the shelf in between the books on police procedures and slipped on her jacket. The wind rattled against the windows, drowning out the sound of the news report on the radio.

'Going somewhere?' McKinley enquired. He stood in the doorway, a battered looking tin reel of film in one hand, and a folder in the other. His blond hair had flopped over into his eyes. It might be fashion, but he badly needed a haircut.

'Yes, I am.' Helen drained the dregs of coffee left in her cup. 'I need to go out to the Borders to see something, then I have a few more questions for Dr Rushmore.'

'Great.' He dropped the tin and file on his desk and brushed his hands on his trousers. 'I'll come with you.'

'I'm leaving now.'

He motioned to the small strip of natural light that leaked through the gaps in the blinds. 'It'll be good to get out there. I just need to put these away.'

'Fine, I'll meet you in the car,' she replied brushing past him. 'Be quick.'

* * *

Helen twisted the key in the engine, and the engine purred into life as the passenger door opened. A red-faced McKinley peered into the Mini.

'Sorry,' he said in between breaths. 'It took me longer than I thought to put everything away.

'I thought you were going to leave without me.' McKinley teased, slumping into the seat.

'I was.' Helen slipped the car into reverse and pulled out of the bay, briefly stopping to let a marked van out. The uniformed officer held his hand up as a sign of thanks. She wound her window down a crack, it was sunny this morning, but the bitter wind destroyed any chance of warmth.

McKinley shrugged. 'Well, I caught you just in time then.' He retrieved a paper bag of hardboiled sweets from his pocket.

'Want one?' He held out the packet, as Helen took the right turn towards Stockbridge.

'What are they?'

'Lemon Sherbets.'

'No, I hate those.' Helen grimaced as she heard the sweet banging off McKinley's teeth.

She slowed passing through Stockbridge as a greengrocer's van pulled out from in front of its shop. Shoppers milled in and out of the various small shops that lined both sides of the street with flats above them. It looked like a nice place to live, but not somewhere that Helen could afford on her salary.

'So where is it we're going?' McKinley asked.

'Have you heard of Biggar?' Helen gripped the steering wheel tightly as the car trailed the cobbles towards the city centre.

A confused look crossed his face. 'I think so . . .'

'There's a house near there that I want to go and have a look at,' Helen replied.

'What for?'

'There's a house there that belonged to my dad.'

She could feel McKinley's eyes on her.

'It's a gift apparently, and it's come as a surprise to me.'

* * *

It took over an hour to drive the thirty or so miles, driven mostly in silence. She could see McKinley glance at her a couple of times, but she kept her eyes fixed ahead on the road. Giving up on that, he flicked through the stations and settled on Radio Caroline, although it gradually became more static than music the further away they got from Edinburgh.

'Do me a favour and get my *A-Z* from the glove box.'

'Sure,' McKinley flicked open the glove box. 'What do you want me to look up?'

'I'm looking for Grigor Drive.'

McKinley made a clicking sound as he skimmed through the book.

Helen followed a farm road that seemed to carry on for miles, churning up gravel that ricocheted against the windscreen. 'Any luck?'

'Right, found it,' McKinley pointed towards the trees on the right. 'Take the next road on the right, then the first one on the left and it should be straight in front of us after that.'

'Thanks,' Helen replied, taking the turning onto a narrow gravel track road. She pulled over into a passing place as a tractor trundled past, spraying dirt onto the windscreen.

'It's quite out in the sticks here,' McKinley remarked. The wheels spun as Helen pulled back onto the road.

'Okay,' he pointed a finger. 'It should be just up here.'

'Oh, how the other half do live.' McKinley commented as Helen manoeuvred the Mini into the gravel driveway. The electric gates were wide open, and a winding path led to an Edwardian mansion with a conservatory on the side. He could see another red gravel path, and a tall oak tree sticking up from the back garden, which no doubt carried on for miles.

'Wow,' he whistled. 'This place is stunning.'

'What?'

Helen wrenched up the handbrake. 'It looks in good condition.' She slipped the key from her pocket. 'Do you want to come in and have a look?'

'Your dad's left you this and mine won't even return my calls!'

Mothballs and damp hit Helen as she crossed the threshold. She stifled a sneeze and held the door open for McKinley.

Double doors led to an open-plan living room. She could see a piano in the corner of the room covered by a dust sheet.

She entered the lounge. From the three dust-coated bay windows, she could see out to the garden where there was a bench and a water fountain that would be lovely in the summer.

'God, this is stunning.' McKinley motioned to the massive kitchen area behind her. 'Have you seen in here?'

Helen peered over his shoulder. Granite worktops and cream-tiled floors and terracotta-brown wall tiles. Two French doors led out to the back garden. 'It's nice,' Helen replied. Her stomach knotted; she was surprised that she hadn't been here before with her father.

She climbed the winding staircase onto the first floor. Straight in front of her she could see a modern avocado bathroom that looked like it came straight out of *Country Living* magazine. On the far right, she opened a door to the master bedroom; a double bed was covered by a dust sheet, along with a cream and brown coloured chest of drawers.

Countryside watercolours adorned the wall above the bed on the baby pink walls.

McKinley followed her. 'Well, this is certainly a step up from your grotty flat.'

'I thought you said that my flat was nice.'

'I was being polite.'

She brushed past him and headed to the room on the far left. It was a study with a mahogany desk and a chair lying on its back. She picked up the chair and slid it under the desk. A yellowed newspaper from 1975 was folded on the desk. A photograph caught her attention, it was her dad along with a blonde woman she didn't recognize and a boy that looked about ten years old. Helen could feel her chest tighten. She put it back down on the desk.

'What are you going to do with this place?' McKinley asked.

'I don't know yet.'

'I bet if you sold it, you would get a lot of money. This place is stunning.'

'You think so.' Helen took a deep breath to steady herself.

'Is that your dad? You have his eyes.'

'Yes, it is.'

'You don't have his hair, thankfully.' McKinley teased.

Helen put the picture back down on the table. 'I've got to get out of here.'

She stood on the grass verge, enjoying the warmth of the sun on her face. Her mind raced.

'Do you know the people in the picture with your dad?' McKinley asked.

She shook her head. 'No, but I'm going to find out.' She locked the front door and headed back to the car.

'I just assumed it was your mum.'

'Well, you assumed wrong.'

'There's probably a reasonable explanation, Helen.'

CHAPTER FORTY

'It's always busy, this place.' McKinley nodded at an elderly woman shuffling inside the flat-roofed building, followed closely by an emaciated toothless man, who looked to be in his sixties, but on a second glance Helen suspected he was a lot younger than that.

'It was the same the last time I was here,' she responded, driving around to the back of the building, where there was a small car park big enough for about four cars. It was empty apart from one vehicle. Parked in the doctor's space was a car that Helen didn't recognize, an olive-green Morris Marina. She could see into Dr Rushmore's office from this angle, but the blinds were drawn.

An elderly man was hobbling into the surgery clutching his lower back, the wind was whipping his wispy hair back and forth.

'Poor bugger,' McKinley muttered clambering out of the Mini. 'Just shoot me if I end up like that.'

'Don't tempt me,' Helen teased.

The reception was empty. Helen scanned her surroundings, then pressed on the small bell on the mahogany counter. She tried to peer over it and into the back room, but it was closed.

'Should we just go through?' McKinley asked.

'If he's here, he might be with a patient.'

'Doesn't look it.'

'Hello?' Helen called over the counter.

The exasperated receptionist emerged from the back room with a pile of overstuffed folders, a look of recognition dawning.

'Is it Dr Rushmore you're wanting?' The receptionist asked, as she dropped the folders onto the desk and wiped her forehead with the blouse sleeve.

Helen nodded.

The woman pointed a chubby finger towards a room down the corridor. 'He's in his office, he's not with anyone, you can go straight through.'

* * *

Dr Rushmore was looking out of the window, arms crossed. He appeared deep in thought when Helen opened the door.

'Dr Rushmore,' she stepped forward. 'We have a few more questions for you.'

'I saw you park up,' the doctor commented, as he turned to face them.

'We won't take up much of your time,' Helen responded.

'Of course,' he motioned to the plastic seats in front of his desk. He moved around and took a seat on the other side.

'I'd also like to say I'm very sorry for your loss.' Helen forced a small smile.

'My loss?'

'Your mother.' Helen exchanged a look with McKinley.

'Thank you, it's my first day back,' the doctor eventually said. 'I'm trying not to think about it.'

Helen gestured to McKinley. 'This is my colleague DC McKinley.'

'What else can I do for you?' The doctor made a steeple with his fingers.

'We're still investigating the disappearance of Moira McKenzie.' Helen stepped forward but didn't bother to sit.

'That's a shame . . . I don't know why you'd bother coming back here though.'

'Right,' Helen responded. 'I think there's a few things you'll be able to clear up for us.'

'I didn't know the woman.' His eyes were fixed on Helen's. 'But if there's anything that I can do to help.'

'Thank you,' Helen replied, 'It's come to our attention that Moira has had electroshock treatment.'

The doctor shrugged.

'Why wasn't it mentioned before?'

'I have no idea. I'm sorry.'

'Of course.'

'Maybe it wasn't in the file then.'

'I had thought that but one of my colleagues picked up the file and it was in there,' Helen countered.

'Did they? Well, I must not have noticed then; I've not been myself with my mother . . .'

'Understandable,' Helen agreed. 'Now, you were at Moira McKenzie's stairwell the day she disappeared.'

The doctor's mouth twitched. 'I don't understand. You've already asked me about this.'

'I wanted to ask you about the house call at the flat below.'

'I can't be expected to remember everything that happens at each one. This is more of a conveyer belt than a doctor's surgery.'

'Is it normal for you to do so many home visits?' Helen asked.

'When a patient is too sick to come into the surgery we have to. We do a lot of them.'

'Isn't the doctor's surgery closed in the evenings?'

The doctor exchanged glances with McKinley and Helen. 'Yes, it is . . . Am I being accused of something here?' The doctor rose to his feet.

'No, not at all.'

'I was working late that night. Patients don't stop getting sick after five o'clock. I have lots to do when I'm not seeing patients. On that evening, Billy's mother called the surgery. Panicking her son wasn't breathing properly.' The doctor paused. 'It was on my way home. I wanted to help her. She has a small baby and no car. I helped Billy then I went home.'

'What time was this?'

'About half seven. I was home for eight.'

'Thank you.' Helen nodded.

'Now, can I help you with anything else?

'No, that's everything just now.'

'Good, because I need to see more patients.' He sighed. 'I'm not even the best person to ask about her, Milton Nairn had more appointments with her than I ever did.'

Outside the surgery, Helen shoved her hands in her pockets for warmth and watched a bus packed with school children trudge past. McKinley glanced back at the building.

'I wouldn't like to be one of his patients.' McKinley muttered.

'Find out everything you can about him.' Helen replied. 'He's shifty and you saw the way he reacted when I mentioned his mother.'

'He also said that Milton Nairn had appointments with Moira, but it was him mentioned in the notes and on the prescriptions.'

Helen massaged her temples and grimaced.

'Are you all right?'

'I just have a headache.'

CHAPTER FORTY-ONE

When Helen got back to the station, McKinley headed down to the canteen for dinner and she said she would meet him down there shortly. She needed to be alone and clear her head first. He'd wanted to talk about the house and her father, and she couldn't face it. A lump sat in the pit of her stomach, she headed into the bathroom and locked herself in one of the cubicles. Closing her eyes, she sucked in a deep breath and held her head in her hands.

Once her breathing slowed, she went to the sink and splashed some cold water over her face and down the back of her neck. In all these years, she'd never heard of her father having a home in the Borders. As a family they'd only been on holiday once or twice, he was always too busy at work. Too busy to take family holidays.

A WPC entered, jolting her back into the present. She stepped back from the sink and slumped down on the bench.

'Are you all right?' The WPC offered a thin smile.

'Aye, I'm fine.'

'It can be a long day sometimes, can't it?'

'Sometimes. I better get back anyway.'

When the office had emptied, Helen dialled her mum's number, but it rang out. She tried it again. No luck. Giving up on that, she plugged in Ted's number and he answered on the fourth ring. Helen tried to control her breathing, but it wasn't working.

'Ted, it's Helen.'

'Helen, I—' She could hear music in the background, a classical tune.

'Did you know what was in the envelope?'

'No, your mum dropped it off. She told me it was a present from your dad.'

Helen dragged the heel of her hand down her face and sighed.

'What was it?' Ted asked.

'A house in the country. A stunning old building with a big garden.'

Helen heard him suck in a breath. 'That's a spectacular gift.'

'I didn't know my dad had a house in the country, do you know anything about it?

'Have you asked your mum?'

'Not yet.'

'She worries about you.'

'She worries about everything.'

'I think you should go and see her. I don't want to say anything out of turn.'

'So, you know something? Ted, please.'

He sighed. Helen rested her head against the wall, her mind was racing and her lips felt dry.

The silence on the line felt never-ending.

'Your mum mentioned to me that your parents had lived separate lives.'

'What the hell is that supposed to mean?'

'This is something you need to speak to your mum about as I don't know much about it. I was only doing what she asked when she wanted me to give you the envelope.'

'Look, I'm sorry to bother you with all this.'

'It's fine, sorry I can't help more.' The line went dead.

She had her hand braced to try her mum's number again but instead grabbed her jacket. She was going to drive over there herself. The house near Glasgow was probably an hour or so's drive, give or take rush hour traffic.

* * *

Helen's heart thudded in her chest and she struggled for breath as she slotted her key into the door. The aroma of fresh gloss hung heavy in the air.

'Mum.'

Silence.

'Mum, are you in?'

'I'm upstairs.'

Helen climbed the staircase and put a hand on the railing for support, feeling the blood rush to her ears. She could hear rustling and muttering coming from her dad's old office. Her mum was boxing up her dad's old things. She was wearing jeans and had her silver hair swept up into a high bun. She also looked like she had lost a little weight since last time. She was wearing a touch of peach blush on her cheeks and mascara, that was a first in a long time.

'I tried to call you but it's just ringing out.' Helen stepped over a cardboard box containing a typewriter and kicked over a paperweight.

'Sorry,' her mother grimaced, 'I think I might have unplugged the phone when I was moving the table.'

'What are you doing?' Helen asked.

'I just thought I'd start to get the house in order. I've got nothing else to do.'

Helen pulled out the envelope from her pocket and dropped it onto the desk between them. 'What is this?'

'I should have given it to you a while back but I just—'

'What was Dad doing with this house?'

Her mum looked like she was thinking of what to say.

'And did Dad have another family?'

Her mum looked momentarily stunned. She stepped backwards.

'There was a picture of him in the house with a woman and a boy,' Helen carried on.

Mum nodded and wiped her brow with her sleeve. 'Your dad *always* did what he wanted.'

'I don't understand.'

'He split his time between there and here.'

'Why didn't you tell me this before?'

'It's not something I was happy about.' Mum looked away. 'Do you think it's something I'd be proud of? Something that I'd want to broadcast?'

'No, of course not.' Helen sighed and looked around the old office. All her dad's photos had been removed from the walls, only the marks of where they had been remained, even his gold velvet curtains had been replaced with nets. Helen could see a pot of gloss on top of a pile of newspapers and her mum had some clippings from home decoration magazines spread out over the desk.

Her mum pointed to the paint tin. 'I'm thinking of selling this place. It's too big for just me. Ted thought I'd get a good price for it.'

'Oh, did he now?' Helen picked up the paperweight from the floor. 'Why didn't you get someone else in to help you? You shouldn't be moving all this stuff by yourself.'

'I need a project to keep me busy,' she smiled. 'It's hard being stuck in here alone.'

'I'm sorry, Mum.' Helen motioned to a couple of the boxes. 'Do you want me to take these downstairs?'

Her mum nodded and tugged nervously at her shirt sleeve. 'Do you want some tea? You look tired.'

'In a minute,' Helen relented. 'But I want to talk to you about the letter from Dad. Why do this now?' She motioned to the keys. 'Why give me these now?'

Her mum shrugged and exhaled a long breath.

'Mum, please!'

Mum shrugged. 'I can't keep living in denial . . . I know your father wanted you to have that house.'

'Where did you get it from?'

'It belonged to your grandfather. It's selfish of me to let it rot there, when you could have use of it.'

Helen's head spun. She picked up the envelope and weighed it up in her hands. 'Who is the woman in the photo and the boy?'

'Does it matter?' Mum crossed her arms. 'That's not important. The only thing you should be concerned about is what you are going to do with the house.'

'But it is important to me, Mum, if Dad had another family. I have a right to know.'

'Family?' she spat. 'No, I don't want anything to do with her.'

'I have a right to know,' Helen countered. 'You don't have to have anything to do with her.'

'I've never met the woman or her . . .'

'Do you have a name for her?' Helen stepped forward. 'I need to know.'

'Why don't you just sell the house and get a new one in town?'

'I don't know what I'm going to do yet but I want to know who that woman is. I'll find out one way or the other.'

'Helen . . .'

'Is it a recent photo?' Her dad was greyer in his sideburns than the last time she saw him.

'I don't know the photograph you are talking about, but I'd guess the boy is maybe twelve or thirteen. Like I said before, I have never met them, nor do I wish to.'

'And is he Dad's?'

Mum nodded, pursing her lips. 'Unfortunately.'

'I really want a name, Mum.'

'Fine, but don't come crying to me when you're left all disappointed. You'll learn that's something your dad was always good at.'

Helen turned to leave. 'I've heard enough of this.'

'Don't go like this. I'll give you her name and I know where she lives . . .'

Helen nodded.

'I haven't spoken to you in so long. How are you?'

'I'm fine, Mum.'

'Ted seemed a bit upset when I called . . .'

Helen made a clicking sound. It was now or never. 'Ted and I aren't together anymore.'

'Oh.' Mum shrugged. 'I thought he was really nice. Is there no way?'

'No, it just wasn't . . .'

'I'm sorry.'

'It's fine.'

'Please stay and have a cup of tea, I've missed you.'

'Fine,' Helen lifted the box at her feet. 'Where do you want this?'

'Drop it at the front door, then stick the kettle on and I'll tell you everything you want to know.'

CHAPTER FORTY-TWO

McKinley broke into a jog to catch up with Helen as she headed along the corridor to the CID room.

McKinley smiled. 'I've been looking all over for you.'

'I've had things to do. I needed to speak to my mum'

'Is everything okay?' He looked concerned and grabbed her arm. 'How did it go?'

'I'm fine,' she tugged her arm free and brushed past. 'Have you found something?'

McKinley furrowed his brow. 'I've tried to find an obituary for Dr Rushmore's mother and there isn't one.'

'Say that again?'

'She's still alive.'

'Are you sure?'

'I've double-checked, then checked again.'

'Great.'

Her name is Orla Docherty, and she's very much alive and kicking.'

Helen opened the door to CID and held it open for McKinley. 'That's very strange.'

'I have all the information on my desk, if you want to see for yourself.'

'I'll have a look.' Helen cut across to McKinley's desk and picked up the slip of paper. 'I think we need to have a wee word with Dr Rushmore and see what his game is.'

'His wife died two months ago.'

'Wife?'

'Yes, she died of cancer.'

Helen brushed a hand through her hair. 'When I offered condolences on his mother, he didn't correct me.'

'I remember.'

'Also, Dr Nairn was the one who told us he was away for his mother's funeral in Aberdeen.' She slipped a glance over at Craven's office. 'Do you know where Jack is? Nairn is married to Jack's ex-wife, so he'll want to know.'

'No idea. He's meant to be on the evening shift.'

Helen crossed to her own desk and flicked open the folder for Tina French's murder. The composite sketch from Eleanor Aldridge's case fluttered out. Helen picked it up and held it up to the light. It was badly drawn in pencil. She turned the drawing to McKinley. 'Does this remind you of anyone?'

He tilted his head to the left. 'Aye, it does.'

* * *

'Right,' Craven sighed, as she explained everything to him. 'Milton has been away for the weekend, but he should be back by now. Let's go and see what he has to say for himself.'

* * *

'We're just about to put the twins down for the evening, Jack.' Liz eyed the pair of them suspiciously, as they stood out on the steps. 'It's not a good time.' She looked flustered and brushed a stray strand of hair from her face.

Craven shrugged. 'I'm sorry Liz, this is business. We need to speak to Milton regarding a case.'

'He told me about that one, the missing woman. Can't it wait until he's back at work tomorrow? He's exhausted from all the driving.'

'I won't take up much of his time.'

Liz gave Craven a look and opened the door wide for them. 'Go into the lounge and I'll go and get him.'

Craven nodded, 'Thank you.'

'Jack, this is a surprise, I would've thought you'd have better things to do than wanting to speak to me.' Milton appeared in the doorway, he had his shirt sleeves rolled up and a glass of wine in his hand.

'Aye, normally,' Craven made a clicking sound. 'This is my colleague DS Carter; I believe you've met before.'

He shrugged and looked her up and down 'Possibly.'

'At the surgery, we met when I wanted to speak with Dr Rushmore, but he was away at his mother's funeral.' Helen added.

'That's right.' He crossed over to the coffee table and put down his glass. 'I'd offer you both a drink, but with you both being on duty—'

'That's fine,' Helen replied. 'About Dr Rushmore's mother's funeral.'

'What about it?'

'Did he tell you how it went?' Craven asked.

'Not really . . .'

'His mother's not dead.'

'That's strange.'

'That's what we were thinking,' Craven added.

'Maybe it wasn't his mother then.' Milton sipped his drink. 'That was probably just a slip of his tongue. It could've been another family member.'

'Are you and Dr Rushmore close?'

'Not particularly, I mean we work together but I wouldn't describe us as friends or anything.'

'Where were you last Friday?' Helen asked looking down at her notebook. 'Between half-eight and half-ten.'

Milton let out a laugh. 'Are you accusing me of something?'

'Not at all.' Helen smiled. 'It's just routine questioning.'

Milton looked Craven up and down. 'If you really want to know, I was enjoying a pleasant evening with my lovely wife.'

Helen could see Craven tense his shoulders. She stepped forward. 'And would your wife be able to verify this?'

'Of course she would, what do you take me for?'

'So has Liz stopped going to her aerobics class?' Craven asked. He went over to the door and called Liz.

Milton spluttered into his wine and struggled to catch his breath.

Liz appeared in the doorway looking flustered. 'Jack, I was reading to the twins. I don't want them up.'

'Do you still do your aerobics on a Friday night at eight?'

Liz nodded, a look of confusion creasing her features. 'You know I do.'

'And does Milton do aerobics with you?'

'Of course he bloody doesn't.'

'Why don't we try again then, Milton?' Craven asked. 'Have another wee think.'

'I must've got my days mixed up. I would've just been in the house.'

'Is there anyone to verify that?' Helen smiled.

'No, the twins were away at my mum's. I was here alone.'

Helen snapped her notebook shut. 'That's everything for now, thank you.'

* * *

'Dad, Dad! I thought it was you!' A little sandy-haired boy with striped pyjamas appeared in the doorway, rubbing sleep away from his eyes.

'You should be in bed, you've got to be up early tomorrow,' Liz scolded.

'Hello, son,' Craven smiled. He dropped to his knees and held out his arms.

The little boy flew into them with a big smile on his face. 'I've missed you, Dad.'

'I've missed you too, son. Where's your sister?'

'She's asleep, Dad. Are you going to be staying the night again?'

Helen could see Milton bristle from the corner of her eye.

'No, your dad has to get back to work,' Milton replied. 'In fact, he better go now or he'll be late.'

'Aye, that's right, son, but I'll come back soon.'

'Can we go to the park again? I loved that, Dad, and maybe we can get ice cream.'

'Of course, we can.' He slipped a glance at Liz, who instantly looked away, scowling.

'Why don't you go upstairs . . . and say good night to Annabelle,' Liz cajoled, turning her gaze to the little boy.

Craven's son guided him from the room, leaving Helen with Milton and Liz.

'I'll go and wait in the car for Jack,' Helen smiled.

'Yes, good idea, you do that,' Milton chimed in. 'I'll show you to the door, shall I?'

'I can let myself out. Good night.' Helen replied.

* * *

'What do you think of that, then?' Craven asked, as he sparked up a fag. He looked back at the house. Liz was still in the doorway. He gave her a wave but she didn't return the gesture.

'He's a bit arrogant but he seems believable.'

'Maybe. He exhaled the smoke slowly. I can't stand him though.'

'I can't say that I'm much of a fan either.'

'Get on the radio and get Dr Rushmore's home address.'

CHAPTER FORTY-THREE

Liz closed the front door as she watched Jack and his colleague disappear around the corner. She could see Milton from the corner of her eye. Milton had his head in his hands and was looking like he was thinking of what to say next.

Liz shrugged then lifted her handbag from the worktop. Her fags were in there somewhere. 'You shouldn't lie to Jack. If he's knows you are, he's like a shark that smells blood.'

Milton scoffed. 'I've got more to worry about than Jack bloody Craven. Anyway, he'll be a thing of the past when we move.'

'Is that why we're moving?'

'No, you know the reasons, don't make me dredge it all up again. I mean, I thought you were on board with all of this?'

'I am, I want a fresh start as much as you do,' she jabbed a finger at him. 'I'm serious, he won't let up. I know that better than anyone.' She reached into her handbag that was on the table and pulled out her packet of Players Number Six.

'I thought you'd stopped; you know I don't like it.'

'I only have one occasionally now.'

'What did little Jack mean when he said, "stayed over again"?'

'I never heard—'

He stared hard at her. 'Those were his exact words. Do you want to explain that?'

'Ach, you know what kids are like.'

'I know what Jack Craven is like.'

'I don't have time for this.'

'If you're going to insist on smoking those things, do it outside, I don't want to breathe that muck in.'

'Fine.'

Milton lifted the telephone receiver.

'Who are you calling?'

'Just someone who I think can help me.'

* * *

'This is a nice place, eh?' Craven said, as he climbed the steps to the Victorian townhouse in Edinburgh's New Town. This house was just a few streets away from Ted's and looked every bit as grand.

Craven rattled on the bronze knocker and took a step back. All the lights were off, and from her position on the stone steps, Helen could see into the drawing room. Empty.

Craven rattled on the door again. 'Is there any way around to the back?' Craven asked.

'No, you'd need to get into the house first,' Helen replied.

Craven peered through the letter box then gave another knock on the door with the side of his fist.

'Can you hear anything?' Helen looked around the street, she couldn't see his car.

He shook his head and stepped back. 'I'm parched. Do you fancy a drink?'

Helen considered this for a moment. 'A quick one,' she eventually replied.

'There's a hotel with a bar just around the corner.' Craven motioned to the end of the street.

* * *

Warmth from the fire and the smell of beer hit Helen as she stepped inside the snug. 'I'll grab that little table, if you can get me an orange juice.'

'Aye, nae bother,' Craven replied, fishing in his pocket for his wallet. He patted his trousers, then sighed.

'It's fine.' Helen reached into her shoulder bag. 'I've got a fiver in here anyway.'

'I think I must've left it back at the station.'

'Don't worry about it.'

A few minutes later, Helen took a long glug of her orange, now realizing how thirsty she was. It tasted bitter and warm. She could feel it coating her teeth.

Craven nursed a pint; he tore at a beer mat and was keeping an eye out the window. From this table, they were able to see a good part of the street. If Dr Rushmore was to return home, most likely he would drive past the hotel.

'How long has Liz been married to that Milton character?'

'Three years or so.'

'That must be hard.'

'It is what it is,' he shrugged, 'it's what she wanted to do. He's a bit of a damp sponge but they seemed to be happy.'

'How did they meet?'

'She knew him from school. He was pretty quick to get himself involved when things between Liz and I went wrong. Suddenly he was sniffing around every five minutes.'

Helen looked away, one of the first things she had heard about Jack was that he was a serial philanderer and gambler. Not to mention the long hours and difficulties that come with working in the police force.

He broke into a hacking cough, nearly spilling his pint. Helen managed to slide it out the way. Craven struggled to take a breath and slapped his chest with the palm of his hand a couple of times.

'Are you all right, Jack?'

'Aye,' he spluttered. 'Just got a cold or something.'

Helen could feel the eyes of the room upon them. He managed to suck in a few deep breaths and that seemed to settle the cough.

'Are you sure you're all right?'

'Fine,' he cleared his throat. 'That happens now and again.'

He noticed Helen raise a sceptical eyebrow.

'It's just a wee cough, nothing to worry about. I was meaning to go and pick up some cough sweets but haven't had the time.' He reached over and grabbed his pint and drained half of it in one go. 'You see, that's better now.' He wiped the foam away from his mouth with the back of his hand. 'Let's go and see if Dr Rushmore has returned home yet.'

'Jack, maybe you need to go home and get some sleep?'

'Why would I do that?' Craven rose to his feet. 'I've got far too much to do for that. Now, are you coming or what?'

After getting no answer at his house again, they drove back to the station. Hopefully the forensic reports would be back. It wasn't long until her shift was over and she had somewhere else that she wanted to be.

CHAPTER FORTY-FOUR

It was just after eight when her shift ended, and Helen drove back down to the country house. In the dark it looked different. Solitary. An owl hooted from one of the surrounding trees, she looked up but couldn't see where it was coming from. The house next door was in darkness and looked in poor repair. Helen slotted her key into the lock and headed inside. She slumped down onto the floral pattered sofa, a plume of dust exploding from it; she stifled a sneeze. From here, she could see out into the front garden and to where her car was parked on the gravel driveway.

She had a paltry amount of furniture in her flat. She closed her eyes and thought about where she could place it in this house. It would be a nightmare commute to work, though, if she was to live here. She crossed her legs and closed her eyes. A thud coming from upstairs felt like electricity through her body and jolted her awake. Maybe she had imagined it. She wasn't sure. Another thud. She scrambled to her feet and backed away. She thought about running out of the house, jumping in the car. No, she took a deep breath to steady herself and took a shaky step towards the staircase, her legs and hands trembling. Her steps were slow. She tried to regulate her breathing. She strained to hear something.

Anything. Nothing. 'Hello?' She placed a hand on the banister and tried to see something on the landing, groping the wall for the light switch.

'Hello,' she gulped. 'Is someone there?' Her heart was beating so fast she could hear it in her ears and feel it in her throat. 'I'm coming up the stairs.' She clenched her jaw and took a deep breath through her nostrils.

Up on the landing the door to the main bedroom was ajar. She patted the wall for the light switch and flicked it on.

'Hello . . .' Sneaking a glance over her shoulder, fists clenched.

She pushed on the door and it creaked open. Holding her breath, she pushed it again, so it thudded against the wall. There was nothing in the room except a teak bed frame and matching wardrobe. She turned around as something brushed against her leg. Something wrapped around her leg. She screamed as she looked down and saw what it was. 'How did you get in here?' She sighed, feeling her heartbeat slow.

She scooped the fluffy bundle up, and it hissed.

'Hey, hey, hey, easy now.'

A tabby cat, young looking and with a protruding rib cage. She scratched under its chin. No collar. 'You gave me a fright, little fella.'

The cat eyed her suspiciously but seemed to be enjoying the contact too much to protest.

'What are you doing in here, eh?' How did you get in?'

She looked around. The window was shut, and she hadn't opened any on her earlier visit either.

'Let's get you outside. I'd give you something to eat but there's nothing in here for you.' Helen scooped up the cat and headed back down the hallway. Its fur felt matted and its body tensed as she pulled open the front door.

Helen dropped the cat out onto the grass outside and shooed it away. 'Go on now, you go home back to where you came from.'

The cat sniffed the grass, then looked back up at her.

She knelt beside it and petted the top of its head. 'I'm serious, little fella, I can't keep you in here. Go on now, go on home. Shoo, shoo!' She waved her hands, but the cat nuzzled against her leg, purring.

'You're a wee sweetie, aren't you?' She picked a couple of stray strands of cat hair from her cords and looked around for where the cat might have come from. Helen unlocked the Mini, reached into her handbag and retrieved her tuna sandwich. The cat followed her interweaving with each step. 'Okay cat, I do have something you might want to eat, I thought it was pretty disgusting, but you might like it.' She tore off a chunk of it and stuck it in front of the cat, who eyed it suspiciously, sniffing then licking before taking a hungry bite. Helen placed the rest of the sandwich down. 'Sorry, little fella, but that's all I have.'

'If you must know, cat, I'm more of a dog person.'

CHAPTER FORTY-FIVE

Terry McKinley was finishing in the shower when the door to the flat unlocked. He was still damp when he slipped his T-shirt over his shoulders and pulled on his boxers and jeans. Sighing, he headed out. Sally was standing in the kitchen, scooping coffee into mugs. He noticed her eyes were puffy like she'd been crying, and some of her mascara had collected under her eyes.

'Sally, what's happened?' McKinley stepped forward. 'Are you all right?'

She shook her head and dabbed at her eyes with a balled-up tissue. 'Everything is fine . . . Do you want sugar in your coffee?' She spoke in a low monotone voice.

He slid the sugar pot out of reach. 'Never mind that, will you just tell me what's wrong?'

She shook her head.

'Please, you're really worrying me.'

'I went to Presto and got some fresh bread and milk. I even got some of those biscuits you like.'

'You didn't have to do that,' he unpacked the carrier bag, and shoved the loaf into the bread bin. 'I didn't hear you go out either.'

'It's fine . . . I like to . . .' She poured hot water into the mugs. 'I've tidied up around the flat too.' She clasped her mug in both hands and blew on it. McKinley noticed her expression change, obviously thinking about what to say.

'Tell me why you're so upset.' He rubbed a hand through his damp hair. 'I'm sorry for the way I spoke to you before, I didn't mean to upset you.'

'It's not you.' She took a loud sip of her coffee. 'I don't want to argue anymore either.'

McKinley sighed and shoved the shopping bag into the cupboard under the sink.

'Is it about Helen? I told you before there's nothing going on.'

She rolled her eyes and took another sip.

'I'm telling you the truth,' he stepped closer, and her lavender-scented perfume trailed up his nostrils.

She offered him a thin smile and sniffed. 'It's not about *her*. Although, I don't know what you see in her. She is such a scruff.'

McKinley groaned. 'I don't see anything.'

'I don't want to argue, Terry.'

'Fine. Do you want something to eat?' He stepped past her and pulled open the fridge, feeling her eyes on him. 'I could make some sandwiches.'

'Do you want me to be here?' Sally asked.

'Why are you asking that?'

'Because of the way you are with me, you've changed.'

'I've never understood why you don't like Helen.' He closed the fridge and turned to face her. 'I've never seen her be rude to you, not once. But you're always having a go about the way she looks, the way she dresses . . .'

'Oh hardly', she scoffed, dragging her eyes away. 'It's not my fault that the woman has no sense of style.'

'That's what I mean.' McKinley muttered.

'When I came back from London, I thought that things would be different.'

'They are different.'

She snorted. 'Well, you won't have to put up with me much longer. I actually thought you would be happy to see me.'

'What are you talking about?'

'It doesn't matter.'

'It clearly does.'

'You remember my friend, Kim?'

'Aye.'

'I'm going to go and stay with her.'

'Sally,' he reached out and pulled her close. 'I didn't mean what I said earlier. I'm just tired with work . . . Helen has gone through a lot and I was worried about her, that's all.'

'Is that really all it is.'

'Do we have to go through all this again?'

'No.' She wrapped her arms around him. 'Do you want to give us another go?'

He puffed out his cheeks, they had been together since school, but there had been a lot of ups and downs since then. More downs than ups. He thought about Helen.

'I take from your silence that you don't want to.'

'It's not that, I don't want to rush into anything again.' He peeled her away from him. 'You were so unhappy with us. What's changed?'

She shrugged. 'I just didn't appreciate what we had before.'

He shook his head. 'I don't know what to think. You were so sure you didn't want to be together before. I can't go through that again.'

'Fine,' she offered a thin smile.

'Just let me have a think about things.'

'I will . . . I was thinking of making some scrambled eggs if you fancy some?'

'Aye, that will be nice.' It wasn't often he had a home-cooked meal.

'Take a seat,' Sally replied, lifting the pan from the drying board.

McKinley sipped water as he watched Sally crack a couple of eggs into a bowl.

'Are you working late tonight?' she asked.

'I'm not sure . . . I hope not.' That used to cause arguments before, never being able to finish on time and when he missed her mother's wedding. There was time when he thought he'd never hear the end of it.

She offered a thin smile as she handed him a plate of eggs.

'Sorry,' she mumbled, by way of apology. 'I'm not much of a cook.'

'No, this is nice.'

Sally nodded as she shoved the watery looking eggs around with a fork but made no move to eat it. 'I've bought you some strawberry tart for tonight, too.' She sounded irritable but tried to smile to hide it.

'Thanks.' McKinley stroked his chin, still feeling tufts of stubble. He badly needed a new blade in his razor. He chewed on some eggs and felt her eyes on him.

'It's not good, is it?'

'It's lovely, I like it.'

'I've lost my appetite.' She slid her plate away, 'I better go and get packed.'

'Don't,' he reached out and placed his hand on top of hers. 'You don't need to make any decisions tonight. Let's just see how we feel.'

'Are you sure?' Sally leaned forward.

'Aye, I mean there's no rush.'

'Thank you, I appreciate that.'

'All right'.

She relaxed. 'Do you want to watch a film tonight? I think there's one on in a little while, *Attack of the Werewolves.*'

'That should be a laugh,' he smiled, sliding his plate away. 'Go get the strawberry tart out.'

'I am sorry . . . You know, for how bad I've been in the past.' She gathered up the plates. 'I didn't intentionally set out to hurt you or . . .'

He sighed and dragged a hand through his hair. 'Do you want me to help you with the washing up?'

'No, I'll do it.'

McKinley slumped down on the sofa; he could hear Sally clattering about with plates. Hesitating, he reached over and picked up the telephone receiver.

* * *

Helen snatched up the phone and slung her jacket onto the sofa. 'Helen.'

'Hi, Helen. It's me.' He spoke in a hushed tone.

'Is everything okay?' She moved over to the window and pulled back the curtains.

'I didn't get a chance to speak to you before you left last night' He sounded hesitant. 'I wanted to speak to you.'

'I'm fine, Terry, I can't talk long. I was just about to make myself something to eat.'

'Right,' he sounded deflated and she heard him draw breath.

'I was out at the country house and I spoke to my mum . . .'

'What did she say?'

'That I have a half-brother and she told me where they live.'

'That's a lot to take in.'

'I don't know what to think now. I was going to go to see them but . . .' She slipped off her shoes and slumped into the armchair.

'Do you want me to come with you?' McKinley asked.

She thought about it. 'I don't think I am going to see them. It won't do any good.'

'You must want to though?'

'I'll think about it.' She felt a little light-headed and looked up at the ceiling tiles.

'I'll come with you.'

'I don't think so, I'll speak to you later.' She clicked off the line and headed into the bathroom. Twisting the shower nozzle, she held her hand under the water until the spray warmed. Steam filled the room. She took a deep breath to steady herself. The address her mum had given her was only a few miles from the country house and, according to the records she had for the house, they were the last tenants. She had thought about driving to their house earlier this evening, but she didn't want to cause any upset and she wasn't sure what she would say or even if they'd want to speak to her. Stepping into the shower, she closed her eyes as the warm water doused her head and shoulders. It was slightly hotter than she'd normally like, but it felt good on her aching muscles. She dug her thumb into her knotted neck muscle until the tension released. She knew exactly what she was going to do with this place and the country house.

* * *

McKinley lifted his coat from the stand. Sally was clattering about in the kitchen.

'I need to go into work now.'

Sally appeared in the hallway, a look of confusion on her face.

'They've just called me out,' he explained.

'Right,' she shrugged. 'Well, I guess, I'll see you later then.'

'Aye, definitely, I'll get back as soon as I can. I just need to go into the office and check something.'

CHAPTER FORTY-SIX

Helen shovelled some instant coffee into a mug while waiting for the kettle on the stove to boil. Her stomach rumbled; she lifted the lid of the bread bin. Empty. The fridge was bare too apart from a knob of butter, and she was unsure how long that had been there. A knock on the front door stopped her in her tracks. She thought about ignoring it but whoever it was rattled on the glass part of the door with more urgency. She couldn't make out who it was from the silhouette. She unlocked the door and shook her head, seeing who it was.

She sighed. 'What do you want?'

'That's rude,' McKinley muttered. 'Especially when I've brought food.' He held up a cotton shopping bag. His blond hair looked freshly trimmed and swept to the side, making him look older. He was also wearing a fitted brown shirt that she hadn't seen before.

'Come in, but I'm getting ready to go.' She headed back into the kitchen; she could feel him follow behind her. The kettle whistled and steam billowed from its spout. She poured hot water in her mug and grabbed another from the draining board.

McKinley dropped the bag on the worktop and removed a loaf of bread and jar of marmalade.

'Home-made this, from my mum.' He ran a hand through his hair.

'My favourite,' Helen smiled.

McKinley placed two slices of bread under the grill. 'I remember you saying.'

Helen took a seat at the table with her coffee.

'I have an ulterior motive for coming here,' McKinley hesitated, turning to face her.

'Have you?' Helen's stomach tightened and she could feel adrenaline in her veins.

He pulled the grill out and dropped the toast onto a plate. He must have noticed her expression because he smiled when he handed her the plate. 'It's nothing bad.' He sat down at the table.

'Are you not going to have any?'

'I've already had breakfast.'

'Come out with it then?'

'I think you should go and see your half-brother.'

'That's it?'

'I was terrified going to meet mine and they're lovely. I would've regretted it if I'd never gone to see them at least.'

She looked down at her toast, losing her appetite. 'I don't want to rush anything.'

'I know.'

'You didn't need to bring me breakfast to tell me that.'

'That's not why I'm here though. I've found the private nursing home where Agnes is.'

'Where is it?'

'It's in Fife.'

'Right, grab that toast — let's go.' Helen said, rising. 'We'll take my car.'

* * *

Forty-five minutes later, Helen parked in the car park of a nondescript building, a council-built pebble-dashed semi.

'Are you sure this is the right place?' she asked wrenching up the handbrake.

'This is it.' McKinley clambered out of the car.

A woman wearing a white shirt and her hair partly pinned back met them at the gate with a smile.

Helen held up her warrant card for inspection.

'Hello,' the woman pointed to the front room. 'She's through here.'

The smell of cooking fat hit Helen as she crossed the threshold. She manoeuvred past a couple of folded-up wheelchairs that had been stored against the wall. Agnes looked up at they entered. She was sipping from a cup with an uneaten bowl of cornflakes in front of her.

'Hello Agnes, my name's Helen Carter and this is DC Terry McKinley.'

'What do you want?' Agnes grimaced and straightened in her seat.

Helen sat down in the seat next to her and took a breath to steady herself. 'We're concerned for your sister's welfare and we're trying to track her down.'

The woman nodded.

'Can you remember the last time you saw her?'

'She came to visit me.'

'When was this?'

Agnes shrugged. 'Last week sometime, I can't remember. I have problems remembering things,' she explained.

'How was your sister when you saw her?' Helen leaned forward.

'She was . . .. fine. Nice, we had a nice time.'

'Can you remember what you talked about?'

Agnes nodded, a smile curling her lips. 'She was really happy and looking forward to the future.'

Agnes looked away and started to tear at a fingernail.

'I know this is really hard for you.' Helen tried to give her a reassuring smile.

'She had a new boyfriend and I'm getting better here. So, I'm going to live with her soon.'

'Is that why you moved here?'

'Yes . . .'

'Did Moira say when she planning to visit you again?'

She considered the question and shrugged. 'She was meant to come yesterday but didn't. I think she must just be busy.' The woman looked at Helen expectantly.

'Of course. Do you know Moira's boyfriend's name?'

'No.' She looked away. 'I'm quite tired now.'

'Do you know what he looks like?'

'I can't remember.' She placed a hand to her temple. 'My head hurts.'

Helen handed Agnes her cup of what looked like lemonade. Agnes offered a thin smile then guzzled greedily.

A short while later, Helen found the nurse in the kitchen area; she was in the middle of buttering bread for sandwiches and wiped her brow with her arm.

'We're finished speaking to Agnes . . . for now.'

The nurse nodded. 'I'll let you out in a moment.'

'Thank you,' Helen replied. 'Can you also give me a ring if Agnes gets any more visitors?'

'Sure.' The nurse pulled open an industrial-sized packet of ham. Helen grimaced at the smell of the pink meat.

'Do you remember the last time Moira visited?'

The woman made a clicking sound as she wrapped a completed sandwich in cling film and shoved it onto the trolley. 'I think so. I wasn't paying much attention to be honest. She wasn't alone though.'

Helen stepped forward. 'Who was she with?'

'A man. I'd say he was in his forties with dark hair. Really nice and friendly.'

'That was the first time you ever saw him?'

'I think so.' She rubbed her hands on her apron. 'He did mention he was a doctor.'

'Would you recognize him again?'

'I don't see why not.'

* * *

232

Outside Helen sucked in a breath of cold fresh air. McKinley stood beside her with his hands in his pockets. He rocked back and forth on the spot.

'What do you think of that then?' he asked.

Helen shook her head. 'We'll be notified if Agnes has any visitors. So, we'll just have to wait.'

CHAPTER FORTY-SEVEN

At the reception, a woman speaking to the staff sergeant slammed her hand on the counter. Helen stopped in the doorway to listen. An overweight man in his late fifties was slumped in one of the waiting chairs, muttered something under his breath at the disturbance, then shifted in his seat. Helen retrieved her car keys from her bag. She hadn't decided whether she should intervene or leave them to it. In her agitation, the woman accidentally knocked the miniature cactus plant on the counter onto the floor with her elbow, and it landed near Helen's foot.

'I've phoned the station several times today. This is ridiculous. You can't actually be telling me you're doing nothing.'

'I never said that,' the officer replied flatly.

'You just take your time then.' The slim, red-headed women drummed her hands on the surface. 'I'm not going anywhere.'

The officer shook his head. Helen thought she recognized the voice but wasn't entirely sure.

'So . . .' she seethed. She sounded Scottish, but there was a twang to the way she spoke. Was it a bit of a northern English accent, maybe? 'You're refusing to help me, then?'

'Am no' saying that at all. I just need to take some details from you.' He took a deep breath then looked up. 'Now, what's your address?'

'Marjorie . . . ?' Helen interjected.

The woman turned around, a look of recognition dawning on her face also. 'I need you to help me.' She turned to Helen. 'I'm being shoved from pillar to post.'

Now that Marjorie was facing her, she could see tear-tracks in Marjorie's foundation.

'Are you going to take care of this?' The officer behind the counter asked hopefully.

Helen nodded and could see the relief wash over his face as he promptly turned his attention back to his reports.

'I can help you,' Helen replied and motioned to the double doors on her left. 'We can have a seat through here.' She pulled open the door to the lobby for Marjorie and hesitantly entered.

After declining the offer of a tea, Helen sat opposite Marjorie at a small table in the corridor.

'It's Reggie,' she tore at a nail. 'He's gone missing.'

'When was the last time you saw him?'

'Two nights ago, he was meant to meet me last night and he didn't show up.'

'Okay,' Helen shrugged. 'Perhaps he was busy or forgot about the meeting?'

She shook her head. 'He wouldn't, I mean . . . He's not like that. I also went to his house, he's not there.' No one's seen him. It's not like him.'

'Reggie is a grown man; it might not be unusual that . . .'

'I know something's happened to him.' Marjorie leaned forward and placed a hand on her heart. 'I know in here. I can feel it.'

'What makes you so sure?' Helen asked.

She took a breath and looked away.

'Marjorie, is there something you're not telling me?'

Marjorie shifted in her seat. 'I need you to take me seriously, I wouldn't have come here if I wasn't desperate.'

'I understand that Marjorie, I do.'

'When I last saw Reggie there was something wrong, he was really . . .' She looked like she was thinking of the right words. 'He was shifty, and he seemed scared. He wouldn't tell me what was wrong. I thought maybe it was something to do with Moira.'

'Thank you, I'll look into it.'

'You need to find him.' Marjorie demanded. 'There was something else.'

As soon as Marjorie left the station. Helen asked the sergeant at the desk to send uniform to Reggie's flat. She was now late for the briefing.

* * *

'Still nothing?' Helen directed her question at Craven.

He shook his head. Most of CID were already sat in the meeting room by the time Helen entered. A couple of constables were chatting about their five-a-side football team and looked up as she shuffled past them and crunched into a spare seat at the top of the table. Wind rattled the window behind her. She looked more closely at Craven as she sat down, he was drumming his fingers on a manila folder, and raised an eyebrow when he met eyes with her. He looked tired and was wearing the same shirt that he'd had on yesterday. She wasn't sure if it was just down to the poor lighting, but his skin seemed to have a yellow pallor that she hadn't noticed before. His brown shirt was crumpled around the neck and the top two buttons were open.

Helen stifled a yawn and leaned back in the seat struggling to find a comfortable position. She closed her eyes for a moment and saw the pool of blood in Moira McKenzie's home and the lifeless body of Tina French lying on the grass verge. She blinked the visions away and felt Terry McKinley's gaze on her. She glanced at the black clock above his head, the briefing was meant to start ten minutes ago, but that was Tam Murphy's style. He liked to keep you waiting. Helen looked across at Randall. He had a stack of paper in front of him, and ran a hand through his thinning hair that had recently gone grey at the temples.

The door bounced off the wall as Tam Murphy entered and the room fell silent.

'Right, boys and girls.' He thumped a dusty folder and a box down onto the table. He looked around and made eye contact with everyone before speaking, enjoying his moment in the spotlight.

'Right,' he made a clicking sound like he was thinking of what to say next. 'As you probably know, we've been inundated on the telephone lines about both cases. We also had a little bit of post this morning. Every mad bastard, it seems, is wanting to take the blame.' He held up a letter that was handwritten in black ink. The ink looked smudged and as though it had been written by a child.

I killed them all.

Helen shifted in her seat to get a better view. The paper looked thick, like drawing paper perhaps or parchment.

'It might just be another idiot with nothing better to do.' Randall shook his head.

'Probably,' McKinley agreed. 'It doesn't help that these newspapers sensationalize everything. Half of these nutters just want to be famous.'

'Aye, or they're just starved of attention,' Randall replied.

Murphy placed a brown purse wrapped in an evidence bag onto the table. 'This was found a few miles away from the McKenzies' address. It contains Moira McKenzie's driving licence and a few coins.'

Helen remembered seeing a purse at Moira's house but that was empty apart from a few receipts.

'When was that found?' Craven asked.

'Handed in about fifteen minutes ago. The man that found it is still downstairs. He's given us a description of the man that dumped it in the bin and a partial of the car. "A white man, mid to late forties, short brown hair, wearing a grey suit." He looked down at his notes. 'He was driving a car, a brown Bentley. No index mark, but new-looking. It was dumped in a bin near a bus stop on Ferry Road, not far from the hospital. He's going through the book of known criminals now, so who knows? He might give us a suspect.'

'Helen, I want you to follow up with him and see if he has put a face to a name, so to speak.'

'Tina French's possessions were also left in the rubbish after she was murdered.' Helen exchanged a glance with Craven then nodded. 'On a separate matter, I also ran into Marjorie Lockwood downstairs. She's worried for Reggie McKenzie. She hasn't spoken to him in a few days and apparently that's not like him. I was going to go and check in on him too.'

'Fine, take Terry with you,' Murphy agreed, as he flicked through his notes. 'Marjorie is also not as clean-cut as she makes out and you know what they say about a woman scorned.'

'We'll head there as soon as I'm finished here. I've got a few things to check first.' Helen remarked. She flicked to the back page of the report.

* * *

'I don't think I'll ever get through this lot,' McKinley remarked as he pulled another folder from the cabinet. He sucked on a lemon sherbet as he spoke. 'Times like this when I miss being in traffic.'

'Keep moaning and I'll send you back there,' Craven remarked. He was standing next to the case board, looking at something that Helen couldn't see.

Randall was sitting at the table next to him skimming through a pile of witness statements. Helen caught him trying not to smirk and shot him a look.

'You better have something worthwhile for me.' Craven spoke to McKinley who had started to blush. 'Since you've got time to moan.'

'I . . . yes, we're . . .' McKinley cleared his throat.

'I've got something for you, Jack,' Randall stood up and handed Craven the folder. 'I've found another case from 1959. This girl, Kelly Montgomery, died of blunt force trauma to the head and had had a chunk of hair cut from the back of her head. She was eighteen, and on her way home from a party. Pretty with long brown hair. Her whole life ahead of her.' Randall raised his eyebrows and pointed to a page that Helen couldn't see. 'Look who was interviewed and then released.'

'Aye but hundreds of men were interviewed,' Craven countered.

'Check if he was interviewed in connection with Eleanor Aldridge.'

'Still, I . . .' The sudden ring of the telephone stopped him in his tracks. Randall snatched it up.

Craven turned to Helen. 'I need to have a private word with you.' He motioned to his office. 'Aye, that's fine. I've just been looking up the address history for Reggie McKenzie. At the time of Eleanor Aldridge's attack, Reggie McKenzie lived less than half a mile from her.'

He perched on the end of his desk and shook his head.

'What is it?' Helen asked.

'Milton Nairn was accused of misconduct with a patient, that's why he wants to get away from Edinburgh.'

'Is this recent?'

'Aye, he says he didn't do it.'

'What does Liz say?'

'She believes him.'

'Do you?' Helen asked.

A knock at the door stopped Craven from responding. Terry McKinley popped his head around. 'Sorry to interrupt but—'

'What?' Craven spat.

'There's something else you need to know.'

* * *

A man in his late fifties wearing painters' overalls looked up as Helen entered the room. He offered a nervous-looking smile and chewed on a nail as he looked through pictures.

'I haven't finished going through these yet.'

'That's fine. I'm DS Carter.' She took a seat opposite him.

'There's a lot,' he spread out his hands, indicating the pictures in front of him.

'I wanted to ask you a few questions about the purse.'

'I was working in the house opposite the bus stop and I noticed this car pull up when there was no one at the bus stop. The guy looked a bit shifty to me.'

'In what way?' Helen asked.

'Just . . . looking around, I guess.' He scratched his bald head. 'It caught my attention anyway, then I saw him slip something into the bin. Once he drove away, I decided to go over and have a look. I fished the purse out of the bin and looked inside, and that's when I noticed the driving licence and remembered her from the newspapers.'

'Was it this man?' Helen took out a photograph of Reggie McKenzie from her file.

Then man took it and shook his head. 'No, the man I saw was . . . I think a bit younger, dark brown short hair. Trouble is, I didn't get a close look at him.'

'What about the car?'

'It looked new, a Bentley T1, I think. Sort of a mustard brown. I wouldn't mind one of them myself.'

* * *

Murphy stopped her as she headed back up to the CID room. He had a packet of sandwiches in one hand and a chocolate bar in the other.

'No doubt Jack the Lad Craven has been bending your ear about me.'

'No, he hasn't,' she replied, taking the steps a little quicker.

'Find that hard to believe. He's always had strong opinions and never knows when to shut his mouth.'

'I wouldn't know.'

'He's done well for himself, considering all the mistakes he's made.'

Helen took a deep breath as she opened the door to the CID room and could feel Murphy's breath on the back of her neck.

McKinley lifted his jacket from the back of his seat. 'Will we go and see Reggie McKenzie?'

Helen nodded and grabbed her jacket; she could feel Murphy's gaze on her, but avoided meeting eyes with him.

CHAPTER FORTY-EIGHT

Reggie gulped down the last of his lager with his feet up on the table. *Coronation Street* was on the telly and he couldn't be bothered getting up to see what was on the other channel. Deirdre was deciding whether to move to Canada or Australia. What a choice, eh? He crushed the can. If it were him, he'd go to Australia, every time. He sighed and flicked the can over his shoulder. It would be good to go somewhere new, start afresh with a clean slate. Maybe once this was sorted, he would. He leaned back in the chair and closed his eyes. Crack. *What the fuck?* Pain shot through his skull. A figure was in front of him. Too fuzzy to see. Whack. Stars flashed across his vision. He reached out. Flailing. Punching. Grabbing flesh. He punched out again. His forehead was wet. Reggie blinked hard, regaining composure. He punched out, feeling his knuckles connect with bone.

* * *

McKinley followed Helen up the stairs to the flat. The scuffed brown door was ajar on the latch. Helen paused, feeling her stomach tighten. She nudged McKinley on the arm and motioned to it.

'I'll have a look.' McKinley whispered and brushed past her and rattled on the letter box, when he got no answer, he pushed the door wide open. 'Mr McKenzie?' McKinley called out. No answer. Peering inside, he called out again.

It was dark. Helen strained to hear any movement coming from inside. McKinley sighed and crossed the threshold. Helen followed. The smell of rotting fruit trailed up Helen's nostrils and it was getting stronger, the further they moved down the corridor. All the doors inside the flat were closed, and Helen could hear the soft murmur of classical music leaking from the bedroom. The floorboards groaned under their weight. The hairs on her arms prickled as she stopped in front of the door. Her hand braced on the handle. This did not look good.

'Mr McKenzie?' Helen asked, twisting the doorknob. 'It's the police.'

A waft of stale air and sweat hit her. The sheets and covers were bunched-up on the bed. Helen stiffened, bracing herself to pull the covers back.

'Oh my god!' Helen stared at the body.

'What is it?'

Helen glanced around the room. A pink lamp had been knocked on the floor and smashed. She stepped aside to allow McKinley to see.

'That's . . .'

'Dr Charles Rushmore.'

'What's he doing here?'

'I don't know,' Helen muttered.

Dr Charles Rushmore was lying face up on the bed, spread-eagle, blood leaking from his mouth. An empty bottle of Valium lay on the bedside cabinet next to him. A fat fly buzzed around. Helen swatted it away.

McKinley manoeuvred around her and opened the rest of the doors in the flat. 'There's no sign of a disturbance in here,' he called out to her from the lounge.

'The front door wasn't locked though,' Helen replied.

She took another look at the body. Defensive wounds trailed his hands and wrists. His nails were filed neatly, with no obvious fibres underneath. She turned his hands over; two red scratches ran across his left palm. They looked fresh, recent.

Blood pooled on the pillow. His lips were blue, and his face had drained of blood. She slipped on gloves and pulled the covers further back. He still had his shoes on. Black fibres trailed the carpet; it looked like he'd been dragged up onto the bed but why?

Helen knelt beside Charles Rushmore. A half-eaten, rotten plate of Spam and chips mottled with green blobs of mould sat on the nightstand beside a glass of beer. McKinley clicked off the radio. A glint of silver peeked out from the blankets. A cross necklace, the same kind as the one belonging to Tina French. She stood up and lifted out a folded bit of paper that had been peeking out of his trouser pocket.

I can't do this anymore. I am sorry for what I've done to Moira. I also killed Tina French. I can't help myself. Reggie.

Helen was about to step away as she noticed Rushmore suck in a breath. A faint, raspy rattle. She felt for a pulse. He had a faint one, but he was fading.

'Terry, get an ambulance, he's still alive! And get me a towel.'

A few moments later, a flustered-looking McKinley appeared behind her with a hand towel.

'Place that over his head wound,' Helen commanded. 'And with pressure.'

McKinley nodded and fumbled to his knees. 'Helen, there is something that I need you to see in the kitchen.'

'It will have to wait.' Helen watched as blood soaked through the white towel. She didn't fancy Rushmore's chances.

He parted his lips and groaned.

'Dr Rushmore, it's Helen Carter. You are going to be okay. Can you speak, can you tell me what's happened?'

His lips parted but no sound came out.

'Stay with me. Keep your eyes open.' Her arms ached from putting pressure on his wound. It felt like hours before an ambulance man popped his head around the door.

Once Charles Rushmore was on his way to hospital, Helen headed through to the kitchen. The room spun as she looked down at the images of herself spread out on the worktop. Polaroid images of her heading into her block of flats. A few more of her at her car.

'He's been following me.' It felt like someone had thrown a bucket of icy water over her when she noticed the ones that had her face cut out of them. 'He's been watching my routine. How could I not have noticed that?'

'We need to find him now.'

Helen nodded, she needed to get out of there. She gasped for breath. Stepping back, she headed through to the living room. No traces of the red pool of blood remained on the threadbare carpet but the faint aroma of bleach lingered in the air. The window was open, rain battered the glass and the water ran down the wall under the frame. She pulled the window shut and whipped the curtains across. The flat fell silent and Helen could feel the pounding of her heart in her chest. She reached into her pocket, clasping her own bottle of pills. She thought about taking one to calm her nerves, her throat tightened, she sucked in a deep breath and held it for a few seconds then released it through her nostrils. As she turned, she noticed Terry McKinley standing in the doorway. His brow furrowed.

'Are you all right?' he asked.

'Why wouldn't I be?'

'Well, from what we've both just seen.'

'I'm fine. You gave me a fright standing there like that.'

'Helen, I'm sorry.'

'We need to catch him, because he's not going to stop otherwise.'

* * *

McKinley was in the kitchen of the McKenzie residence; the worktops were cluttered with open tins and dirty plates. The ashtray on the scuffed table was overspilling with butt-ends and ash.

'Reggie wasn't the one that was doing the housework then,' McKinley stated.

'No,' flies fluttered above the stuffed bin. Helen lifted the lid, nothing unusual. Egg shells, yoghurt cartons and old newspapers.

'I think this is strange, there's a lot more to this than meets the eye.'

McKinley nodded. 'Marjorie has history and maybe she thought with Moira out the way she and Reggie would be together, but he obviously had other ideas.'

'We need to find whoever dumped Moira's purse, that wasn't Marjorie.' Helen countered.

McKinley shrugged. 'There's that too.'

'She seemed genuinely upset when I spoke to her at the station. She was worried for Reggie's safety.'

'Or maybe she just wanted us to find him?'

'We need to speak with her again.'

* * *

Reggie slumped back into the driver's seat of Rushmore's car. He angled the mirror towards himself. An angry welt stuck out from his temple. Gritting his teeth, he pulled away a few strands of stray hair that had stuck to the wound. He knew Moira wouldn't have been smart enough to fake her own death, but he hadn't counted on her having help. And from the doctor, of all people. He'd seen her with a man a few weeks before she vanished, but it wasn't that Rushmore character. Moira was nothing but a dirty little scrubber.

'Fuck's sake,' he muttered and reached over into the glove box. Rushmore's driving licence was in there, under a small map book. He flicked the driving licence open. Dundee wasn't too far away and that's probably where he'd find Moira.

CHAPTER FORTY-NINE

'My poor Reggie's dead, isn't he?' Marjorie was waiting for Helen and McKinley in the interview room. She looked different from their earlier conversation, all her make-up had been washed off, and her red hair scraped back. Her green eyes were puffy from crying, and she wiped a trailing tear away with the palm of her hand. She had an untouched mug of tea in front of her. 'I can tell, I can't believe this.' She sobbed.

Helen nodded. 'What makes you think that?'

'Did he hurt himself?' her face drained of all colour.

'We don't know where Reggie McKenzie is at the moment, but he may be hurt. Do you have any idea where he may be?'

Marjorie covered her hand with her mouth, and it looked like she was going to retch. 'No, I just always thought he would come to me. You know, if he needed help.'

Helen took a moment to let the news sink in. The stuffy little room had no windows and barely fit the table and four chairs. Marjorie was wearing a sweet perfume that hung so heavy in the air Helen could practically taste it.

'Marjorie, I need to ask you some questions now,' Helen replied.

Marjorie sniffled.

'You were worried about Reggie, so worried in fact that you came into the police station.'

'I did, I mean I was, and I was right.' She sought confirmation from McKinley. 'I did the right thing.'

'Did you go to Reggie's flat?'

'Yes,' she wiped another tear away. 'There wasn't any answer.'

'When we went to the property the door was ajar.'

Marjorie exchanged a look with Helen, then shrugged. 'I don't know.'

'Are you sure?' Helen flicked to another page in her notes.

'It was closed when I was there.' She furrowed her brow. 'It was locked, and he didn't answer.'

'How was Reggie when you last spoke to him?' Helen asked.

Marjorie looked up at the clock on the wall and sighed.

'Marjorie, we are just trying to understand,' McKinley said, keeping his voice soft and low.

'He was . . .' She looked directly at McKinley, her voice breaking.

'Take your time,' he smiled.

'Well, I thought we were going to be together and he basically broke up with me. He said it wouldn't look good for us to be together with what happened with Moira. I just thought that I would need to give him time.'

'Maybe you were upset at him for not wanting to be with you?' Helen pressed on.

'I was . . . but . . . you think I've hurt him? I can't believe this.' She looked at McKinley pleadingly.

'I do have good reason to ask these questions,' Helen carried on. 'Well, you have been charged with assault previously.'

'So?' Her voice was cold. 'That has nothing to do with Reggie.'

'I don't know . . . A woman scorned, a woman who's quite handy with her fists when the mood takes her. Maybe when things didn't go your way . . .'

'That was a long time ago, I'm not the same person any-more. I was young and it was an accident. You know Moira wasn't this loving wife that the newspapers make her out to be. She was having an affair and wanted a divorce from him. Maybe you should be looking for that man.'

'Reggie told you that?' Helen asked.

'Aye, we used to talk about it in the pub, that's how we got together, he was heartbroken about it. Heartbroken at first anyway, he felt like she was making a fool out of him.'

'Do you know who this man was?'

'I don't. I think he was successful and had a lot of money. Reggie wasn't the type of guy that I would normally have gone for, but he was nice to me, it's not something that happens often, you know. He'd listen to me, and just be with me.'

'Do you know anywhere that Reggie might go? Any friends even?' McKinley asked.

'No, I don't.'

'Do you know a Dr Charles Rushmore?' Has Reggie ever mentioned him before? Helen looked back down at her notes.

'No, I can honestly say I have never heard of that name.'

* * *

'Hello, my darling Moira.' Reggie smiled, as the door opened. She tried to shut it, but he stuck his boot in the gap and shouldered it open, knocking her to the ground. His head pounded and felt sticky to the touch.

'I would've made an effort; you know, dressed nice. But Rushmore ruined my shirt when he smacked me over the head with a mallet.' Reggie shrugged. 'That was a bit rude, was it not?'

Moira staggered backwards. 'Reggie, please don't . . . where's Charles? What have you done to him?'

'What have *I* done to *him*?' He motioned to his head. 'What has he done to me?' He made a grab for her and she

249

recoiled. Her eyes darted round the room, seeking a way out. 'I've driven all this way, and this is the welcome I get?' He shook his head.

'Where's Charles?' she demanded.

'You don't need to worry about him again. Ever. He's dead.'

'No!' Moira shook her head, tears bursting from her eyes. 'I don't believe you.'

'I don't care.' He grabbed her by the shoulders and felt her body sag. 'You'll never escape me,' he whispered in her ear. 'Only I get to decide when and how this ends.'

He gave her a shove that sent her sprawling towards the fireplace. She landed on the hearth with a thud — so hard it made her whimper.

Reggie walked towards her. 'You're weak. Pathetic. Stupid.'

She turned her face up to look at him. 'No, I'm not.'

He wound a handful of her hair around his fingers and yanked her up.

'You don't scare me,' she spat. 'No anymore. What else have I got to lose?'

CHAPTER FIFTY

An annoyed-looking Craven was standing outside the inter-view room, arms folded, when Helen emerged. He motioned for McKinley to head down the corridor in the direction of the CID suite, while Craven himself hung back to speak with Helen. McKinley hadn't looked pleased with that. Craven was wearing his tweed jacket, she noticed, its shoulders damp with the rain. His hand gripped an unlit cigarette.

'What is it?' Helen asked.

Craven smiled bitterly. 'I don't know if I'm making a mistake, but you're the only person that I think I can trust with this.'

'You're starting to worry me now.' Helen stepped for-ward, closing the gap between them.

'Like I said, it's probably nothing.'

Helen shrugged. 'Let me be the judge of that.'

He glanced around the empty corridor, then leaned in closer. 'The brown Bentley that was driven by the suspect who put the Moira's purse in the bin?'

Helen nodded.

'I know who drives one.'

'Who?'

'Milton Nairn.' Craven snorted.

'Are you sure?' Helen thought back to meeting him at the doctor's surgery. 'He wasn't driving a Bentley when I met him, and I haven't seen one at the surgery'

'Well, I know he has one because he showed it off to me,' Craven shrugged. 'Maybe it's his weekend car?' Craven carried on, 'I saw him pick up the twins from my flat in it.' He scoffed, 'He even tried to show me the leather interior.' He paused for a moment. 'What do you think?'

'He also fits the general description of the man who dumped Moira's purse.' She blew out a sigh. 'But it's a very vague description.'

Craven dragged a hand down his face. 'This man is living with my children.'

'It's probably nothing. I wouldn't jump to conclusions just yet.'

'That's what I'm hoping, I didn't want to tell anyone up there. They'd act like a bull in a china shop. This is something I need to look at myself. If I'm wrong Liz will move away with the children and I'll never see them again.'

'What do you want to do?' Helen asked.

'We need to go speak to Milton.'

'Agreed,' Helen nodded. 'The doctor's surgery will be closed now.'

'I know where he'll be.'

* * *

When Liz opened the front door, she looked ready to slam it shut again. 'Jack, now is not a good time and I would appreciate it if you wouldn't keep bringing your colleague here too.' She gave Helen a look.

Craven took two quick drags on his fag before speaking, then flicked it onto the path. 'Is Milton in?'

'What do you want to speak to Milton for? If it's about the job, he's already accepted it so . . .'

'No, it's not about that.' He tried to look past her. 'I need to come in, where is he?'

'Jack, what has got into you?'

'Milton,' he called out.

Liz sighed and opened the door. 'Come in if you must, but make this quick. He's cooking dinner in kitchen. The kids are at his mum's.'

* * *

Milton was frying steaks and sipping at a glass of wine when he noticed Jack and Helen standing in the doorway. 'I . . . this is a surprise, Jack. There's not enough for you and your companion, I'm afraid.'

'We're not here for the food,' Craven replied.

Milton gulped and slipped one of the steaks onto a plate. 'Well, we're just about to have dinner so . . .'

'How's that new Bentley of yours?' Craven asked.

'The what?' Milton drained his glass of wine. 'Liz, can you carry on with the steaks?'

A look of concern furrowed Liz's brown. She exchanged a look with Craven and Milton.

Milton forced a smile. 'Jack has a car problem he wants my advice on.'

'What do you know about cars?' Liz asked, making a face.

'This won't take long.' Craven replied to Liz.

Milton placed his wine glass on the worktop then motioned to the side door. 'You know the way,' he said to Craven.

Milton led them out into the garage where a car, presumably the Bentley, was parked underneath a grey cover. The garage door wasn't fully shut, and Helen enjoyed the cool breeze.

Milton closed the door that led back into the house and stood in front of it. 'Right, what is it you want?' He spoke through gritted teeth.

Helen noticed Craven's shoulder tense, so she stepped in between the men. 'A man matching your description was seen in a brown Bentley putting a purse in a bin. A purse belonging to a woman we presume murdered,' Helen replied.

'There's lots of men out there that look like me.' Milton chuckled.

'This is nothing to laugh about.' Craven stepped forward.

'I have nothing to do with that. You've had a wasted trip.' Milton had his hand braced on the door handle. 'Is this really all you have Jack? I must say this is desperate.'

'I know it was you,' Craven stated bluntly

A smile spread over Milton's thin features. 'No, you don't. There's no proof and lots of people will have a car like mine. That means nothing and you know it. You just want it to be my car.'

'Okay,' Helen nodded. 'This is easily sorted. Where were you at eleven this morning?'

Milton rolled his eyes. 'I was working.'

'We will need to verify that.' Helen spoke slowly, making sure that he was understanding the seriousness of the situation. 'Do you have anyone that can corroborate that?'

'No, that was before my first appointment, so I was alone in the office.'

Craven brushed past Helen and grabbed Milton around the scruff of his neck. Milton flailed his arms and tried to pull away, but Craven kept a tight grip. He spun him around and dragged him to the front of the car, shoved him onto the bonnet and pressed his forearm onto Milton's neck. Milton clawed at the arm and gasped for breath. He kicked out, his face reddening.

'Let go of him, this isn't the way to do it.' Helen stepped forward. 'Please don't do this.'

'Are you going to start telling the truth?' Craven asked.

Milton looked pleadingly at Helen.

'Jack, he can't breathe.' Helen grabbed Craven's arm as he released the hold.

Milton slid to the ground and broke into a coughing fit.

'Start talking.' Craven knelt beside him.

Milton rubbed his neck. 'I'll have you done for assault.'

'Assault? I haven't even started yet.'

'I haven't done what you're thinking.' Milton spoke in a hoarse whisper.

Craven levelled a boot at Milton's stomach, and he crumpled. 'I can go all night, so you are going to start speaking, one way or the other.'

'Fine! Fine! Please!'

Craven lifted his boot for another blow.

'Don't.' Helen stepped in the way.

Milton spat blood onto the ground. 'Okay, I dropped the purse into the bin, but I didn't kill her.'

Craven raised an eyebrow. 'I'm supposed to believe that, am I?'

'It's the truth. I had nothing to do with anything.'

'You'll need to do better than that.' Craven warned.

'I'm telling you the truth.'

'Where did you get the purse?' Helen asked.

'I think you've broken my tooth.' Milton flinched as he felt around his jaw.

'A woman is probably dead, and you think I'd be bothered about your tooth? You're lucky I've no' knocked them all out.'

Milton shot Craven a look. 'My colleague found the purse after you had been asking questions.'

'Why not hand it in?' Helen shrugged. 'You know the seriousness of the case.'

Milton dropped his eyes. 'Charles was worried you would suspect him. We thought it was safer to just get rid of it.'

'Safer? This is a murder investigation and I'll tell you it's not looking good for you,' Craven sneered. 'I think you did it.'

'No, no, I swear. I had nothing to do with it. I don't know anything that happened to her. I wouldn't! Charles told me that she had left it at her last appointment, and he'd forgotten all about it until you both showed up asking questions about her and he panicked. He was worried about how you would act.'

'You've tried to destroy evidence.' Helen warned. 'That's a crime.'

Milton shook his head 'It was stupid, but I just tried to help a colleague. I shouldn't have agreed to it, but I was worried this would happen, that if I handed it in you wouldn't believe me. I know you hate me Jack and I don't blame you, but I love Liz and I wouldn't do anything to risk that.'

Craven grabbed Milton and pulled him up to his feet. 'Where does Dr Rushmore go when he is not in Edinburgh?'

'I don't know.'

'Think.' Craven shook him. 'Or maybe I go back into the house and ask Liz what she knows about this.'

'You can't tell Liz.'

'Can't I?' Craven smiled. 'I think she has a right to know.'

'Don't. I have an Edinburgh address, and one for his country home near Dundee. They're in my address book in the hall'

I don't know if he'll be there, but it's worth a try. He's had the flu and not been working the last couple of days.'

'Get that and then you're coming with us.' Craven pushed him towards the door.

'Please don't tell Liz. I swear that I'm telling you the truth.'

'Why should I do anything to help you, eh?'

'Because this would break her heart and you know it.'

* * *

Liz was sitting at the dining table with her head in her hands. She had the two plates of Steak Diane untouched on the table. She looked at Craven. 'What's going on? What's he's done?' Her mascara was smudged and clumped under her bleary eyes. Helen slipped a glance at Craven who looked like he was thinking about what to say.

'Milton has offered to come down to the station with us to help with some enquiries,' Helen answered.

Liz swallowed hard. Is this true?' She directed her question to Craven. 'Are you serious?'

'Aye, it shouldn't take too long.' Craven shrugged and turned towards the door. He was no doubt worried that this would affect him seeing his children.

Milton appeared behind them with a small red book. 'I won't be long.'

'What about your meal?' Liz asked. 'I never thought you would sink this low Jack.'

Milton forced a smile. 'Put it in the oven and I'll have it when I get back.'

Liz stood up. 'Please. Can this wait until tomorrow, Jack?'

'No, we need Milton's help tonight,' Craven replied.

'Well, should I come with you?' Liz asked, stepping around the table.

'No, Liz, there's no need. You eat and watch television. Try and relax.'

Helen caught Craven rolling his eyes.

They walked back in silence to the car. Helen could see Liz watching in the doorway from the corner of her eye.

Milton was the first to speak as he clambered into the back of the Granada. 'Thanks for not telling her, Jack.'

'I didn't do it for you.' Craven slipped off the handbrake and pulled out into the road before Helen had even had time to fasten her seatbelt. The tyres screeched, as he slipped the car into second.

'Jack, I promise that I haven't done what you think I have. What benefit would I get out of that? I haven't even met the woman.'

'I don't know what goes on in that sick mind of yours,' Craven countered.

'You know me, you wouldn't have let me live with your children for three years if you really thought that about me.'

Craven pressed on the accelerator and Milton was thrown back into his seat.

'You know, Charles told me you questioned him at the doctor's surgery, asking him why he was at Billy Hutchinson's house. He was just scared that he was going to get blamed for something that he hasn't done.'

'Where did he say that he found the purse?' Helen asked, as she finally managed to get her seatbelt on. Milton shook his head.

'Well, she didn't have an appointment, did you see her at the surgery?' Helen prompted.

'No . . . I . . .'

'It's just not adding up, is it?' Craven interjected.

'I didn't think that much about it. I was just trying to help a colleague.'

* * *

Moira stared back at Reggie. Her eyelids swollen and her features knotted in a mask of defiance. She held her fists bunched at her sides.

'I'm going to bring you back home,' he told her. 'And you can tidy up the mess you left behind.'

'You'll never get away with this,' Moira hissed back at him. 'Even you must realize that much.'

'Or maybe I'll finish the job.' Reggie's voice was full of loathing. 'Kill you right here. Make it look like Rushmore did it, then came to our flat to finish me off . . . but I got the better of him. I'd be a hero.'

'You're delusional,' Moira scoffed. 'A delusional fool if you think you'd get away with that. Have you even thought about the evidence, forensics . . . ?' Moira moved towards the fireplace.

'I can start a new life — the life I've always wanted in Australia. Marjorie will be there by my side. I'll be a poor widower.'

'It's never going to happen.' Moira lifted a bronze statue from the mantlepiece. She chucked it and it connected with his forehead.

His knees buckled and he fell forward. She made a run for the back door. Rage boiled in his stomach. She would pay for that.

CHAPTER FIFTY-ONE

'Do you think Milton is telling the truth?' Helen asked Craven once they got back in the Granada after dropping Milton Nairn off at the station to be interviewed. Craven was staring hard out of the window, puffing on a cigarette.

'I don't know.' He considered the question for a moment. 'He doesn't have an alibi and I wouldn't trust him as far as I could throw him.' He flicked his cigarette out the window and turned the engine. 'Let's get going.'

'Fine,' Helen gave a sharp sigh.

Fifteen minutes later, they pulled out onto the A90, rain peppering the windscreen. Craven had been flooring it all the way and Helen thought better of telling him to slow down.

She wasn't too sure of the route, but Craven seemed to know the way.

'We might need to stop for petrol shortly,' Craven eventually said, as he fished in his chest pocket for his cigarettes. He flicked the packet open with his thumb and placed one to his lips. 'There's a place I know up here if we do.'

'Maybe we should leave this, and get local uniform to visit the house instead?' Helen shifted uncomfortably in the passenger seat, her seatbelt digging into the side of her neck.

Craven shook his head. 'No, I think we should get up there.'

'You think Moira could still be alive up there? Up at this house?' Helen asked.

'I think that's a possibility and we still don't know the whereabouts of Reggie either.'

'If that's not the case, it's two hours in the car when we could be questioning—'

'Let him sweat in there,' Craven muttered. 'It's nothing that he doesn't deserve.'

'That's not the point—'

'I don't care.' He made a clicking sound. 'Well, I can drop you off here, if you want.'

'You don't need to do that and we're about fifty miles from the station. I can hardly walk back.'

Craven sighed and pushed down on the accelerator. 'If Moira is still alive, she could be in danger.'

'But it's a big "if" . . . How do you explain all the blood we found at their flat?'

Craven shrugged. 'There's a map in the dash. I know we turn off soon, but I'm not sure where.'

As the rain died away, the last of the late-evening sun sat low in the sky. Helen slipped down the visor to avoid the glare. They drove the rest of the way mostly in silence. Helen took the time to prepare herself for what they might find. The sight of a solitary stone cottage on the horizon made her straighten in her seat.

'At least we know someone is home.' Helen pointed to the smoke trailing from the chimney stack.

Craven took the left-hand turn towards the building. The single-track road was poorly maintained with bits of broken branches and rubble strewn across it. The car rattled and wobbled as it crossed the debris. Craven revved the engine to take the bump.

'As soon as we drive further up the road anyone in there will see us coming,' Craven remarked.

'What other choice do we have?' Helen asked.

Craven pulled into a passing place and brought the car to a stop. The cottage's wrought-iron gate was now in view — but still a safe distance away. Craven lit his fag and took a long drag. 'All those branches on the road look deliberate to me.'

Helen stared ahead. She could see another car parked out front. A brown one with a vinyl top. 'That looks like Dr Rushmore's car parked up there.'

'Reggie could have taken it.'

Helen thought for a moment, then pointed to the dense woodland that surrounded the house. 'Why don't you carry on without me, up towards the house? The car is unmarked so he may not realize it's a police vehicle. Reggie also knows that I drive a Mini. He's never seen this car before.'

'I don't know.' Craven stubbed his fag out on the dash and flicked it out the window.

'Look—' Helen pointed to a clearing between the trees — 'that looks like a back way up to the property. I'll head up that way and meet you at the house. That way he can't make a quick exit.' She unclipped her seatbelt.

'Nah, it's too risky.' Craven shook his head.

A blood-curdling scream filled the silence that hung between them.

'What the hell was that?' Craven spoke first.

'It sounded like it came from the woods. I'll see you shortly.'

'I think I should go with you.'

'We need the car up there.'

Craven nodded. 'Just be careful.'

* * *

Maybe this wasn't such a good idea after all. Helen could hear distant howls, but she couldn't make out where from. She was surrounded by overgrown trees obscuring her view of the house. She could only follow the path in its general direction. Adrenaline surged through her body and her heart raced. She sucked in a deep breath, shoving branches out of her way to find her footing. The ground was soft and clay-like from the recent downpour, and her boots sank into it with every step. *Bloody brilliant!*

She pulled a boot free and felt that her socks and the hem of her trousers were now soggy. The car journey back to the station was going to be pleasant in this state. A branch snapped behind her. Helen bristled and whipped around but she couldn't see anything. She shoved her foot back into her boot and tried to pick up the pace, moving further down the path — all the while wishing for a little light and scanning for any sign she wasn't alone. As she pressed ahead the trees seemed to grow taller and the path narrowed with bulging roots protruding from the dirt. Wiry branches snagged her hair and scratched at her arms. Almost like they were closing in on her. It couldn't be much further, surely . . .

There was a burst of what she first thought was torch-light, then she heard a car spark into life and pull away. Another *snap* and she jerked her head towards the noise. But it was useless — she could see only shadows. She pressed on, and let out a ragged breath. Finally, she reached a gap in the trees and the house came into view. Orange light flickered from a window on the top floor, giving her a direction to follow.

She'd need to move quickly — Craven would be nearly there. A second piercing scream filled the silence and Helen flinched. It sounded like it came from in front of her, maybe from the house. *Damn!* The wind had picked up and with all the rustling from the trees, she couldn't be sure. She knew she needed to keep going, just a couple of hundred yards to the house—

Whack. She fell to the floor with a thud. Ice-cold pain shot through her left ankle and knee. Grimacing, she turned to see she had tripped over a tree root. She scrambled back up to her feet, using a tree trunk for support and shaking off the pain. No blood — that was something at least. She tested her weight on her injured leg and it held. She slipped a glance over her shoulder, unable to shake the feeling that she was being watched.

She could see the back of the house. There was a small wooden fence with a gate, which swayed open in the breeze — and a path leading directly to the back door. Helen stopped in her tracks. She could see footprints in the mud, made by a pair of feet about the same size as hers. Helen sucked in a breath to steady herself, swallowing down the anxiety that threatened to crush her chest.

The tracks seemed to lead uphill from the house and away from the road. Helen followed them, flinching as her left knee protested with each step. Icy panic trailed up her torso as a shape up ahead caught her eye. Helen thought it was a rock at first — until it moved. Helen froze. It was a person, dressed in black, crouching in the bushes. Helen stepped forward, but the figure didn't move. It wasn't so dark in this clearing and Helen realized that the person hadn't seen her coming. Whoever it was seemed to be focused intently on the house. Helen let out the breath she had been holding and moved closer, trying to tread as softly as possible. She grimaced as a twig snapped under her foot. The figure whipped around. It was only then that Helen got a look at the face.

CHAPTER FIFTY-TWO

Jack Craven pushed open the door and was hit with a cold draught. Inside, the house was a lot smaller than he'd been expecting and sparsely decorated with a solitary wicker sofa and an antique coffee table. On the wall above was a glassy eyed stag's head. There was a bookshelf on the left side of the room, but that too was empty. He crinkled his nose, scenting the stale air, which was thick with dust and mothballs. It was obviously not a place that was lived-in. The floorboards groaned as he stepped further into the room and looked around. A cough burst from his chest, and he was annoyed at himself for the involuntary action. If there was anyone here, they'd have to be deaf not to hear him. He sucked in a rattly breath as he pushed open a second door.

He batted away a cobweb as he investigated the kitchen, which was barely big enough for a white hob and a couple of blue cupboards. A pot sat in the sink, but it looked dry and unused. He listened for any other noise in the house. Silence.

Back out in the living area, he moved over to the fireplace, where he noted a stack of charred logs. Warmth still radiated from them. Someone had been here very recently. A speckle of red on the stones in front caught his eye. It looked like blood. He kneeled and brushed it with his finger.

* * *

'Who are you?' The woman wailed, a look of surprise twisting her features. She was wearing a brown suede skirt that was torn and muddy, and her blouse was ripped at the collar. Her cheeks were pink, and her almond eyes swollen and wild. 'You've got to help. He's coming for me.' The woman pleaded, her mucky, bloody arms outstretched.

'Moira?' Helen retrieved her warrant card from her pocket. She looked thinner than the pictures Helen had seen, and her hair had been cut to just under her ears and dyed auburn. 'Who's coming for you?'

A sob burst from her, and she fell forward into Helen's arms. Trembling.

'Who's coming?' Helen repeated forcefully, grimacing, as she tried and failed to hold up Moira's weight. 'Moira, you need to work with me here.' She helped Moira to the ground and the motion sent a bolt of pain through her left knee again.

'I should have known,' Moira muttered.

'Reggie?' Helen asked. 'Is Reggie after you? I can't help you if you don't tell me.'

She nodded, tears rolling down her cheeks. 'He's going to kill me.'

'Do you know where he is?' Helen glanced around the woods. They were surrounded by overgrown grass and trees. The remnants of mist made it impossible to see back down to the house.

'He'll kill you too.'

'I won't let him.'

'He'll find us,' the woman sobbed. 'He'll kill us both.'

Helen's mouth was dry. 'You just need to keep calm.' She said it out loud for her own benefit as much as Moira's.

'He's capable of anything.'

'We need to get back down to the house.'

'No . . . No, I can't.' Moira pushed Helen away.

'I have a colleague down there. He can help us.'

'I can't.'

Helen grabbed her by the shoulders. 'You have to. This is the only way.'

'No.'

'What's the alternative? Wait for Reggie?'

'He might be at the house.'

'Maybe. But my inspector is down there and he has a car, so we can get away.'

Moira swallowed hard.

'Why? Why did you run away like this?' Helen questioned.

'Because he would've killed me.' Moira slumped forward. She was sobbing again.

Helen's shoulders tensed. 'How do you know that?'

'Because he's a murderer,' she wailed. 'He was hardly going to let me leave, was he?'

'I know this is hard, but you need to stay calm.' Helen lowered her own voice, fighting the urge to pull Moira to her feet and shake her. Instead she settled for, 'Why didn't you go to the police?'

'What, "Nutty Moira"? Aye, sure you lot'd believe me. Last time I called you after Reggie battered me, you turned me away. Told me it was my own fault.'

Helen persisted, 'You say that he's a murderer. Who has he killed?'

'I don't know how many, but I think he killed the woman in the papers, Tina French. He can't help himself. He even gave me her necklace to wear. Charles helped me, and now Reggie has killed him too. Things were good before our son died. Really good, then not long after he had an accident at work, and he changed. It made him so angry, so cold. He started to beat me. He became obsessed with death.'

Helen shook her head. 'Let's just get to my colleague.'

Moira shrieked and backed away. Helen swung around as the mallet connected with her forearm with a sickening crack, knocking her to the ground. Pain shot through her ribs and spine as she landed on a stone. He raised the mallet again, this time at her head. She swerved to the left. The mallet landed next to her head, spraying mud onto her face. Then it swung down again. She swerved to the right then kicked out with all her might. Her assailant yelped in pain and clutched his shin. *Reggie.* She kicked again and again. His knee buckled. Helen fumbled in the soil snatching at anything that she could turn into a weapon. Her fingers connected with a rock. She threw it and watched it crack off his forehead.

He was momentarily stunned. 'That hurt, you bitch!'

Helen shuffled backwards, trying to make some space between them.

'Now I know which one of you will be the first to die.' He wiped blood from his head with the back of his hand.

'Stop this, Reggie. There's no way you can get away from this.' Her arm was numb, she shook it to get the blood flowing again. 'You've already assaulted a police officer, don't make this any worse for yourself.'

'When I'm finished no one will find you.'

Moira made eye contact with Helen. She had shuffled out of Reggie's line of vision and laid hands on a stick.

'Reggie, you'll never get away with this. I'm not alone out here. I brought back-up — a colleague.'

'I don't see—'

Moira screamed and swung at the back of Reggie's head with the stick. It connected with a clunk and Reggie fell forward. Helen scrambled to her feet, retrieving her handcuffs. She stuck a knee in his back then secured his hands.

Moira looked like a wild animal. 'Is he . . . ?'

'No, he's still breathing, just knocked out.' Helen gingerly touched her ribs. They didn't feel broken. She looked up as footsteps approached. 'You're late to the party,' Helen smiled, flexing the fingers of her injured arm.

'Well—' Craven gestured to Reggie — 'looks like you had it all in hand.'

'Barely.' Helen blew out a sigh and motioned to the mallet that was lying near Reggie's head.

He held out a hand and pulled her to her feet. 'Are you okay?'

'I'll be fine. Let's just get him out of here.'

* * *

After regaining consciousness Reggie was guided into the back of a police car by a couple of uniformed officers. His eyes met Helen's. His face contorted with hate. He muttered something that Helen couldn't make out and she wasn't interested in hearing. Helen looked away as she escorted a trembling Moira around to the front of the house where an ambulance was parked with its doors open. Scenes of crime officers were examining the house, although Helen wasn't sure they'd get much from it. Moira's legs buckled and she crumpled into a heap, nearly taking Helen down with her. As Helen tried to pull her to her feet, she was scooped up by a uniformed officer who offered Helen a broad smile.

'Thanks.' Helen sighed.

'No bother,' the officer shrugged. 'I could see you struggling.'

Helen looked down and noticed what the officer was carrying in his free hand. The mallet wrapped in an evidence bag.

Helen's smile faded. She felt the colour drain from her face.

'I'll help her to the ambulance,' the office offered.

Helen nodded, relieved to be free of helping Moira. Nearly every bone in her body ached.

Craven offered Helen a small wave as he approached. 'How's the arm?'

She shrugged and peeled up her sleeve showing a blue-green welt that spread down her forearm. 'It's not broken. Just badly bruised.'

268

Craven shook his head. 'That could have been a lot worse. You're lucky.'

Helen scoffed. 'I don't feel lucky.'

He nodded towards the ambulance. 'Are you not wanting to get checked out?'

Helen shook her head. A lengthy wait in hospital, only to be sent home to rest — it was the last thing she wanted right now. 'Moira claimed that Reggie murdered Tina French and others. We'll get more out of her once she's back at the station.'

'What a night.' Craven shook his head and stifled a cough. 'I need a drink. My head's thumping.'

'I just want to get home and sleep.'

Craven looked her up and down. 'Judging by the state of you, I'll do the driving.'

CHAPTER FIFTY-THREE

'This isn't Moira's fault.' Charles Rushmore muttered the next morning from his hospital bed. His head was bandaged, and his face bruised and bloody. 'You need to let her go.'

'Do we now?' Craven sat down in one of the visitor seats with his arms crossed.

Helen remained standing. Sitting aggravated the pain in her knee.

'It was all me,' Charles persisted. 'Arrest me but not her.'

'Why do you say that?' Helen's arm still throbbed, so she shoved her hand in her pocket to try and give it some support.

'He was going to keep on killing. If I hadn't—' He looked up at Helen as he blinked back tears. 'Moira told me that he'd killed a woman and she was terrified of him. I had to do something.'

'Is that why you went to his house?' Helen asked.

'Yes, I was going to kill him, but he got the better of me. I was going to make it look like suicide.'

'Why didn't you speak to us?' Helen tried to keep her voice low.

He seemed to be considering the question.

'Who has he killed?' Helen carried on.

'Women, Moira told me he was compelled to . . . You ask me why I didn't go to the police? You had done nothing to stop him before. I didn't want him to get away and hurt Moira. I had to protect her.'

Helen flicked to another page in the file. 'Why was all the blood left in the flat for us to find?'

'I couldn't take the chance that Reggie would kill Moira. I wanted him to think she was dead, to give her freedom. She had told me that he would rather kill her than let her leave.'

'How did you do it?'

'I . . . well,' he cleared his throat. 'I took blood every time she visited the surgery. It wasn't long before . . . Before I had enough that you would think she was dead.'

'So, if Moira finally had her freedom from Reggie, why kill him?'

'It didn't work. I thought it would shine a spotlight on what Reggie was, but it didn't and more importantly he didn't believe she was dead. He came into the surgery asking questions, then he visited Moira's sister, asking about Moira's whereabouts. I had no choice.'

'How did you do it?'

'I used Moira's keys to get into the flat, then I was going to suffocate him with a pillow while he slept but he was eating so I took my chance and tried to knock him out.' He shifted in the bed. 'The man deserved it, and I don't regret it. Moira helped me when my wife was dying. She gave me something to live for and I wanted to do the same for her.'

* * *

Coffee and shortbread in hand, Helen took a seat by the window in the station canteen. A couple of pigeons bathing in a puddle caught her attention and she watched until one of them flew away. A moment later McKinley sat opposite and tore into a cheese sandwich. He spoke in between bites.

'Are you sure you won't see a doctor?'

271

Helen shook her head and tried not to flinch at the pain the movement caused her.

'Sally is leaving. She's going back to London.'

Helen nodded and bit into the shortbread. Her stomach ached, and it had been hours since she'd eaten anything. 'She's left before though,' she heard herself saying.

'I'm quite happy about it to be honest,' he rubbed his mouth with the back of his hand.

'Well, that's something.'

'I didn't mean to make things awkward.'

'It doesn't matter. I've just got a lot on right now. I can't think about this.'

'I know but—'

'No, you don't. I've just got out of a relationship. I've got a half-brother that I didn't know existed a week ago.' She drained her coffee. 'The last thing I need is to talk to you about this.'

'I really like you, Helen.'

She stood up and grabbed her jacket from the back of the chair. 'I really can't do this now.'

'Can we not just talk? I can go with you to see your dad's family.' He shrugged. 'I know what that's like.'

'Thanks for the offer but I just want time to think things through.' Her heart started to pound in her chest.

'You don't need to do this alone.'

Helen shook her head. 'The boy in the photo looked the spitting image of my little brother. I need to go. I'll speak to you later.'

Helen struggled for breath as she climbed the stairs, the familiar tightness in her chest and arms. She gripped onto the handrail for support. Gasping for breath, she disappeared into the bathroom and the tension tightened around her throat. She managed to stagger to the sink and splash icy water on her face and back of her neck. She reached into her pocket and slipped out her pills as stars blotted her vision. She swallowed one and scooped some water into her mouth.

She looked away, avoiding her gaze in the mirror. The door opened.

'Are you okay?'

Helen turned to see a blonde woman who she'd seen around the station a couple of times, but she didn't know her name.

'Are you okay?' The woman stepped forward, concern furrowing her brow.

Helen shoved the pill bottle back into her pocket. 'Never better.'

The woman crossed over to the lockers. 'Are you sure? You don't look it.'

Helen turned off the tap. 'It's been a long shift.' Helen forced a thin smile and took a seat on the bench. 'You know what it's like?'

'Tell me about it, that's been eight hours for me. The woman slipped her feet from her heeled shoe then wiggled her toes. 'These are absolutely killing me.'

'Are you finished now?' The woman asked.

'No, not by a long shot.' Helen took a deep breath, feeling her heart slowing.

'Shame.'

'Anyway,' Helen replied, standing up, 'I better get back.'

'Good luck! I'm Sophie by the way.'

'Thanks,' Helen said, heading for the door. 'I'm Helen.'

* * *

Liz held her mouth and shook her head. 'I don't know what to say.'

'I'm just glad that you're not leaving.' Craven sat next to her in the garden, despite the bitter wind that whipped through his shirt.

'Milton was always safe, I didn't need to worry when he was going to be home, what he was up to . . .' Liz wiped a tear away with the back of her hand and sniffed.

Craven nodded and looked away. 'I'm sorry.' He couldn't think of anything else to say. Nairn's career would be over and he'd probably be looking at jail time.

'I don't think he knew what he was getting into with Charles Rushmore and one stupid decision . . .'

He retrieved his hip flask from his pocket. 'This will warm you up.' His hand brushed hers. 'Just like the old times.'

'I'm not sure.'

'I wasn't thinking.' He looked away. She'd had a problem with the drink, but that had been a long time ago.

She took it from his hand.

'Do you always carry this around?'

'Aye.'

Liz gave him a thin smile before taking a hesitant swig. 'What is that?' She grimaced, stifling a cough. 'It's like firewater.'

'Did you know Charles?'

'Milton and Charles trained together. I knew he was unhappily married for quite a long time, but he didn't want to divorce as she was ill. Milton had said he has met someone else and seemed really happy.'

'What are you and Milton—'

'We're not. He had some many opportunities to be truthful with me. I can't help thinking that maybe he knew about Moira all along.'

Craven shrugged. 'He says he didn't.'

'I don't know.'

'It never gets any easier. I had to go tell a poor woman that we had found her niece's killer. You should see the state of her. I doubt she'll ever get over it. The woman had a young son too, not much older than the twins.'

Liz puffed out her cheeks and passed the flask back. 'I think you need this more than I do.'

CHAPTER FIFTY-FOUR

Reggie sat in the interview room with his hands in front of him, looking bored. He had a bandage over the left-hand side of his temple and a purple bruise on the other side. He smiled as Helen entered the room followed by Craven. He motioned to her arm, 'I bet that hurts. I gave it a good whack. Mind you, I was aiming for your head.'

Helen took a seat in front of him and looked down at her notes.

'I thought you lot would have wanted to speak to me sooner, I have been waiting here for ages.' He looked at his solicitor for confirmation. The middle-aged brief looked away sheepishly.

Helen sucked in a breath to steady herself.

'How is that slapper that I call my wife?' He motioned to his injuries. 'I hope the pair of them will be done for assault. I think they were trying to give me brain damage.'

Craven slid a picture across the table. A post-mortem picture of Tina French. Reggie made no move to look at it. Instead, he stared at Helen.

'Look at the photo. Do you recognize the woman?' Craven said.

'You know I do. Just don't ask me to name them all.' He winked at Helen. She looked away and from the corner of her eye, she could see Craven clench his fist.

'And what do you mean by them all? Craven lent forward.

'You know exactly what it means.' Reggie rolled his eyes. 'Aye, I killed her.' He smiled as if remembering a fond memory. 'There's so many more, too. You're going to be busy, pal.'

'Why would you do that?' Helen asked, surprising herself at her own forcefulness.

'Death was all I could think about since I lost my son and I enjoy it.'

Helen shook her head. He spoke like he was talking about going to a football game.

'It took over. Don't get me wrong, I knew I wasn't going to get away with it.'

Craven added another photo to the table. A picture of Eleanor Aldridge and her injuries.

'You attacked this woman, before your son died.'

Reggie shrugged. 'I don't remember.'

'You're pathetic,' Craven seethed.

'I'm not going to be forgotten though, am I? I am somebody now.'

'I think we're done for now,' Helen replied, watching the smile drain from his face.

'It's such a pity that I didn't get to sort you out,' he sneered. 'I should have killed you when I had the chance.'

Helen rose to her feet. 'You're a right charmer, aren't you? We're done here.'

CHAPTER FIFTY-FIVE

The next day, Helen wrenched up the hand brake outside the address and peered out the window. It looked like a lovely family home, and less than a ten-minute drive from her father's country house. That must've been handy. There was a small wooden swing in the front garden and a red Panther pedal bike leaning against the gate. She unclipped her seatbelt, as a blond boy emerged from the house with a football under his arm. His knees were scraped, and his white T-shirt was grassy and muddy. She found herself holding her breath. He could almost pass for her brother's twin. This boy was maybe a little thinner and taller, but even his hair flopped onto his forehead in the same way. She blinked hard a couple of times to ease the stinging in her eyes. A woman in a green dress followed behind him, carrying a wicker picnic basket. She looked younger than Helen had envisaged from the photograph. She couldn't have been much past forty, with flowing auburn hair. Taking a deep breath, Helen climbed out of the car. The woman stopped on the path.

'Hello,' Helen mustered. 'I'm Helen, Helen Carter.'

THE END

Thank you for reading this book.

If you enjoyed it please leave feedback on Amazon or Goodreads, and if there is anything we missed or you have a question about, then please get in touch. We appreciate you choosing our book.

Founded in 2014 in Shoreditch, London, we at Joffe Books pride ourselves on our history of innovative publishing. We were thrilled to be shortlisted for Independent Publisher of the Year at the British Book Awards.

www.joffebooks.com

We're very grateful to eagle-eyed readers who take the time to contact us. Please send any errors you find to corrections@joffebooks.com. We'll get them fixed ASAP.

Printed in Great Britain
by Amazon